Break on Through

Break on Through

Jill Murray

DOUBLEDAY CANADA

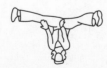

Doubleday Canada and colophon are trademarks.

Library and Archives Canada Cataloguing in Publication

Murray, Jill, 1977–
Break On Through / Jill Murray

ISBN 978-0-385-66490-5

I. Title
PS8626.U775B74 2008   jC813'.6   C2007-90559-2

This is a work of fiction. Names, characters, places, and incidents are products of
the author's imagination or are used fictitiously. Any resemblance to actual events
or locales or persons living or dead, is entirely coincidental.

torontod**arts**council
An arm's length body of the City of Toronto

Cover image: M. Spendlove
Cover design: Jennifer Lum
Line drawings: Jill Murray
Printed and bound in Canada

Published in Canada by
Doubleday Canada, a division of
Random House of Canada Limited

Visit Random House of Canada Limited's website: www.randomhouse.ca

TRANS   10   9   8   7   6   5   4   3   2   1

For all the b-girls

ᴏɴᴇ

I can see myself winning when I close my eyes.

It's March. I'm at the final round of the Hogtown Showdown, the most important b-boy battle of the year in all of Toronto. My crew, Rackit Klub, is up against the legendary Infinite Jest. Some of them have been breaking since before I could walk. Not only did they start this battle, they've won it eight times, not to mention all the titles they hold in New York, L.A. and every far-flung cipher and circle around the planet. They've been in the newspaper. They've been on TV. Their videos have made the top ten of almost every b-boy website there is. Sponsors give them free clothes. When local MCs want b-boys in their videos, Infinite Jest gets called up first. All that's left is for someone to name a shoe after them.

Meanwhile, me and the boys of tha Rackit Klub have trouble getting practice space at school. We can't even get an invitation to the sessions that Infinite leads. So far, nothing we do grabs their attention. Or anyone else's.

Until today.

You can feel it in the air. Something amazing is going to happen. The crowd knows it too. As we're called to the floor, everyone—b-boys, fans, photographers—they all rush to the side of the circle. Some use their elbows to get to the front.

Infinite jokes around with fans and makes fun of the DJ—a personal friend. By now, anyone who's anyone in this scene and not jealous is a personal friend of Infinite Jest.

I'm terrified, but my nerves are helping me focus. That's one thing about me. I like pressure. The cash prize is close to $5,000, but more than that, I'm driven by the chance to show what I can do next to the best of the best.

I'm wearing my lucky pants today. (The grey cargoes my mother hates—too faded.) I am also wearing my lucky shoes (too expensive), lucky shirt (too tight) and lucky hoop earrings ("How do you dance in those?"). My hair is twisted up under my lucky bandana from my Mexican grandmother (too ratty), beneath my lucky hat with the patch from my Jamaican grandfather (makes me look like a boy). Even my bra feels lucky today. (Don't even get me started.) It's a silver bikini bathing suit top but you can only tell if you're looking harder than you should be. I am hot. I am tough. I am a superhero in camo-print sneakers. I can melt you with my eyes. I can shoot lasers from my hands. I don't just have my game face on; I *am* the game.

The rest of my crew is bugging-out nervous. Encore and Recoil are pacing back and forth, bumping fists and reviewing strategies. I listen to the music and force my brain to quiet down; no easy feat with Sean, a.k.a. Ruckus, a.k.a. my boyfriend, hopping around beside me, cracking his knuckles and muttering under his breath. If we can beat Infinite Jest, the money won't even matter. A victory here is like an automatic upgrade. If we beat them, we'll become the crew to beat. We'll be in.

The DJ drops the needle and the battle begins.

Our two crews face each other, tensely stepping from one foot to the other, each daring the other to go first, like it's a game of chicken. The crowd starts to clap the beat. On our side, Recoil finally gets sick of waiting and leaps into the ring, opening big with a series of power moves, more like gymnastics than dancing. The room goes wild. I cheer with Sean and Encore, but on the inside I wince. I wish Recoil would do some actual dancing before getting into the big tricks. The judges are looking for foundation moves and creativity, not just brute acrobatics.

I'm pretty sure this is why I'm always second in the running order. Mr. Ruckus and the boys of tha Klub figure that by burying me here, they're playing it safe. They can still open big and close big and as long as I don't screw up, the fact that I'm a girl won't matter, 'cause at least I'll have the basics covered for the judges. I hate the way they try to pass off sexism as strategy, like there's nothing I can ever do to match them. But I take my battles one at a time, and right now, I need to stick with the program and nail this round. The best way to win is to win.

Mephisto throws down for Infinite next. He kicks off his run by ticking off every move Recoil did on fast-forward, as if to ask, "Is that all you've got?" Then he drops down and fills in everything Recoil missed, ending with a couple of tricks he invented himself.

This is what I have to follow. If I think about it, I'll either panic or ask for an autograph. Instead, I keep my head down, try to focus on what I do best.

As the crowd gathers closer, I open with a few funky dance steps—Bronx and Brooklyn Rock, light on my feet, playing with the music, riffing off what's going on in the song. I work through some intricate footwork—6-steps, CCs and other variations, focusing on the essential foundations of the dance. The guys are always bitching at me to learn more power. They won't be happy until they see my feet flying around in the air. But when I'm doing these moves, I feel connected to the start of it all, back in the day, somewhere in the Bronx in the seventies. I hit everything nice and tight, toss the crowd something a little unexpected but save some strength for later. I don't want to burn through my best stuff like Recoil, who is still panting on the sidelines even though his turn is long over.

"Yeah! Lady Six!" a fan shouts from the crowd.

We go back and forth like this until we've all gone twice, and at the end of the final, the crowd erupts in chaos. Some people are chanting for Rackit Klub. Some people are chanting for Infinite Jest.

It takes forever for the judges to announce a winner. When the MC finally steps up to the mike, the room gets so quiet you can hear a bandana drop.

"And the winner of the Hogtown Showdown is . . ."

No way!

It's a tie.

The judges could have split the prize money and called it a night, but the crowd won't rest till they declare a champion.

The room gets loud again. A fight almost breaks out. Bouncers struggle to keep people apart. The MC has to yell into the mike.

"The judges request that each crew sends one man forward."

I can't believe my ears. There's going to be an extra round—a one-on-one battle—foundation only. No power moves. No backflips. No amount of spinning will help.

Sean grabs his face in his hands. I know he wants to put himself in but he went all out on his last run and popped his knee. Recoil hasn't practised foundation in, like, a year. Encore steps forward like he's ready to take on the job like a man, but then Sean sends him back.

"Sorry, man," he says, "I know you want to battle but I have to think about the big picture. It has to be Nadine."

I am blown away. All the times he acted like I wasn't strong enough, all the hours he spent making me do it over—he saw my true potential all along.

Encore looks mad for a second, but then he thinks about it.

"It's true, dawg, it's true," he says. "Nadine's our only hope."

"Amen," says Recoil.

"Six Sky, Six Sky," they start to chant as I step into the circle. Mephisto stares me down but I am not afraid. I breathe deep and summon the spirit strength of the warrior queen who is my b-girl namesake. I am Lady Six Sky.

The DJ drops the needle, and "Treat 'em Right" by Chubb Rock bursts through the speakers. I leap into the circle. None of this waiting stuff for me. I have to be first. No way am I letting the judges think the other guy might be hungrier. I don't care how much experience he has. I don't want to hear about upper-body strength. This one is *mine*. His crew might be legendary, but I've trained for this. I have talent, I have energy, and more importantly, I want it more.

The music rips through my body, pushing me to move. I'm not thinking. I'm not even in control of my limbs. Within twenty counts, I'm down on the floor. My hands and feet twist and wind around each other with familiar flow, weaving my body through illusions of contortions. The crowd cheers louder the deeper I get. I feed off their energy.

When the timing feels right, I unwind from a windmill, track into a headstand, fake like I'm going to end my run right there but then pop up into a hollowback handstand, my shoulders stretching, back arching so far that I can feel my feet reaching for the ground. I freeze there for a gravity-defying lifetime of seconds. The crowd sucks in its breath, then lets out a cheer as I land back on my feet in a proud b-girl stance. I brush the imaginary dust off my shoulder and toss my hair at my opponents.

Sean is waiting for me on the sidelines. "Baby, I am so proud of you." The guys grab me and lift me over their shoulders.

Mephisto finishes his run and the judges dive into a quick huddle. The MC steps up to announce their decision.

"And the winner is—"

Sean squeezes me tighter. Encore and Recoil have their fingers crossed.

"Rackit Klub."

He says it again 'cause no one can believe it.

"Put it together for Rack-it Klu-uuuuuub!"

The entire building loses its mind. People jump on top of us in a giant heap, cheering. A hundred strange hands pat me on the back. I'm carried across the club by a tidal wave of fans, to a podium where Ender from Infinite is waiting to present Rackit Klub with a cheque for $5,000, Ed McMahon style.

"That was amazing!" he says. "Have you ever thought about teaching a class?"

Before I can answer, a reporter from my school newspaper shoves a mike in my face.

"Lady Six!" a voice calls behind me. I turn around and Sassy Sam from Grüv TV is standing there with a camera. A whole line of little kids ignore her and wave pens at me, begging for my autograph.

Infinite brings around a rented stretch Hummer to

escort us to their private winners' party, and the day ends with the flash of a hundred cameras.

We've unseated the champions. At the age of fifteen, I am the youngest Showdown winner in over a decade, and the first girl ever.

But forget all that. It's just a stupid dream that's never going to happen now.

two

When I got home from school today, my parents were sitting in the living room with some white guy in a suit. I wasn't even expecting them to be home, and my dad never lets people from his new job see where we live, so it was really weird to find this strange dude in the living room.

Suit guy smiled at me with toothpaste-commercial teeth and said, "This must be Nadine. Are you excited, Nadine?"

I tried to act natural as I put down my bag and stepped into the living room. Excited about what? My parents hate it when they tell me stuff and then I forget it and they have to tell me again. But it's the end of the school year. It's so hot, I can hardly remember to go to class, let alone care about random crap my parents think is important.

"Am I?" I answered.

My father cleared his throat. "Nadine, this is Bill. He's our real estate agent."

Who? Since when do we have real estate? We have lived in this Parkdale apartment for seven years. Somehow I don't think that counts.

I looked over at my mom. She was grinning ear to ear and rocking back and forth like she had to pee.

"Bill just sold us our *new house!*" she finally squealed, like she was giving away a prize on a game show. "We didn't want to tell you until it was final, so you wouldn't get disappointed if it didn't work out."

Everything went blank for what felt like an hour. I didn't know we needed to move. I didn't know they wanted to move.

Bill reached into his attaché case and handed me a glossy folder with a picture of a house on it. The house had a name: the Wood Dove. It was a big grey thing with two storeys and a yard and more space between it and the next house than between our building and the high-rise next door. Something dropped right through me from my chest to my feet.

"It's in Rivercrest!" my mom practically screamed.

My dad beamed. I waited for the punchline. Rivercrest is like a hundred years away from Parkdale. The subway doesn't go there. The LRT doesn't go there. The bus after the LRT after the subway doesn't even go there. My hands started to shake and my chest clamped up.

"If this is a joke, it isn't funny."

That's all I remember. I must have fainted.

This moving thing is like the fiftieth or sixtieth surprise my parents have sprung on me since spring. They live in a secret world where all information is classified. They're afraid that if I know too much, I'll end up like them. They're still embarrassed because they had me when they were sixteen, but I don't see what the big deal is. There are worse things to do with your life than give birth to a superstar b-girl, the likes of whose Pumas any b-boy would be lucky to touch.

My friends always think it must be so cool having parents who are so young, but they are so, so wrong. My parents are as cool as suspenders and as young as acid-wash jeans, both of which my dad has been known to wear. Together. At the same time.

I think they were hoping I would turn out to be some kind of studious, pink-sweater-set wearing, churchgoing saint or something. The fact is, I'm the opposite of everything they would have wanted if they'd sat down and thought about it, used a condom, and then waited, like, a decade, instead of going at it like rabbits in the back of my grandfather's Lincoln for an entire fall semester.

Maybe there's a curse where whatever you're like, your children will turn out opposite. I'm going to keep that in mind when I have kids. If they join the AV club or Up With People, I won't blame myself. I will trust them not to do exactly the same dumbass crap my parents did, and I will tell them things.

Like the real reason my dad got a new job last spring.

He used to do bookkeeping for a bunch of different stores in Parkdale. Now he's a tax analyst for some company off Bay Street. Not exactly exciting, but good news, right? That's what I thought when they finally let me know about it. But then he started working late all the time, and whenever he was home he would have more work with him. He got so busy, he stopped walking me home from practices after work and stopped asking about school every five minutes and then he even seemed to forget about Sean, who he practically hates. He started wearing suits, even on weekends, and then it was like, yo, who's this stranger in my house and why does he only come here when I'm sleeping?

I asked my mom why Dad had to work so much and she said it was to make a good impression at his new job. So I asked why he couldn't go back to his old job, and she told me not to be silly.

I guess it was because of money? I don't know what Dad was making before and I don't know what he's making now, but it seemed like he used to be around more. It's not like we were starving. It didn't make any sense to me that he would kill himself working when we were already doing fine.

I didn't know my parents had *plans,* and after a while, I let myself get used to things again.

Then this spring, my mom finished her social work degree and got promoted to day manager at the women's shelter. I was proud of her. She'd been working on that degree almost my whole life.

After the grad ceremony we went out for dinner in Little Italy to celebrate. It was the first time the three of us had hung out together like that in a long time. My parents were weirdly cuddly—they kept touching each other and looking at each other and smiling, which was pretty gross but it almost seemed normal considering the occasion.

Then I started to notice all these funny little things. Like my dad had wine, but my mom had milk. And she ordered pizza with olives, which she usually hates.

While we were waiting for dessert to come, my dad put his arm around my mom and we sat there staring at each other for a while, me on one side of the booth and them on the other, me feeling like I shouldn't really be there at their romantic celebration dinner. That's when they decided to tell me.

They're having a baby. Or, as they put it, I'm getting a little brother or sister.

I didn't know what to say. They waited for me to get really excited, but I kept thinking, *a baby? Why? They're old.* Well, OK, not old. But they're parents. *My* parents. So what gives?

And now we're moving.

—

When I came to, my mom was standing over me saying, "Nadine, don't be silly. Your father and I have careers now. You didn't think we could keep living here after the baby came, did you? Where would she sleep? You're going to have to accept that this is the best solution for everyone."

Yeah. Everyone except me.

"What about breaking? What about Sean? What about my life?"

I didn't mean to yell. It just came out like that all at once. Bill winced like he was afraid I'd blow his toupée off. My father sat with hands in lap staring at the floor.

I ran down the hall and slammed my door so hard my shelves rattled. I jammed on my headphones and lay on my bed with my eyes closed, mouthing angry MOP lyrics until my parents burst into my room and yanked the 'phones off my ears.

"You know, Nadine, we would have hoped you'd be excited for u— to have a new home."

Nice save, Mom. As if any of it has anything to do with me.

My father pointed his finger in my face. "How dare you embarrass us like that in front of Bill."

How dare they get mad at me when I was already mad at them!

"You are acting selfish and childish."

"Me? Did I just drop horrible news on you? Am I telling you how to feel about it?"

My mother narrowed her eyes. "Think about the baby. It's a beautiful house in a safe neighbourhood. And the schools are wonderful."

"What's wrong with this neighbourhood? I like my school."

"Are you serious? You complain about school every day. I worry every time you leave the building. This apartment is falling apart at the seams. On the news, they talk about drugs and gangs. And your grades— Nadine, won't it be nice to be somewhere quiet, with fresh air and room to move?"

"The news? They exaggerate everything. They don't know how it really is. This place was safe enough for me to grow up in. Those are my initials carved in the sidewalk out front. Why is that not good enough all of a sudden?"

She threw up her hands. "Nadine, I grew up here too, but this is a great opportunity for all of us and we might not get another one. Your grandma Karina would be so proud. The least you can do is give Rivercrest a try before hating it."

My dad shoved the stupid house folder back at me, forcing me to open it. Inside there was a page listing the many exciting activities Rivercrest has to offer. I could join the equestrian club or enjoy all the golf my heart could ever desire. And team sports, oh, the team sports! Rivercrest High School leads the league in every jock sport you can imagine, not to mention cheerleading.

"My spirit fingers are tingling just thinking about it."

My mother got that look she gets when she knows that child abuse is wrong but she can't remember why. Then she smiled her scary, scary "work" smile—the one she uses to "mediate situations" in a "respectful" way that "promotes non-violence and mutual understanding." It's totally fake. She learned it at school.

"Sweetie, turn the page. See? The house has a renovated basement where you can hang out with all your new friends."

That's when it hit me.

"New friends? Oh, I get it. You *want* to ruin my life. You're trying to break me and Sean up and force me to stop b-girling. That's what this is all about. Great idea, Mom, I'll never figure it out. It's totally going to work."

I ran down the stairs (much faster than the ancient elevator) and tore down the street as hard as I could. I didn't even know where I was going. I just needed to get out.

I imagined myself running to Sean's, slipping into his room through his basement window and climbing under the covers with him. That would show them.

But I wasn't ready to tell Sean about Rivercrest. Not really ready to sneak into his room either. And his mom is probably the first person my parents would call anyway.

I picked a direction and ran as far as I could into my horrible, not-good-enough-for-the-new-baby, unsafe neighbourhood.

three

I wake up tired, and I drag my feet to school. It's practically the last week of school. I should be fidgety and excited and running around trying to start water fights like the rest of my class, but instead I walk slowly through the halls before homeroom, everyone blending into the green lockers around me. I'm a zombie.

I track down the guys in the courtyard at our usual picnic bench. It's a million degrees hot out, but Encore is practising one-handed handstands in a brand-new fleece hoodie, trying to catch the attention of some girl. Sean is critiquing his technique, barking advice that is unwanted, judging by the expression on Encore's face. Recoil lounges on a bench, smoking and carving a half-assed tag into the red and yellow paint with his keys.

It always amazes me how dancers can smoke. Or singers. Anyone, really, but seriously, you'd think that people whose very passion depends on their lungs would want to cut that ish out.

That's exactly what I wish Sean would realize about Recoil: b-boying is not his passion. It's just another pose for him, like the way he's sitting with his back to the guys, with his afro shooting out sideways from under his trucker hat and a blue bandana poking out of his pocket like he thinks he's a Crip.

Sean sees me coming from across the courtyard and reaches out his hand. I smile despite the two-ton weight in my gut. I had a huge crush on him before we started going out, and I still feel like a dippy idiot anytime he does anything to confirm that yes, he likes me and it's not my imagination.

He wraps me in his arms, scoops me off the ground and kisses me. Behind us, Jazmin starts to drum her plastic nails on the table. That girl is always lurking around, waiting for an opportunity to get between us. I know she's trying to get with Sean. It's spelled out so clearly, I don't need to call it intuition. If she was really just "into the crew, you know, a supporter," she would be my friend too or have settled for Encore or Recoil a long time ago. Those two would fall all over each other just to be able to share.

But no. She hates me and only hangs around with them so she can keep tabs on Sean. She follows us to all our practices, where she sits around, bigging up the guys and laughing her ass off every time I mess up. She has all kinds of stories about how she used to take sooo many "serious" dance classes. She tries to prove this by arching her back and doing weird stretches like a stripper. She calls the calluses on my hands "disgusting," and if I get a bruise, she goes on and on about how she could never let her appearance go like that. She's always saying things like, "I just don't think girls should break or rap. It looks stupid."

She's not smart enough to notice that when she puts girls down like that, she's insulting herself. What I really want to do is walk over there and give her a shove.

I pull Sean a little further out of listening distance and tell him we need to talk. He hugs me and starts to play with my hair.

"What's the matter, baby?"

I don't really like being called baby, but somehow I don't mind when Sean says it.

"It's my parents."

"Don't worry about them, baby, we can hang out at my house. I told you. My mom's working late this week. Your folks don't have to know. Tell them you've got detention."

I look around the courtyard. Everyone is staring.

"It's not that. Can we talk in private?"

A collective "ooh" travels across the courtyard in waves. Someone heckles, "Preggers!" Jazmin kisses her teeth and mumbles something about the lesson she would teach me if she was my mama.

I lead him around the corner.

"My family is moving to Rivercrest."

He takes a step back from me. "You're kidding."

"Nope."

"What are we gonna do?"

"I don't know. The Showdown—"

"Forget that. How am I going to hang out with you every day, Nadine?"

"How are we going to practise?"

"Don't even worry about that right now. We'll figure something out."

"Really?"

Getting into the Showdown is crazy hard. The whole thing started one year when Infinite, who rep the Junction, called out Gr8 Xpct8shnz, from Regent Park. A whole whack of crews showed up to watch and a bunch more battles came out of that. Now the whole thing is this big deal where Infinite personally invites twelve crews and then there are four wildcard spots open for any riff-raff who want to fight to get in. If you want to get invited back the next year, you have to battle your way out of the bottom of the barrel. We came so close last March. We qualified for a wildcat spot, but then didn't advance to the next round. Back to the bottom. We have to do better next year. It's the only way anyone is ever going to notice us.

Sean notices the look on my face and pulls me back into a hug.

"Baby, it's in February. We have time. We'll figure it out."

He kisses the top of my head, then sticks his head around the corner and calls Encore and Recoil over.

"Guys, bad news."

Recoil rolls his eyes. "Great. What did the bitch do now?"

Sean slaps him upside the head.

"I'm not being funny. This is serious. Nadine?" He gestures for me to spill it.

"I'm moving to Rivercrest."

There's a deadly pause. Then Encore laughs so hard, his chocolate milk shoots out his nose.

"Rivercrest? Aw man, Sean, didn't I always tell you there was something wrong with this girl?"

Sean lunges forward like he's going to slap him again, but I stop him. I can stick up for myself.

"Hello? It's not like I want to go. My parents didn't exactly ask for my opinion."

Encore throws up his arms. "Yeah, Nadine, and you never asked for ours."

I'm not even sure what that's supposed to mean.

"Ooh-la-la, Rivercrest," Recoil needles. "Guess you're not going to want to come around here no more. How could we possibly measure up?"

"Measure up?" Encore says. "You've got to be kidding. Rivercrest is lame. One week in that place and she'll forget she was ever here. She'll be too busy golfing and listening to Kenny G."

"Yo, yo, guys, that's enough," says Sean. "Go back to your cages."

He looks at me again. "It's not the end of the world. We'll find a way to make it work."

The bell rings. No one reacts until a teacher comes out and starts to personally snuff out people's cigarettes and escort them inside.

Sean kisses the top of my head again and stalks across the courtyard. Recoil follows, giving me the finger as he goes.

Jazmin jumps up from the picnic table and runs after them, face flushed with excitement, ugly blond corn braids rattling behind her.

Tha Klub is my crew and crew is like family, but it wasn't always easy in the beginning.

I first met Sean after I had been breaking a year, maybe a year and a half. It was my obsession. Every day, I did dozens of 6-steps beside the b-ball court at lunch, and at home in the living room before my parents got home from work. Every week, I downloaded how-to clips from the net and found new music. But I was always practising by myself, judging myself and encouraging myself. It was good, but after a while, I started to realize I'd learned as much as I was going to learn on my own.

I posted on message boards and started going to practice jams around town. I didn't think anything of it at first but soon I noticed that wherever I went, guys were always giving me excuses why they didn't want to teach me. Either I was too young or not strong enough or I danced too much "like a girl." They'd make me audition with moves that required more strength than skill—moves I'd need a whole other body to do right. Or I'd show up to a session and they would act like I wasn't there. I felt like I was learning even less than when I was practising alone. At least the guys in the videos danced at my command.

When I finally met Sean, it felt like a miracle. It was the second week of school. I was looking for a spot to practise. Usually I would stay away from the courtyard because I got a weird vibe from the smokers who seemed to own the space. But I was desperate. Someone had dropped a hot dog on my usual spot out back, and lunch was half over already.

So I slipped through the doors at the south end as quietly as I could and ignored the smokers even though I could feel their eyes on the back of my head as I scoped out the area for a practice spot.

There wasn't much coverage in the courtyard—just a few benches and tables and a couple of sad shrubs that people had used for ashtrays. I managed to find a small clear space between a dead bush and a bench with no seat, and keeping my back to the courtyard, I created my own mental privacy tent.

I practised a few light moves—just some footwork and some air freezes. I'm not prissy, but I wasn't about to put my face down on the ground with all the old gum and cigarette butts.

I'd been at it maybe five minutes when suddenly a shadow spread across the 6-step I was working on. Sean.

He waited for me to finish, and then threw down opposite me. He was good. I noticed right away. Smooth, strong, creative—and he didn't have anything to say to me about being a girl. He didn't say anything to me at all. We just went back and forth like that for three rounds in total silence, our hands and feet generating the beat, no one speaking a word. The smokers craned their necks to see what was going on.

Then a door slammed open, and Sean's boys showed up. He jumped to his feet and ran off to join them, but then turned and jogged backwards a few steps.

"Your 6-step would be tight if you didn't lean so far back. Watch your form."

Maybe if the whole thing happened now, I'd be insulted—like, who is this stranger coming in here, telling me what to do? But he was kind of right. And besides, here was a living, breathing b-boy who, although he knew he was a better breaker than me, would actually practise with me. And he was hot.

To impress tha Klub, I did everything I could to act as unlike a girl as possible. I pulled my hair back tight under bandanas. I took back all the school clothes my mom bought me and traded them for baggy shirts and guys' track pants.

But it didn't work. Sean didn't seem to care what I wore, and Encore and Recoil made fun of every move I worked on by challenging each other to do it better, or faster, or knock more of them off with their eyes closed.

Once it was clear that guys like that were never going to give me a chance regardless of how baggy my pants were or how many times I grabbed my crotch, I started wearing earrings again, and normal-sized T-shirts.

That's when Sean finally asked me out. I was shocked because I'd been hoping it would happen for so long, I'd pretty much given up. But it turned out that even though I liked him first, and he's almost two years older than me, he was shy—he couldn't get up the nerve to talk to me about anything but my moves.

I got this call one day from Encore. He was like, "Yo, you know Ruckus likes you, right?"

I knew if I didn't keep cool, I'd blow it, so I was like, "OK, and?"

Encore said, "So do you want to go out with him or what?"

And I was about to say "OK, I guess," when Recoil came on the line and said, "Yo, Nadine, I like you too, wanna give me a blow job?"

And then I heard Sean yell, "Hey!" and then there were some shoving sounds and then he called Recoil an idiot and took the phone himself and said, "Yo, Nadine, ignore that."

And I said, "OK," 'cause I kind of was already.

Sean said, "Want to come to my place on Tuesday after practice?"

And I said, "OK."

And he said, "A'ight. Peace."

And that was that. The next Tuesday, I went over to his place, and we sat and watched b-boy videos with the guys and then he gave them this look and they left and he made me show him a move we'd been working on and he gave me some pointers and I took his advice. Then we made out for a while until his mom came home, then we had supper and we were officially a couple. That was before my parents knew about Sean and I was banned from hanging out at his house.

After we'd been working together in private for about a month, Sean convinced me I was good enough to try out for the crew, even though I didn't meet their "official standards." Whatever that meant. There were only three of them in the crew at that time, and Sean was starting to get antsy about wanting to enter four-on-four battles, to prepare for the Showdown. But the three of them had this weird thing where they all lived on Lansdowne, or just around the corner on West Lodge, and they'd been friends since they were little, and they agreed they'd only let Lansdowne people in their crew. The fact that I lived two blocks away on Jameson was too extreme for them, like they had to rep not only their neighbourhood but their exact block, as close to their exact postal code as humanly possible. "North of Queen Street only," they said. They were making it up just to keep me out.

So I called them out. The battle happened that Friday at Broderick Community Centre.

All battles are different. There aren't even standard rules. This one was me against them. One against two. I had hoped to battle Sean, but he sent his boys in for him.

I already knew what they were going to bring: power moves. Neither of them has enough respect for the foundation of the dance, in my opinion—being on-beat, good footwork, creativity. They had loads of confidence (overconfidence, even) and lots of big moves, but that left huge holes in their basic technique. I just had to ignore their insults and dance through those holes.

I'm not saying it was easy—two against one, with the crowd against me to start, and Encore and Recoil actually giggling when I tried to pull bigger moves. I was nervous. Sean's training might have helped get me there, but he made it clear before the battle: he was on no one's side. He watched the whole thing with his arms crossed over his chest, giving nothing away, watching the crowd more than the battle itself.

But the more Encore and Recoil heckled, the more confident I acted. The more tired I got, the more I focused on battle strategy, pushing myself harder and harder and harder.

At the end of ten minutes, I was about ready to pass out and Encore and Recoil had barely broken a sweat. Because they didn't respect me, they didn't even try to bring it. They prejudged. Then the impossible happened: the crowd started coming over to my side. While I didn't let myself think for a second I was winning, every cheer gave me a fresh burst of energy.

Sean let the crowd pick the winner. It was close, but the crowd picked me, and that's all that mattered. Tha Klub had to let me in then, or risk losing the respect of the whole scene.

Until that moment when the whole crowd started cheering for me, I never really knew if I was any good or not. But getting into the crew gave me so much confidence. B-girling always made me feel free before, but this was like next level.

I'm not about to give all that up now just because my parents have other ideas.

four

The movers come for our stuff and it only takes an hour to cart it off. That's how much we don't have.

I stand in the middle of my room, staring at the faded spots where my posters used to be. New people will come and this apartment will forget me. Then Parkdale will forget me and then there will be no more me. The Rivercrest house is always going to feel as empty as this apartment does right now.

It doesn't help that my parents are ridiculously cheery today. They were up at five, getting ready for the movers. My dad dragged me out of bed for a big early breakfast at the Over Easy and practically skipped all the way there. When we got back, the movers were half done.

My mom, who can't eat breakfast these days without throwing up, was standing in the middle of the living room, beaming and crossing things off a checklist.

Every step I take today feels like the end of something. I keep telling myself, "This is the last time I'll ever get dragged out of this bedroom." "This is the last time I'll see the sun rise at the end of our street." (Maybe the first time, too, now that I think of it.) "This is my last sausage in this booth." "The last time I'll ever walk through this lobby." This move is my execution.

Sean was supposed to meet us at breakfast. My dad was even prepared to pay for his eggs, but he was a no-show.

Probably he had to help his mom with something at the last minute.

I sit on the front steps playing with my phone and waiting. I can't get through to him. His line just keeps going straight to voice mail.

I hear the elevator thud open down the hall, through the open door behind me. My dad comes out, carrying my mom's suitcase.

"Get your stuff together, kiddo. We're leaving in fifteen."

"But Sean—"

"Nadine, he's two hours late. We have to go."

I stare at the ground and wait for him to go back in the building.

"Yo, Nadine!" I look up and it's Sean, running down the sidewalk.

"Sean!" I jump down the front steps, run down the walkway and give him a big hug. "What happened to breakfast?"

He rubs his eyes. He's out of breath. "I know. I'm sorry I'm so late. You know how it is—my mom— But I have a surprise for you."

I almost let myself get a little excited for a second.

He brings his hand out from behind his back and hands me an old plastic bag wrapped around . . .

"Oh. My *Jurassic 5* CD."

He laughs. "Do you like it?"

I look behind his back to see if he's hiding anything else. Maybe the CD is just supposed to be funny? He shrugs and takes the empty bag back, stuffs it into his pocket.

"Baby, what's wrong?"

I don't know what I was expecting. Flowers? A poem? I don't really care about that.

"I don't know. I guess I just thought we'd have more time to say goodbye."

He puts his hands on my waist again. His fingers slide under the bottom of my shirt, against my skin. "Let's just enjoy the time we have."

He kisses me again. I close my eyes and try to ignore everything except the warmth of his breath and how tiny I feel when I'm pressed up against him. It mostly works, until my dad crashes through the door.

"Sean, nice to see you," he yells loud enough to wake up half the neighbourhood.

Sean practically flies off me into the bushes.

"Hey, Mr. Durant," he mumbles, wiping his mouth.

My mother comes down the path and forces a smile. "Sean."

"Hi, Mrs. Durant."

He turns back to me. "Looks like this is the big goodbye."

"No way. I'll call you as soon as I'm unpacked. I'll see you at practice on Saturday."

He smiles. "Deal. We'll set something up for sure. Don't worry."

"Later!" I say, like I'm just going down the street.

"A'ight, lates," he says.

I manage to get in the tiniest peck on the cheek with my parents watching, and then he chickens out and walks away backwards down the sidewalk, waving.

My eyes sting, but only until I blink it away. I need to just suck it up already. I am not going to let my parents think they are winning.

It starts to rain as my dad finishes loading up the car with the last of our luggage. I stand on the front walk and stare up at our building. My parents yell at me to get in the car. So long, Jameson Mansions. Joke's on me. It's just a typical Parkdale apartment tower. Nothing mansiony about it. It's probably got nothing on the Wood Dove. Pieces of brick probably don't wash away every time it rains on the Wood Dove. We probably won't be able to hear the kid next door screaming when we try to watch TV in Rivercrest. Our neighbours on Treemore Lane are unlikely to be evicted for running a grow-op.

But so what? This is how we improve our neighbourhood? By getting the hell out the second we find some cash?

"*A'ight!* Let's go home!" my dad says, smacking his hands together. I want to kick him but he gets in the car too fast.

As we drive down the street, I lean my head against the window and watch the neighbourhood roll away through the rain: down the street, past my school, onto the expressway. If you told me a month ago that I'd feel sad about leaving my school behind, I would have laughed.

We drive along Lakeshore Boulevard, past the old factories and new condo towers, the green expressway rising and falling around us, till the CN Tower looms over us like a warning. *Turn back. Last chance.* But we turn up the DVP anyway, past the glowing Beemer dealership, and wind our way north with the city shrinking in the rearview mirror. I feel myself disappearing with it. I lean my head back and close my eyes. By the time we reach the 401, I am drifting off to sleep.

When I wake up, we are in a strange place, East of Scarborough, where all the houses look the same and there's a strip mall every five hundred metres. After a while, the houses start to taper off. Then, once we're so far into the middle of nowhere that no one can hear me scream, my dad rolls down the car window and inhales deeply.

"Smell that air! So fresh! So clean!"

Never mind that we're in the centre lane of a ten-lane highway. I hope that was not supposed to be a reference to vintage OutKast.

Eventually, signs of life start to pop up on the side of the highway again: billboard ads for the same pukey-perfect subdivisions like the one we're moving to, gas stations, a warehouse.

My mom claps her hands. "Look, Nadine! That's your new school!"

"Yippee. Now if I try to skip, I'll end up roadkill."

They really did think this through.

We exit the highway and drive through a part of town where everything is spelled with an extra *e* on the end, including the word *towne*. We turn a corner and then there's a giant grocery store and about thirty streets with rows and rows of houses that all look the same. Everything is so new; I can hear it squeaking from inside the car. There is no graf anywhere. No posters or newspaper boxes. No people out on the street, either. It's so normal, it's weird—like *The Stepford Wives* or one of those creepy movies where the call is always coming from inside the house.

Turns out the neighbourhoods in Rivercrest are organized according to the alphabet, which is good, because otherwise you'd never be able to figure out where you were. Our street, Treemore, is a long way in—after Sycamore but before Umbra, down Trellis Lane, near Thistle Court. I'll probably never find my way out again. I'll miss practice next Saturday because I'm lost somewhere in the Ks.

Finally, we turn into the driveway of the most normal-looking house on the street. There is an actual picket fence beside the driveway.

My dad makes a big production of taking the shiny new key out of his pocket. He actually pauses to point out how shiny it is, and then does a putting-the-shiny-key-in-the-shiny-lock-and-turning dance. I'm so embarrassed, I'm almost glad we're nine hundred miles away from anyone I know.

My mom takes me by the hand and drags me from room to room, pointing out the tile and the carpet, oohing and aahing. But the carpet is scratchy and the tile is cold. Every room stinks like polyester and paint, and there's a layer of fine dust on all the windowsills. I sneeze. So this is what buying now and paying later smells like.

The kitchen is full of shiny white appliances that are so big, they could have eaten our old appliances. This is supposed to impress me.

"Wow, Mom, thanks for making it so much easier for me to stick my head in the oven."

"Don't be funny, Nadine."

"I wasn't trying to be funny."

She smiles her scary work smile.

The living room is more of the same. There's a shiny new couch, easy chair and TV that look like they came as a set. The chairs have handles on the sides that you can pull to make a footrest pop out. They're made of like vinyl or something.

My dad beams.

"Do you like it? We wanted it to be a surprise!"

I roll my eyes. "Dad, enough with the surprises already. I am going to hate surprises for the rest of my life, guaranteed."

My mom swoops in with her work voice.

"Well, Nadine, we know you're uncomfortable with change, so to make you feel better, we kept the ratty old living-room set for you downstairs in the lounge."

Right. The lounge, where I'm going to hang out with all my new friends as long as they are studious and none of them are male.

My footsteps sound hollow on the stairs as I go up to my new room. It feels like if I lean too hard on the wall, my hand will go through.

The first thing I notice when I open my door is that they have replaced my bed. I don't even get to sleep in my own bed tonight. I'm so mad, I punch the bed and kick it over and over again until it starts to thump against the wall and my dad calls up from the kitchen.

"Nadine? What's going on up there?"

"Nothing."

I bite into my pillow instead of screaming.

If you can believe it, my new room is actually smaller than my old room. It has two windows. One of them looks out over the front lawn, which is brownish and half dead. The other one faces the brick wall of the neighbours' house, also brownish. Like everything else in the house, my walls are beige. The same scratchy carpet from the living room is in here too. There is a flat, square ceiling light in the centre of the room, and in one corner, a big closet with mirrored sliding doors. My old bedside table has not been trashed, so it's beside the bed. My desk at home was actually built right into the wall to save space. Here, there's a small white desk that looks like it came from Canadian Tire. Not exactly my taste, but then again, neither is homework. My DJ table somehow survived the move too. It's disassembled and stashed at the back of the closet, like a suggestion that maybe I should give up spinning and start reading more.

I wander into the baby's room. It's maybe a little smaller than mine, but it has more light. It's totally bare. No furniture, no blinds, not even paint on the wall. I can't imagine a whole new person living here. It's been just the three of us for so long.

When I was little, my parents always told me that none of this Rivercrest stuff mattered—that you didn't need a big house or a fancy car or a lawn to be happy. The important thing was to have your family and work hard and be a good person. Maybe they were only telling me that because they had no choice and didn't want me asking for stuff.

My grandma Karina thought that education was the most important thing in the world, so we lived in her basement and she took care of me while my parents went to school and worked. My dad always had part-time jobs. When he finished high school, he went straight to college for accounting stuff. My mom finished high school a year later and then started working. I remember some days, my dad would come home and we would do our homework together, then my mom would come home and I would have my bath and she would read to me. Once in a while, when my dad dropped me off at school in the morning, I would see other parents whispering about us, but our life was normal to me.

Grandma Karina was my favourite person in the whole world. She was an amazing cook and she knew how to sew and she would tell me stories about when my parents were little. My first word was "gamma." When I was eight, she died of a heart attack. She wasn't even fifty. My parents say I was sad for a year. I almost didn't pass grade three.

That year, we moved into our first real apartment as a family. Mom worked nights, so she was home during the day. She also went to university part time, studying for her social-work degree. Dad worked mainly during the day, at a sports store. After my homework was done, he and I would go for walks around the city and get takeout roti as a special treat. "Your mom doesn't have to know about this. It can be our special secret," he would say. The rest of the time, it was scrambled eggs and frozen vegetables or hot dogs and beans from a can.

Why does everything need to be different for the new baby? My mom keeps complaining that the kid is pressing on her bladder, but I think it's her brain that's getting the squeeze. I don't know what my dad's excuse is.

While my parents unpack and get supper ready, I try to rearrange my room so it's more like me. I move my bed to the opposite wall, under the front window, just because I can. I shove the desk in a corner, and stack all my records along the far wall, next to my turntables. I find my posters and cover every bare space until I can barely see the beige paint underneath. It feels good to sink pushpins into the spongy new walls. I'm determined that my room will be the one beige-free zone in the house.

Dinner is microwaved soup from a can, in mugs because the dishes and pots are still lost in a box somewhere. I sit across from my parents and we eat in what would be silence if my dad didn't keep looking around the kitchen and sighing like it's the best meal he's ever eaten.

After supper, I sit on the front step and watch the neighbourhood. At least, I think I'm watching the neighbourhood. It's a little hard to tell because nothing moves. All the trees are exactly the same size and shape. It's too quiet. There's no wind. There are barely any lights on in the other houses. It feels like an abandoned movie set.

I am going to hate this place forever.

ꟻive

I spend the July first long weekend helping my parents unpack the rest of our junk, and then on Tuesday, I call Sean. It goes straight to voice mail, so I leave a message on his cell.

He doesn't call me back right away, and later that day, I call his house and his mom says he's not there. I ask her to tell him I called and she says she will, but I know how she does: she'll forget to tell him, or she just won't, 'cause she'll think it's not important, no matter how nice I am on the phone or how important I say it is.

"Sean! Your secretary does not live here! You must have me confused with somebody else."

I don't know how many times I've heard her say that.

On Wednesday I call again, and he answers on the second ring.

"Hey, baby, 'sup?"

"Did you get my message?"

"Yeah, I got it. Sorry I couldn't ring you back. It's long distance and my moms was like, 'Sean! Do you think we're all made of money now?'"

"What's that supposed to mean?"

"Nothing. You know how my mom is."

True enough. I once saw her yell at a homeless chick who was listening to an iPod while begging for change. "I don't have no iPod. You want my change? How about instead you give me your change?"

"So what time do you want to practise on Saturday?" I ask him.

He sighs. "Is that the only reason you called me? What are you wearing right now?"

"Jeans and a hoodie."

His voice gets lower. "No, Nadine, what are you *wearing* right now?"

"Sean!"

He laughs. "OK, fine. Saturday. I haven't thought that far ahead yet. Let me talk to the guys. I'll text you back."

I can't wait for Saturday. I'll get to see Sean. I'll get to practise. I'll get to see my real neighbourhood and pretend I have a life.

There is nothing to do here. There are activities to sign up for, but there are no people around and there's nowhere to go. Every street is as boring as the next. There's not even a corner store or coffee shop in our whole neighbourhood.

You'd think that with all the wide open space that's around here, and with nothing else to do, I'd be getting a lot of practice in, but it's more like I'm dying of thirst in the middle of the ocean. This house has a lot of rooms, but none of them are very big. My room can barely hold my record collection. There's not enough space to practise full out in the lounge without putting a foot through the TV.

If I wake up early enough, I can run to the park and do footwork on the tennis court before the crack-of-dawn tennis people chase me away. Those old women in the white skirts can be really mean!

If I wake up late, I can go to the parking lot behind my new school, but it's cement, which is hard on the hands, which is fine—if it was good enough for the originals, it's good enough for me—but I can't do backspins on it. I tried doing the old-school thing and getting some cardboard but it kept sliding all over the place and blowing away. I don't know how that's supposed to work. It's too far to drag a giant roll of linoleum, if I could even get a giant roll of linoleum.

I checked at the community-centre gym but all their time is booked up with kids' programs and basketball for dads. They told me I could rent it for sixty bucks an hour. Great. I could sell a kidney online, but then what would I do the second time I wanted to work out?

By Thursday, I still haven't heard from Sean, but I find a train schedule online. There's a bus that leaves Rivercrest at exactly 11:04 and connects to a train that gets to Exhibition station, a few blocks from our old place, just under three hours later. So if I'm going to make it home for dinner, which my parents are going to insist on before they'll even let me go, I have to be back at the station by four. That only leaves two hours for practising, and it's going to cost me fifteen bucks, but I'll do it.

I find my dad and ask him if he can drive me to the bus stop on Saturday morning.

"Really, Nadine? That's more than half your allowance. Are you sure you don't want to save it for a movie or something? New shoes?"

I roll my eyes. "Right. I'm going to skip practice for some dumb movie."

His eyebrows come together like they do when he's worried. "Let me go with you this time, so I know you'll get there and back safely."

"Nooo . . ." I try to say like I'm not panicking. "You don't have to. What are you going to do while we practise?"

This image of my dad watching us—or worse, showing off his Humpty Dance—pops into my head. I'd rather never dance again than see that happen even once.

"I'll go into the office for a while. Anything for my little girl."

He ruffles my hair, and my vision of hanging out with Sean and chilling in the old neighbourhood starts to evaporate.

"Dad. I'm fine. You don't have to do that. Just drop me off at the bus station in the morning."

The corners of his mouth start to twitch like they do when he thinks we're having a "good, spirited debate."

"I'll come with you at least this once, Nadine, or you won't go at all. The lawn needs mowing. If you don't like it, you can stay home and do that instead. Don't push me on this."

I cross my arms. "Fine."

But by Friday night, I still haven't heard from Sean.

I wake up to the sound of lawn mowers on Saturday morning. It sounds like four of them out there, all at the same time, whining like the crappiest electronic dance beat of all time. I keep waiting for a cheesy drum machine to kick in. When it doesn't, I drag myself downstairs, half asleep. My dad is already up and showered. The lawn is mowed. His breakfast is eaten. My mom is drumming her fingers against the table, anxious for Dad and me to get on with the day and out of the house. It's going to be a "me-time" day for her, which will probably mean thumbing a magazine in the bath, and then falling asleep for three hours. She keeps complaining about how she can't nap during the week when she's at work. The baby is stealing her life force.

I walk into the kitchen, skip the fridge and the good mornings and make a beeline for the phone.

"Sean?"

"Nadine? What time is it? I was sleeping."

"It's ten. Sorry. I just need to know where we're practising. If I don't make it to the bus by eleven, I won't be able to come."

"Oh yeah. Didn't you get my email?"

"No . . ."

"Yeah, that fell through."

"What do you mean, it fell through? What's going on?"

"It just didn't work out with the guys."

"Why not? If we're going to qualify at the Showdown, we really have to work at this."

"Nadine, we've got, like, almost a year to practise. I think it'll be OK if we miss just one."

"I guess. Do you want to just hang out instead?"

"I can't today. Nadine, I'll call you when I wake up for real, OK?" He hangs up.

I stand in the kitchen staring at the phone, my dad watching me, jingling his car keys.

I bite my lip. Shit comes up. It happens. There's no point getting disappointed about it. I don't need to hang out with Sean. I can talk to him on the phone later. We'll have other chances to hang out. And practise—I'll just have to try harder to find a practice spot.

My dad clears his throat and shoots a sideways glance at my mother, who frowns.

"OK, you know what, Nadine?" he says. "I've changed my mind. You're not getting on that train. I don't want to spend the day in the office when it's nice out. I know you want to practise with da boyz, but I make the rules around

33

here, and today, you are hangin' with me. Let's get out of here and find out what all the other kids are up to."

He's trying, but it's not working.

"Dad, I don't want to 'hang.' I just want to practise."

"I know you do, Nadine, but have you thought about finding another activity out here? It might be hard for you to find anyone to practise with in Rivercrest. And these guys from your crew . . ."

"It's not an 'activity.' It's my life. How can you even say that to me?".

I can't believe my ears. I was with my dad when I discovered breaking. He was *there.*

We were at the Ex. That was always my reward for not being too much of a nuisance all summer. It used to take my mind off the start of school, which always makes me nervous.

We had spent the whole day riding the midway rides and I was pretty tired and strung out on sugar. I was twelve— old enough to know better—but I was so hepped up on cotton candy, I was actually walking between my parents, holding their hands. My dad was singing "Every Little Step I Take" by Bobby Brown. Ew. My mom was laughing. And if I'm not mistaken, we were *skipping.* I would shudder to remember this moment if not for what happened next, which was that all of a sudden, this guy came running out of nowhere and did a flip and landed on his back right in front of us. We stopped. I screamed. My dad even stopped singing. Then we noticed a crowd had gathered and there was this whole crew of guys dancing on the boardwalk. It was probably Infinite, now that I think of it, but I didn't know anything about the scene at the time.

This one guy was doing this thing where he moved like he was under a strobe light. This other guy was so on-beat, it was like he was finding new beats in between the beats that I didn't even know could be there. Then this third guy did this thing where he pushed up from a headstand into a handstand and I thought to myself, *these people are super-heroes*. It seemed impossible that an ordinary body could move like that. Had they not heard of this thing called gravity? My next thought, half a second later, was, *I want to be a superhero too*. I must have completely spaced out because next thing I knew my parents were tugging at my shirt and laughing at me.

"Nadine," says my dad, jingling his keys to get my attention again, "your world is too small."

"Yeah, well, so's your mind," I tell him.

He looks like he's about to bark at me, but then my phone beeps. I grab it out of my pocket. It's not Sean. It's just a text message about some stupid contest from the phone company. I put it to my ear anyway.

"Hey, baby," I say to no one, and run upstairs to my room to "take the call."

SIX

I haven't been back to Parkdale to practise in like a month. It's killing me.

My mom came downstairs before work this morning and told me that if I don't stop "moping around the basement" soon, she's going to send me to summer school.

"For what? I passed everything this year."

"Just barely," she said.

"Yeah, but I'm well rounded."

She glared. I shrugged.

"Do I not have both b-girl and DJ experience?" I asked. "That is two of the four elements of hip hop right there. I don't need to MC, and you probably don't want me doing graffiti, so—"

"I'd prefer if you did really well in even two of your seven classes."

"Whatever."

"Do you know how much I would have loved to have the opportunities you have? When I was your age—"

"I know, I know . . . you were 'pregnant out to here' and sooo upset that you couldn't go back to school in the fall. You've told me a thousand times. I get it."

"Are you going to leave the house today?"

"Yes! I go out every day."

"OK," says my mom. "If you do go out, please be back by dinner. I'm bringing home something important to show you."

Yuck. I know what that means. Ultrasound day. For weeks, my parents have been making a big deal out of getting our next look at the new baby, but I don't want to talk about mucus while I'm forcing down Hamburger Helper.

My dad kisses me on the head on his way through the kitchen. "Have a good day, sweetheart."

Finally they disappear into the garage. The car starts. The garage door rumbles down. Alone, at last.

I run downstairs and begin the first of what I plan to be forty-five headstands. This is what I've been reduced to. No flow. No creativity. I have to be happy that I'm building the muscles in my neck.

When I've had enough of that, I grab my running shoes and go for a run. There's nothing like actually battling to build stamina and endurance—I can always push myself further when the pressure is on—but I figure running is probably the next best thing. I know how to do it. It's cheap.

I come home, have a sandwich and a shower. Then I nap for a while. It's about three o'clock when I wake up. I hate this part of the day. It drags. I'm done practising. There's nothing on TV besides stupid soap operas and shows for little kids. Even if I had somewhere to go, I shouldn't because I have to be back in time for dinner.

I go back downstairs and reach behind the couch, through the tear in the upholstery, and find the stack of old disks Sean burned me from our practice sessions. Whenever my parents think I'm hiding something, my room is the first place they look. In the closet, under my mattress . . . but I figured out this couch trick back at the old apartment, and they never caught on. Technically, there's nothing on the disks my parents can't see. There's just a lot I don't want them to. Like all the parts with Sean. Everything he does, they always find a way to twist it so it looks bad.

I find the disk marked "Nadine's First Windmill," from last September, when we first started going out. He dotted the *i*'s with little hearts.

Windmills are the move where you're spinning on your back and shoulders and your feet are flying around in the air, like a windmill. When I started b-girling, I thought I'd never be able to do them at all because I had the upper-body strength of a T. Rex. But when I met Sean, he was like, "Stop making excuses. It's about the momentum from swinging your legs. You can do the move." So I had to try.

It took me forever to get even one rotation down. I kept smashing my hip into the floor. I was bruised for a month.

Once I figured out how to get my legs around, I was only halfway there because then I couldn't understand how to plant my hand to go into the second rotation. It's not much of a move if you can only get around once. They don't call it a continuous backspin for nothing. But Sean didn't give up on me then. He stood over me, practice after practice, yelling, "Now, now, now," trying to get me to hit it in time. He'd get so frustrated, veins would pop out on his neck. I'd be swearing every time I missed and by the end of every practice, we practically wouldn't be speaking to each other. But then finally, finally, I nailed the move. I was so surprised, I forgot what I was doing and collapsed halfway through. But Sean was so happy he picked me up and spun me around the room until I got dizzy from the spinning and the laughing so hard.

That's where the video stops—where I rewind it and watch it again from the beginning.

I'm halfway through the video for the second time when I hear a thud from the window behind me.

44

My first thought is that I'm home alone in the middle of nowhere and my parents are at work and I'm trapped in the basement and I refuse to die in Rivercrest.

I kill the light and the TV, and I crouch down behind the couch while I look around the room for some kind of heavy weapon-like object. The only liftable thing around is the old blanket my grandma crocheted. Not exactly deadly.

I hear the noise again. This time, it's more of a scratching against the glass. I ease myself up so I can see over the back of the couch.

A pair of tan workboots and the cuffs of some baggy dark blue jeans are framed in the window. My heart thumps so hard, my future killer can probably hear it on the other side of the glass. I run for the stairs.

Yo Psycho starts banging on the window again, and yelling something. Something-een. Something-een.

Before I reach the top of the steps I stop for a second to get one last look at those boots—they're going to be all I have to describe to the police, if I can even get to the phone in time.

Suddenly the guy ducks down so his head is in the window.

I scream and bolt for the door.

He yells louder.

"NADINE!"

I stop. He yells again. I slowly back down the stairs until I can see his face.

"Sean!"

I run back up the stairs, out the front door and around to the back of the house.

"Sean!"

I run to him and jump. He catches me. I give him a big hug.

"Why didn't you just ring the doorbell?" I ask as he puts me down.

"What if your parents were home?"

I lead him back around to the front door and we make out for like fifteen minutes in the front hall, until he stops and looks into my eyes and says, "You got any food?"

He takes his boots off, and we go into the kitchen, where he grabs my ass while I make him a sandwich—Kraft slices and cold cuts.

"So, how's the crew?" I ask.

He shrugs. "Fine. The usual."

"Have you been practising?"

"Hell yeah. We're gonna clean the floor at the Showdown next year. You been keeping up your end of the bargain?"

"Yeah . . ."

"But?" he asks, like he doesn't believe me.

I hand him the sandwich. He crams half of it into his mouth at once.

"It would be good to practise with you guys some-times."

"You will," he says through a mouthful of food.

"When?"

"We'll set something up. Don't worry. It's all a part of my strategy."

"Your *strategy*?"

"Yeah. For the Showdown. I got it all planned out."

"Cool. What is it?"

He smiles mysteriously. "If I told you, then it wouldn't be a strategy."

"No, Sean, that's a secret."

"What?"

"Do the guys know about this *strategy?*"

"Oh yeah," he says, wiping the Miracle Whip off his face. "They know."

"So why can't you tell me?"

"Well, they know. They just don't *know*. You know?"

"No."

He finishes eating.

"What were you doing downstairs?" He traces his fingers lightly over my wrist. I get goosebumps.

"Watching b-boy videos."

"Cool, let's do that."

Topic changed. I lead him by the hand to the basement, where we snuggle into the couch.

I choose an old "Freestyle Sessions" disk I bought. I don't want him to think I'm some freak with nothing better to do than watch videos of us all day. But he grabs the one I was watching before.

"Hey, what's this? Is this the one I made you?"

"Yeah . . ." I mumble into my own armpit as I set up the DVD player.

"Let's watch this one instead."

"Geez, Sean, I didn't know you were so sentimental."

"Why'd you think I made it for you?"

"So I could see what was wrong with my mills?"

"Nah. Come here, give me that." He pats my empty seat on the sofa and reaches for the remote at the same time. "Put your feet up."

I wiggle down to one end of the couch and put my feet in his lap. He starts massaging them. He has really strong hands, but gentle. I close my eyes. I hear his voice on the TV telling me to do the move again, do the move again. There's that edge to his voice like he's trying not to get angry.

My eyes pop open.

"Why are you being so nice to me all of a sudden?"

He stiffens a little, but moves his hands up to my ankles. "What do you mean? How do you want me to be?"

"This is good. But on the phone last week, you sounded bored. You seemed like you were mad at me."

"I don't know what you're talking about," he says, moving to my calves.

"OK," I say, closing my eyes again.

The me on the video tries the move three more times and smashes into the floor three more times. I've seen it so often, it doesn't even make me wince anymore.

"Look, look," says Sean, working up the backs of my knees. "This is my favourite part."

I open my eyes again. It's the part at the end where I get the move and he hugs me, and everything is good.

I smile. "Me too."

I sit up, and kiss him on the cheek. He kisses me back, hard, and I melt back into the couch. He climbs over me, kissing my neck, my ears, my lips. I feel like I am drowning, but in a good way, like I have no control but I never really wanted it. He presses his hips between my legs and I can feel him hard through our jeans. I push back against him. My hands, working on their own, unbutton his shirt, slide under his undershirt. His chain bumps against my chin. He rips it off and throws it across the room. His breath is hot on my collarbone.

How many times have I imagined this? I wonder as my fingers get caught in his belt loops. Watching him from across the gym at school. The first time we went to a battle together. The day he asked me out.

But in my imagination, he never has mayo on his

face. We go out first. He's happy when I call. I don't have to check to see if he's mad at me first.

He unhooks my bra, under my shirt. I can feel myself starting to worry, getting less carried away by his fingers on my skin, and more distracted by the smell of lunch on his breath.

Get over it, Nadine, I tell myself. You're just chicken. He can't help it if I moved and it's harder to hang out now. You can't really expect him to be perfect all of the time. You should be able to accept him as he is.

Jazmin's face pops into my head. "You're such a baby."

Encore and Recoil: "You think you're better than us now."

My mom, wringing her hands: "When I was your age—"

Now I'm thinking too much.

"Stop!"

I push him off me and practically jump to an upright position on the couch.

Sean's eyes flash angry. "What's wrong?" he asks slowly, breathing deeply, enunciating each word.

"Nothing's wrong." I sigh, covering my face with my hands. "Something just isn't *right* now."

"Then when, Nadine?" He flops back on the couch, angrily buttoning his fly. "Sometimes I think you don't even like me."

"No! It's not that, it's just—" I hear a low rumbling sound.

"It's what?" he asks sharply.

"Shh!" I hold up my hand. "Did you hear that?"

"Hear what?"

The rumbling turns into a clunk. There's a pause. Then it starts up again.

"The garage door! My parents are back!"

He grabs his shirt and heads for the stairs.

"Not that way—they'll see you." I look frantically around the room. "The window! Go!"

"Nadine—"

"They're called escape windows for a reason. Go! Escape!" I push the ottoman under the window.

"My shoes—" he says, pulling his undershirt over his head.

I'm starting to hyperventilate now. "Just go. Hide behind the deck. I'll figure something out."

His feet disappear through the window. I slam it after him and tear up the stairs. I grab our shoes and run out the front door barefoot before my parents even make it through the kitchen door.

I find Sean kneeling behind a bush on the side of the house, crouched like a burglar for the second time today. His socks are black with mud and the knees of his jeans are soaked right through. Damn automatic sprinklers. We stuff our feet into our shoes and run down the street faster than we've ever run before, me smoothing my clothes as we run.

"Well, Nadine," he says when we finally reach the main road and slow down. "You really know how to show a guy a good time."

I wince. "Sorry."

But then he starts laughing. "'They're called escape windows for a reason.' You're funny, you know that?"

He palms my head like it's a basketball. I heave a sigh of relief.

"I guess I should call Encore to come get me," he says. "He's sleeping in the parking lot at the Tim Hortons."

I frown. "I don't want you to go."

He stops walking and wraps his arms around me. He kisses me on the head. I can smell my perfume on his neck. Suddenly I regret making him stop. Suddenly everything seems right again.

"I know. But I should go. Maybe I can even talk the guys into practising if I get back in time."

"OK." I squeeze his hand and walk with him down the long road towards the highway until we see the car in the distance. It's totally unmistakable because of the giant pizza on the roof.

"I'll be back soon. I promise. I'll call you," he says as he gets in the car.

I watch them drive away. He waves goodbye through the window until the car vanishes onto the highway.

Dammit, I'm an idiot. I kick the gravel. Dust flies everywhere.

I check my watch. It's later than I thought—nearly six o'clock. My parents are going to kill me if I'm not back in the kitchen, eating dinner in exactly eleven minutes.

I run as fast as I can until I make it to the edge of our neighbourhood. Because the stupid roads are like a maze here, I can see the back of my house from where I'm standing but I'm not sure which street will get me to ours fastest. Every second I think about it, I can feel my parents getting more and more pissed.

I figure I can wander around for half an hour, trying to find the right path, or I can just cut through three back yards and be home in a minute. Easiest decision I'll ever make. I jump the fence in front of me and jog across the lawn. I jump the next fence and get halfway through the back yard when this woman two houses over starts yelling at me.

"What are you doing? Who in god's name do you think you are?"

"I'm Nadine, I live in that grey house over—"

"I know this neighbourhood and you are no neighbour of mine. The last thing we need around here is cigarette butts and graffiti everywhere. Get off my grass right now."

Before I can explain, she lets her dog out after me—a German shepherd. Next thing I know, I'm running even faster than before. I tear straight across the next street and onto the next lawn. Suddenly, an alarm goes off. A get-the-hell-off-my-grass alarm. I didn't even know they made those.

All at once, neighbours are pouring out of different houses. I lose my mind and climb the first runty apple tree I come across. (That's how far in the middle of nowhere Rivercrest is. Fruit grows here.) I'm surrounded by shouting adults. The alarm beeps like I've stolen a car. This dog is trying to chew my tree in half. Then this guy comes out of the house, rubbing his face like he just woke up from a nap.

"Whoa, whoa, whoa . . . What's going on here?"

He gets them all to stop shouting, tells the dog to lie down and helps me out of the tree.

"Charles Henderson," he says, offering his hand for me to shake. He doesn't look like a psycho. He's maybe ten years older than my parents. Looks like some kind of business guy. I shake.

"Nadine. I live at 68 Treemore. I got lost. I was just—"

"That's OK," he says. "I don't know what they were thinking when they mapped out this neighbourhood. It's like a maze. Drives me crazy."

He walks me through his back yard, to his gate, which has a door in it, leading to my street.

"Your family new around here? You don't look familiar."

"Yeah. We've been here about a month."

I wait for him to close the gate, but he insists on walking me the rest of the way home.

"It's OK, Mr. Henderson. It's just over there."

But he says he wants to meet my parents, so he walks me to the door and rings the bell.

My mom looks surprised when she opens the door, but she manages to find her work smile in a hurry and pretend she's all happy to see me, and delighted to meet Mr. Henderson, even though I'm half an hour late and I can see it in her eye that as soon as he leaves, she's going to kill me and then move the new baby into my room like nothing ever happened.

"Looks like your daughter got in a bit of a scrape this afternoon, Mrs. —"

"Durant," she says, smiling and shaking his hand.

"Is that Nadine?" asks my father, coming around the corner from the kitchen.

"Yes," says my mother, grinning so hard her cheeks must hurt. "And she's brought a neighbour for us to meet."

My father's eyes light up. "Charles!"

"David! Good to see you again! I had no idea . . ."

"Isn't that a coincidence?" says my dad, patting my mother on the shoulder. "I met Charles the other day at the garden centre."

"How's that fertilizer working out for you?" asks Charles.

I slowly back away and creep through the living room, through the kitchen, to the basement.

I find Sean's chain under the chair and stash it in the back of the couch with the DVD. I fold up the blanket and double-check that the window is closed properly.

I hear the front door close, then my mother yells from the hall.

"Nadine! You come up here this instant."

I walk back upstairs as casually as possible, yawning as I step into the kitchen. My parents pounce on me.

"Nadine, we've had enough of this."

"You're sullen."

"You're disrespectful."

"You're always late."

They don't care that I was almost devoured by a dog today.

"How dare you embarrass us like that in front of Mr. Henderson."

"And the whole neighbourhood!"

"Don't you understand that we're new here?"

"People don't know us!"

"What are they supposed to think of us now?"

They keep coming at me, yelling over each other so I can't get a word in. Then they drop the sucker punch.

"What's going to happen when you go to school, Nadine?"

"I don't even want to think about it!" I say, starting to feel sick to my stomach.

My mother sighs. "Nadine," she says, gentler now, suddenly remembering her mediation training. "You have to stop being so negative. This is a chance for you to start over. Get your grades back up. Broaden your horizons."

"Yes," says my father. "I'm tired of watching you moon around. This is ridiculous."

"Oh!" I yell. "So now my life is ridiculous? I'm ridiculous? Well who made me ridic—"

He cuts me off. "Nadine, you need to be more open to

new experiences. Your life is not always going to be the same day in and day out. This family is going to change."

My mother pulls the ultrasound out from an envelope on the counter and shoves it in my face. "We are trying to create a positive environment for the baby, Nadine. Think about what's important."

The kid isn't even born yet and they're already worried about me corrupting it. I'm never going to get them to listen. When they were my age, they had each other, but I'm on my own here. No one is going to take my side.

"The baby, the baby, the baby! I'm so sick of hearing about the baby!"

"Nadine! That is no way to talk about your sister."

If it weren't for that baby, none of this would be happening to me. I would still be in Parkdale. I would still have my friends. My parents would still like me. Tears burn in my eyes. "Let me see that."

I snatch the ultrasound from her hand and stare at it as hard as I can. All I can see is black. I hold it up to her face. "I *hate* this baby."

Her mouth drops open and her face turns red. She reaches for the ultrasound. Before I can stop myself, I take it in both hands and tear it straight down the middle, then do it again. I toss it back in her face in four jagged pieces.

Next thing I know, my face flashes hot.

I don't know what hurts more—the slap or the surprise. She's never hit me before.

My dad steps between us. "Nadine, I think you'd better go to your room."

I look at him standing there, controlling.

"Don't worry. I'm halfway there," I say, and storm up the stairs.

—

After they go to bed, I can hear them arguing for hours. About me. Every so often I catch a stray word.

"Adjust."

"Unacceptable."

"Overreacting."

"Teenager."

Very subtle. I consider yelling a few words back just to make a point: *Walls. Thin. Nadine. Hearsyou.*

They're still at it when I finally fall asleep with a pillow over my head.

seven

At breakfast, my parents give each other warning looks when I come downstairs.

I chew my bagel almost slower than humanly possible, just so I can test how long it's going to take them to figure out their next move.

I'm already rinsing my plate in slow motion when my dad finally clears his throat and says, "Nadine, we realize you're . . . upset . . . but change is a natural part of life. You don't have to like it here, but you do have to live by our rules, and you absolutely have to respect us *and* your future sister."

He glances at my mother, who nods slightly. She approves.

"OK," I say, because I can see it's going to be the easiest way out. "I'm sorry."

It's not a total lie. I'm sorry they're never going to see my side. I'm sorry I don't get a say. And I actually am sorry I ripped the ultrasound. The hurt look on my mother's face felt good at the time, but I shouldn't have lost control. You can't win a battle you don't control.

Apparently satisfied with my apology, my mother puts on her "new beginnings" smile. "So, Nadine, I was thinking that next Wednesday I'd take the afternoon off so we can go shopping for school clothes. Classes are going to start up again before you know it."

My mom would rather go naked than shop on a Saturday.

"If you give me money, I can go by myself," I say. I'm not interested in a Rivercrest makeover.

"I was thinking we could have a girls' day. I need to do some shopping too. I wore the same dress to work twice this week. All my pants are too tight now."

"Well, can we go on Queen Street?"

"No. It's too expensive."

"The Dufferin Mall, then? I can come into work with you in the morning. I'll help with something. I'll be really quiet. Or I can go practise at the gym . . ."

"No, Nadine."

"Why not?"

"They have the same clothes here. We can find out what your new friends are going to be wearing and—"

"Mom, no. Forget it. I don't even need new clothes. I'll just wear what I have. Don't bother."

I stare down the drain—where my life is going. I hate this part of the year. I always have, but this year it's way worse. "Can't I just go back to Cuthbert-Deller? I could go in with you when you go to work."

"It doesn't work like that, Nadine. You know that."

"What about home schooling?"

"No, Nadine."

I groan. When I get to school, everyone will already have their little in-crowds sorted out, and their secret rules about who to avoid picking as a lab partner. High school is bullshit, but my mom's not buying it. She's so stuck on the idea that she would have loved high school if she'd been able to experience it fully. She thinks I'm just not "grateful" that the world is my "oyster." Oysters, to me, are all about food poisoning.

"Just be yourself, and you'll make friends in no time," she says.

"Yeah, right. And smoking doesn't make you cool, and it's what's inside that counts."

She laughs. "Nadine, you're making these kids into monsters. They're just like you."

I restrain myself from smashing my head against the counter.

"They're not like me. I bet they don't even listen to hip hop."

"Then find some new music to listen to."

"Mom!"

"Nadine, you are starting school in Rivercrest in two weeks, and that is final. If you can't make the most of it, you have only your own attitude to blame."

She leaves the room and I go sit down in front of the TV. Another thrilling summer day in the R-C. I flip channels. There's nothing on. Grüv TV doesn't actually play music videos anymore. I hate game shows. I don't care about sharks or makeovers.

I'm considering going out back and dragging all the patio furniture onto the lawn so I can do footwork on the deck when the doorbell rings. I peek out the front window and see Mr. Henderson standing on the front stoop, leaning on a bicycle. I open the door.

"I found this bike just now while I was cleaning the garage—exciting vacation, huh?"

"Tell me about it."

He laughs. "Do you suppose a bicycle might help you get around easier? My ex-wife left it behind and it's just taking up space at my place. Looks like it might be your size."

He rolls it towards me. I take it by the handlebars. It's all right. A little beat up, and the tires need air, but the brakes seem to work.

"Thanks. This is . . . actually cool. Thank you."

"No problem. I know how it can be around here without a car."

"Yeah. Thanks."

He cranes his neck to look in the front door. "Your dad around?"

"No. He's at work."

"All right. Give your parents my best. And don't get into too much trouble with that thing. I don't want them upset with me."

"OK."

He walks back to his house.

I look at the bike. All right. It's better than what I was doing five minutes ago.

I walk the bike to the gas station halfway across Rivercrest and get the tires inflated. Then I climb on and wobble down the hill to the main road. It's not that I've never ridden a bike before, just that I haven't ridden one in a really long time. I think my last bike had pink streamers on the handlebars.

Now what? There's a whole section of town I've never been to before because it's too far to walk, and there's no shopping there, so my parents just don't go that way. I cross north over the freight tracks and ride east towards the fields at the far edge of town where pavement is older and there's no sidewalk where the street meets the grass—just crumbly earth.

So this is it? As rough as it gets in Rivercrest?

I turn down a street that looks like it's going to dead-end—Argyle. But when I reach the place where I expect it to stop, it actually keeps going, until it crosses an old bridge. It's hard to tell because there's not even a stop sign or anything leading up to it, and the guardrail is practically buried under long grass. I don't think anyone has needed to drive to this side of town for any reason for a loooong time.

I get off the bike and rest it on its kickstand. I push the grass aside and walk to the middle of the bridge. It's so quiet, I feel like I'm in the Twilight Zone. I lean up against the metal guardrail and look down. There is nothing there but an uneven, dry trench, maybe three feet deep. I follow it with my eyes until it seems to stop at the ass end of my neighbourhood, in the Z streets.

Seems like a weird thing to build a bridge over.

I look over the other side of the bridge. The trench stretches in a wiggly line as far as I can see, until it disappears into what looks like a dead forest.

It hits me. Is this it? Is this the trench that put the river in Rivercrest? I was wondering where the water was.

I pick up a handful of gravel and toss it over edge, one pebble at a time, skipping each one across the hard mud.

The plonk of the last one hitting the ground is answered by a scuttling sound from under the bridge. I lean over the railing to see what's there. Local wildlife? Snakes? It seems pretty quiet. But do I notice there's a staircase winding down the far side of the embankment.

I run to the other side of the bridge and find where it starts. Except for the top step, which is totally hidden, it's surprisingly free of grass and mud. I tiptoe down the stairs, unsure of what I'm going to find at the bottom. If this was home, someone would be living here, for sure. There used to be a spot like this just down the street from school, and it was a secret tent city until they kicked everyone out and built condos on it.

But there's no one living here. It's deserted, except for the hot, dry wind. Under my feet is a long, wide concrete landing. There's about a six-foot drop from here down to the river, like it must have been a lot deeper at some point. I crouch down and touch my hand to the ground. It's cool and smooth, like the concrete on the floor of my garage. I test it out with some footwork. My heart starts to race a little faster.

I could practise here.

I do a quick turn to come back up standing, and a splash of red on the wall just above my head catches my eye. It's paint. Drippy. It spells something in smudgy letters—T-Y-P . . . Typ0. It's . . . a *tag.* I rub my eyes. A tag! In Rivercrest!

I climb back up the steps to examine it closer. Who made it? Where there's a tag, there's a tagger, right? How long has it been there? I lean over to touch it. It's fresh!

I look each way down the river trench. I don't see anyone. I run back up the stairs, hoping to catch some sign of where the tagger went, but everything is totally still.

And my bike is not where I left it.

I panic for a second—kind of a dumb way to feel about a bike I didn't even own this morning—but then I see it leaned neatly up against the guardrail on the other side of the bridge.

I guess this place isn't quite as deserted as I thought it was.

I hide the bike behind some bushes and go back down to the platform. At least if the tagger ran away, then probably no one is going to bother me.

All of this space is mine, I tell myself, stretching my arms out wide. I can do anything I want with it. No one is going to interrupt. No one will look at me funny. No one will ask me to leave. I will practise here, by myself, and I will return to Parkdale, a stronger, flyer, more invincible version of myself, and astound tha Rackit Klub with my new skills. They will work their asses off trying to catch up. We will win our spot in the Hogtown Showdown, and we will owe our victory to this crappy bridge over this crappy trench in the middle of crappy nowhere.

I take a few deep breaths like a gymnast preparing to vault, then run through some experimental steps. In the silence, each one rings out like thunder.

I listen as the squeaking of my sneakers alternates with my breathing, and I alter my steps to carry the rhythm forward, mixing my own beat out of the swishing of the fabric of my track pants.

I do it over and over again, perfecting it each time, refining the rhythm, adding style. Then I drop to the ground, dancing harder and harder, layering beats after beats, beats over beats, beats between beats, my hands slapping the floor between my feet, my body winding around itself, exploding outward, flipping, twisting.

The frenetic rhythm builds and builds until finally I swish upwards into a shoulder freeze and hold it there for I don't know how long, breathing hard, not thinking, just taking in the scenery from this weird sideways-upside-down perspective.

I sit on the cement, out of breath, blood draining back into my body. This is how it should be. Every day, every night. You don't just practise this stuff. You live it.

eight

The first day of school comes too quickly.

I ignore the alarm when it goes off. My mother bangs on my door. I roll over on my face and pretend I don't hear. She barges in, walks straight over to the bed and starts shaking me like I don't already know she's there. I'm not deaf, I'm protesting. I'm not going back to school without a fight.

"Get out of my room!" I yell.

She rolls her eyes. "Be downstairs in half an hour, or else."

Before bed last night I picked out a slammin' outfit. I've got my Triple 5 pants, my shirt from the Gang Starr concert, fresh new Nike kicks, and thunderbolt earrings to top it all off. I even ironed. People are going to *know* not to mess with me when I walk into that school. They don't have to like me, but they are going to respect me. I am going to show them a thing or two about style.

There's a school bus that goes right by our house, but my parents insist on driving me and calling it quality time. They are happy, happy, happy in the car because they're excited for me to go back to school. My dad won't shut up about how good new school supplies smell. My mom shouts questions back at me over the radio, which has been tuned to news-talk since the day we moved here. Suddenly, they care about traffic.

"Are you excited, sweetie?"

No.

"I think this is going to be a really good year for you."

Whatever. I'm dreading showing up in homeroom and meeting all the young Riverclones.

I put my headphones on until my parents notice I'm not talking and make me take them off. Then I slouch and listen to the weather report on the radio—cloudy, cloudy, cloudy—and they glance back and forth at each other across the armrest like "oh, Nadine's being a silly teenager again," as if I don't know what they're doing and it's not their fault to begin with. Then my dad rubs my mother's stomach and she kisses his hand and they relax again.

Barf.

As we pull up to the school, I pull up my hood so no one can see my face. But it's not necessary. As far as I can see through the inch of space between the bottom of the car window and the top of my hood, having overprotective parents is what everyone does here. All the little Britneys and Skippers are hopping out of BMWs and kissing Mummy and Daddy goodbye. A few seniors pull up in their own cars. I spot a couple of Lexuses and a Civic or two. When the bus pulls up, it's half empty. No one walks.

Girls are screaming and hugging 'cause they haven't hung out all summer, even though they probably live a block away from each other. Guys are checking them out, bumping fists, trying to edge their way in on the hugging action.

RHS is brand new and twice the size of my old school. The atmosphere out front is like a fashion parade with only three outfits, worn seven hundred times each. Everyone is divided into very clear groups. There are the preppies— cheerleader types, joiner/yearbook people and jocks, all kind of muddled together in circles according to what year they're in. Way off to the side, there are your hardcore nerds, who look like their moms dressed them, and the rockers with greasy hair, a whole three of them—a guy, a girl and one kid who's not giving anything away.

That's it. The rest of the school is awash in a sea of khaki. I try to find the hip-hop heads but there don't seem to be any. I'm not surprised and yet I am. Aren't we meant to believe that the suburbs made hip hop when all the cute, privileged people tried to piss their parents off by listening to the scary rap music about "urban" people shooting each other?

Oh no, wait, one. One head. Some guy. He points at my shirt and smiles as if I'm going to think he's any different from the rest of them just because he's black. He'd be cuter if he wasn't from Rivercrest.

I summon the spirit of Lady Six Sky, walk straight up the front steps and ignore the whole scene.

The morning is all about me trying to find a quiet seat, mind my own business and keep a low profile. At lunch, I find a place in the cafeteria, in a corner. I've got my headphones on and I'm trying to visualize myself doing halos. A bunch of girls at the next table are watching me and whispering.

I'm right here, I want to tell them. *I can see you. You're wearing so much perfume, I can't even smell my sandwich and I can practically hear you through my headphones.* I turn the volume up higher.

Next thing I know, one of them slides down the bench and attaches herself to my right arm. I guess she's the leader, because before I know it, I'm surrounded. The girl gestures for me to remove my headphones.

"Hey, you're new, right?"

I make a note to myself: the leader isn't bright. Then she touches my head.

"We've been trying to figure it out all lunch. Where on earth did you get this gorgeous hair?"

I'm caught off guard. She has a point. I have good hair. It's dark. It's curly. It's so big, it needs its own postal code. No, let me rephrase that. It *deserves* its own postal code. But I don't like to have strange people touching me. I think she might be in my English class. Maybe that's why she thinks she knows me. When she's done petting me like I'm a stray puppy she found hiding under her daddy's Benz, she speaks again.

"Where are you from?"

"Toronto. Parkdale."

She looks at me like I'm not understanding.

"No, like, where were you *born?*"

"Women's College Hospital," I tell her.

She laughs. "No, silly. Where's your *family* from?"

"They're also from here."

She rolls her eyes. "No. Where are they from *originally?*"

"My mother's parents were Mexican. My dad's mom is Jamaican and his dad was French."

She stops frowning and presses her hands together like I've made her day. "Oh, so you're Latina?"

"No . . ."

Suddenly, I realize what she's been getting at all along. I should have cut her off while I had the chance.

Where are you from?

My mother's vagina.

"So what language do you speak at home?"

I speak bitch, like you, I want to tell her. But instead I say, "The same thing I speak everywhere else. English."

"Oh."

I've disappointed her. But as a citizen of Rivercrest, it's her duty to be perky all the time.

"Well, it's super-nice to meet you. I'm Madi."

"Nadine."

"Welcome to RHS!"

And then she and her posse abandon the table and giggle away.

They're every bit as lame as Sean said they would be.

nine

By the third week of school, people no longer think I'm exotic or mysterious. They do not ask me to repeat things in Spanish or Arabic. Now that they know I'm not a refugee or a terrorist, they have stopped giving me leeway for my taste in clothes and music.

The people here make Encore and Recoil look like geniuses. My parents think I'm overreacting, but they're not at RHS every day to see how it is. I would reject me too if I knew I lived here.

Like today, I'm washing my hands in the west-wing bathroom when this Ashley girl from my grade comes in to fix her makeup.

I've never talked to this girl before. Something about her just makes me know to stay away—some kind of bad vibe she gives off. She's not as preppy as the rest of the girls here. Her whole wardrobe looks like something you'd wear out clubbing with a Hilton, and although she always has five girls hanging off her every word, her best friends all seem to be guys. I think even some teachers are afraid of her. She gets away with skipping classes and smoking on school property. If this was a movie, she would definitely be played by some-one almost as old as my parents.

I'm almost safe, I'm just reaching for a paper towel, when suddenly she speaks.

"So you're from Toronto, right? Like actually *in* Toronto?

Like, Rexdale or something?" she says. It takes me a second to register that she has spoken to me and not to the mirror.

"Parkdale," I tell her.

"Right, same thing."

I wince.

"So you, like, must have seen some crazy shit, right?" she says, applying a fresh coat of mascara to her left eyelashes.

"Like what?" Infinite dancing on the pier? Crazy man with no teeth riding his tricycle on the sidewalk? Jazmin trying to adjust her fishnets with a fresh coat of orange polish on her fake nails?

She leans in closer. "You *know,* like parties . . . and stuff? I know how you city girls are," she says, narrowing her eyes. "It was *off the hook,* right?" She tosses her hair and tucks the compact away. The scent of her shampoo fills the bathroom.

"Uh, sure, I guess . . ."

"So you must still hang out with people there, right?" She takes out a cigarette and starts to shake out half the tobacco on the counter.

I shrug like it's no big deal. "Yeah."

She looks over her shoulder. "Can you help me out with something?" She extracts a tiny metal can of mints from her purse and opens it. It does not contain mints.

"Like what?" I ask.

"Can you hook me up with some stuff?"

She makes a little funnel out of an old receipt from the bottom of her purse and proceeds to empty the contents of the can into the cigarette.

"What do you mean?" I ask her.

"Oh my god, you are so funny," she says, shoving my

shoulder a little harder than playfully. "You know. *Stuff.*" She brushes some of the tobacco off the counter, back into the cigarette, and tamps it down against the counter before popping it back into her purse.

I stare at her like she's on crack. "I don't have anything like that," I tell her. "That's not my scene."

"Oh yeah, right," she says.

Next thing I know, she's making a grab for my backpack.

"Hey!"

My bag flies open. Makeup, books, brush, tampons, wristguards for practising crab freezes, an earring, my phone, iPod, headphones—all my stuff crashes to the tile and scatters all over the bathroom floor.

"You're serious?" says Ashley, digging through the bottom of my bag.

I stare her down. She shrinks a little, then seems to grow taller.

"You're even more pathetic than I thought."

She throws the empty bag at me, steals my iPod off the floor and storms out the door.

"Hey! That's mine!" I chase her into the hall.

Classes are just getting out, and she's hard to follow through the crowds of kids streaming into the hall.

"Get off me, you freak," Ashley squeals as I try to wrench the player out of her hand.

That Madi girl hears and runs down the hall.

"Oh my god, Ashley, are you OK?" She looks like a hall monitor, in her perfect kilt and knee-highs, squeezing her books to her chest.

"No! She—she attacked me!" says Ashley.

"Oh my god," says Madi before I can defend myself.

"Yeah, oh my god," says another girl, rushing to Ashley's side. We are gathering quite an audience.

"Oh my god," says a third girl.

They collapse around Ashley in a defensive group hug.

"Thank you, girls," she says, dropping my iPod to throw her arms around them.

"I guess I was wrong about *you*," Madi spits at me. I have no idea what she means.

"Watch your back, bitch," says one of their friends as I stoop to grab the pod from under their feet. Great. The casing is cracked.

"At this school, we take *care* of each other," says Madi.

And then they shuffle Trashley into the nearest staircase, leaving me to collect my things from all over the bathroom floor.

I don't go to my afternoon classes. I duck out a side door and walk the long way around town to the bridge.

TypO has been busy. There are grey lines sketched across the wall under the tag for what looks like the start of a mural. But I can barely bring myself to care, I'm still so mad.

After I've done about four hundred sets of push-ups and so many sit-ups I feel sick, I start to calm down. I walk home along the trench and take my time finding my way back to the house, staying out of people's yards this time.

"How was your day, Nadine?" my mom asks when she gets home.

"Fine," I tell her like usual.

"Are you sure? You look down."

"Yeah. Geez. Leave me alone."

I'm not telling my parents about Trashley. I already know what they'd say.

Nadine, don't exaggerate.
Try harder to fit in.
What do you expect with the way you dress?
Well, sport, you just have to prove her wrong. Join a club!
Turn it around with good grades!

It's amazing how little it takes to start a rumour at RHS.

Within twenty hours of the Trashley incident, I start to hear all kinds of crazy things about myself. By homeroom, I have been given a whole new personality. By lunch, I find out that I was kicked out of my last school for starting a knife fight.

I am late to fifth-period English because someone jammed my lock and I can't get my notebook out of my locker.

I ask the girl beside me, a Britney, if she can spare a piece of looseleaf. I know that she is no friend of Trashley's—her star is just not that bright—but instead of opening her binder and giving me a sheet, she turns around in her chair to look at her friend, who gives her this *look*—this horrible *don't even think about it* look, as if I'd just asked to borrow her boyfriend. So Follower Britney shuts her binder and tells me, "I think you should learn to bring your own school supplies from now on."

From there, it only gets worse. Idiot jock guys pelt me with lacrosse balls while I try to practise handstands out back. Girls dump their drinks on the ground right where I'm working on my footwork.

At the end of the day, I can't get out of school fast enough. While the last bell is still ringing, I leap out of my seat and rush out the front door.

My phone rings. I scrounge through my bag and somehow manage to answer on the very last ring. I don't recognize the number.

"Hello?"

"Nadine!"

"Sean?"

It's been weeks since I've heard from him. I was starting to wonder if he'd forgotten about me.

"Yeah. Who did you think?"

"Oh my god, am I happy to hear a friendly voice! Where are you?"

"Uh," he says. "Buddy's place. Recoil's cousin. How you doin'?"

"Awful. But I don't want to talk about that. I'm just so happy to hear from you. I miss you. What's new?"

"Oh . . . you know . . . nothin' much."

"How's the crew."

"Good."

"What's happening in the scene?"

"Oh, I don't know. We haven't really been battling. We've just been chillin', you know."

"You haven't been going out at *all?*"

"Naw. You know how it is with the guys' work schedules."

I know what that means. It means the Showdown is now only six months away and they're not doing anything to get ready. I clear my throat.

"So, um, I was thinking . . . Since it's so hard for you to get the guys together to practise at home, maybe y'all could come out here once in a while instead."

There's a noise on the other end of the line like the phone being moved around. He disappears for a second and I hear him say something muffled to someone in the background. When he comes back on the line, it's like he didn't even hear my question.

"Sorry, Nadine, food just got here. What were you saying?"

"Practise. Here. I mean . . . if it's easier. I found this great new spot and—"

"Nadine," he snaps. "You think I can't control my own crew? The Showdown is not going to be won in Rivercrest. Rivercrest doesn't want people like me and Recoil."

"Or me," I remind him. "I'm not asking you to live here. I'm just talking about practice."

"Look," says Sean. "I didn't call you for this. I don't want to fight. Can't we talk about something a little more romantic?"

He says it all gentle, but it feels more like a kick in the stomach to me.

"I'm not in a romantic mood, Sean. I told you, I had a crap day, and you're making it worse right now."

He laughs through his nose. "What's that supposed to mean?"

"I'm getting tired of this," I tell him in a voice so quiet I'm not even sure he can hear.

"Tired of what?" he almost yells.

"You avoid my calls, you stand me up, you won't practise, you can't answer a straight question."

"Well, maybe I'm getting sick of it too," he says. "*When are we practising, Sean? When are we practising, Sean? When are we practising, Sean?* You're a broken record. What about *us*, Nadine? What about *me*?"

"I don't feel like I know anything about you right now, Sean. That's my point."

Someone yells something in the background.

"I gotta go. I'll call you when you're in a better mood."

The phone goes dead.

ten

I get through the next day by slamming things. The car door in the morning; my locker, once the janitor cuts off my lock; my books on my desk; the chalk against the blackboard when I'm called to "share my answers," a.k.a. make stuff up while people giggle at me under their breath.

My teachers hate me. All day, it's "Nadine, sit up straight. Nadine, pay attention. Nadine, speak up more. Nadine, did you study? Nadine, the notes are on the board, not out the window."

At lunch a Tiffany and her follower friends make fun of my *R.I.P. Left-Eye* shirt, so I ask them if they all got their outfits off the same page of the Sears catalogue. They actually look like they all shopped the same page of J. Crew, but if I told them that, they wouldn't know they were supposed to be insulted.

"Watch your back, bitch," they say before sneaking down the back stairwell to smoke. They have as much flava as a tray of ice cubes, but man, are they touchy about their khaki.

I have phys. ed. right after lunch. We're playing lacrosse. At Cuthbert-Deller, we had basketball, floor hockey, track and volleyball, but nothing that needed a really big field, so in my first gym class the teacher, Ms. Bundt, had to take me out in the hall and show me how to catch and throw, remedial style.

I get picked last when Tiffany[3] and Brittany[2] choose the teams. I'm like, "I can throw now. You don't have to keep me on the bench all class." But even the girl with the cast gets picked before me. I get stuck on defence. Second line. Trashley is not in this class, but that doesn't mean she's not running things.

I slam my body down on the bench and toss my stick to the floor. My teammates edge away from me and huddle together like I'm going to give them rabies.

This is the worst day ever.

I also have the worst team ever. Not even ten seconds after Ms. Bundt blows the whistle to start the game, the other side scores. I still have my face in my hands thirty seconds later, when they score again. I figure that the goalie got picked because she's dating Brittany[2]'s brother or something.

Eventually, almost by accident, one of our supposed star attackers gets the ball, and what does she do with it? She runs halfway down the gym, takes a wild shot on net and gets the ball stuck in the ceiling. Wicked.

Finally, Ms. Bundt blows the whistle for the lines to change.

I stand up and stick my hand out to high-five the girl I'm subbing. The bitch sucker-punches me in the stomach. Everyone laughs.

Whatever. I play better when I'm mad.

I take my position. I know how gym class works. As soon as that girl notices I'm good, she'll pretend to be nice 'cause she'll want me on her team. I'll take over her position, then go after the attackers.

Just one problem. First, I have to be able to get in on the game, and people are not passing to me.

I see my chance when one of the opposing players trips and loses the ball right in front of me. I reach for it, but one of my own teammates dives in front of me to steal it. And misses. The other team grabs the ball back and charges on the net. As the score climbs to 90,087 to 0, I start to clue in to the fact that no one is going to let me touch the ball if they can help it.

I do my best to run around like I'm at least following the game.

Eventually, there's a skirmish at the other end. Madi, who's on the attack for the other team, breaks free and dashes down the centre of the field. You wouldn't guess it from the way she follows Trashley around and dresses like she's eighty, but she's tough and fast. My team can't stop her. They're stuck in the far end, racing to catch up from behind.

I realize that this is my moment. I am the only thing standing between the net and the goalie, and that's about as good as the net being wide open.

I run up the field to meet her. She dodges left. I block her. She dodges right. I block her again. She reaches over my head to pass and I check her stick so she can't. She pivots and tries to pass around the other side of me but I'm already there waiting for her. Then out of nowhere, she turns again and slashes at my shins. The pain is dizzying.

I check her hard. Her own stick hits her in the face. Before it even touches her, she screams and falls to her knees, grabbing her face with her hands.

"My eye! My eye!"

Blood trickles down my shin.

Ms. Bundt blows the whistle like thirty times to stop the game.

Next thing I know, one of Madi's friends leaps on top of me and pulls my hair. I grab her wrist and twist her arm around behind her head.

Ten more girls pile on top of me. Bundt stands there watching and blowing her stupid whistle.

"Let me go," I yell. "She hit me first. It was an accident. She's faking."

They're yelling back.

"Bitch."

"Ho-bag."

"Get out of here."

"Go back to the *ghetto*."

I try to shout back, but I can't think of anything awful enough to get back at them. Nothing will hurt enough.

I grasp at the face of the girl in front of me and try to get a grip on her cheek with my nails, but another girl kicks me in the side. I fall face down on the floor. A third girl brings her heel down on my fingers.

Finally, Ms. Bundt stomps over to us, waving her arms, bellowing. I make out the words "office," and "detention."

I bite the leg of the girl who's grinding my hand into the floor, and she jumps back with a screech. I manage to stand up before she can kick me in the face. People grab my arms and start to tug me in two directions at once. I feel my shoulder pop out of its socket. Through pure rage, I find the strength to kick the legs out from under the girls who are dragging me. I pry myself free and run the hell across the gym.

As I stumble into the hall, I pop my shoulder back into place with a stomach-churning crack. The pain subsides almost immediately. I notice there's blood on my shirt. I think the third finger on my right hand might be broken. Miss Faker lets go of her eye and watches me leave.

In thirty seconds, when I get expelled, I'm going to be *so* happy.

"Whoa. Are you OK? What happened?"

Yo hip-hop guy is sitting in the office when I report for sentencing.

I cough up half a laugh and my ribs hurt. "What? You don't already know? Guess you'll just have to wait five more minutes and find out with the rest of the school."

"Must be a good story, then," he says. "Five minutes—that's a long time at this school." The corners of his mouth turn up. I notice he has dimples. But is he making fun of me?

I glare at him.

"What are you doing here?" he says. "Shouldn't you be at a clinic or something? That doesn't look comfortable." He points at my arm, which is swelling in three places.

I close my eyes and lean back in my chair, ignoring him.

A second later, the secretary calls my name. I step up to accept my destiny.

"Be careful in there," curious boy says with a mischievous wink.

He's nice to me now, but after he hears the whole story tomorrow, he'll hate me just like the rest of them.

I am expecting a serious talking-to from the vice-principal, but instead I'm greeted by the guidance counsellor and escorted to the nurse's office.

"Nadine Durant," says Mr. Winkley as we walk down the narrow corridor. "Nadine Durant," he says, not like it's a question, like most teachers do, but *"Nadine Durant,"* like it's a serious condition.

I'm looking forward to explaining myself—maybe

getting Miss Faker tossed out on her ass with me—but I'm not expecting any miracles. At least when I get expelled, I can go back to my old school and get on with my real life.

But this Winkley guy has other ideas.

"Well, Ms. Durant, I don't know if you know how we do things here at RHS, but it looks to me like you're overdue for a lesson in sportsmanship."

Sportsmanship? I am the queen of sportsmanship. Lady Six Sky picks beef only where beef is due. And even then . . . I never touched a hair on Jazmin's greasy head. If that doesn't make me a pacifist—

"Tell me," he says, "is there anything wrong?" He gives me a look, which I think is supposed to mean something.

"Yeah, something's wrong," I tell him. "I was just attacked by eleven girls in broad daylight."

"No, I mean at home."

"No," I say. "None of those girls knows where I live."

He frowns. "You, missy, need a long think to find a better attitude." He hands me a pink slip. "Detention. Three-thirty sharp."

The nurse comes in the room and shuts the door behind her.

"Well, Nurse Jefferson, she's all yours," says Winkley. "Good luck."

He's gone before I can even give him the names of the real perps.

When the nurse is done with me, I go to math class with no Advil, one Band-Aid and an ice pack, and fail a test because I don't actually answer the questions. I just stare out the window, icing my shoulder. At the end of class, I hand in my blank answer sheet and leave, ignoring the teacher when he tries to call me back.

—

My shoulder is killing, and to be honest, I'm not that thrilled about the idea of walking home alone with half of Rivercrest out there wanting a piece of me. So I do what I try never to do, and *call my dad.* At work.

"What's wrong?" he wants to know on the first ring.

"Nothing," I say, on reflex. "Can I get a lift home from school today? I'm going to be in the library for about an hour so by the time you get—"

"Can't today, Nadine. I promised your mother I'd—"

I hear someone say his name and drop something on his desk. He puts the phone on hold, and I'm left humming "The Girl from Ipanema."

"Nadine," he says, finally coming back on the line. "I gotta go." And just like that, he hangs up on me. He hangs up on me and leaves me sitting outside my locker at school with a busted face and my shoulder burning so hard it's about to fall off. I sit there, just feeling the burn, until the hallways are completely quiet and the janitor comes by to shut off the lights in the west wing.

I stand up slowly, sliding my back up my locker, using my good arm to pull myself up, gripping the lock like a handle. I limp to the back door, and when I make sure the coast is clear, I leave the school and walk home, watching my back the whole way.

On Main Street, a car squeals by and someone yells "Bitch!" through a rolled-down window. I duck just in time to dodge the apple core that flies at my head. After that, I stick to side streets. It takes longer, but not even Trashley would attack me on her own grandma's front lawn.

I picture my parents, safe and warm and listening to Nu Jazz in the car—my mom with her seat back and slightly reclined to make room for the baby, boxes of paperwork spread out across the back seat. *Thank goodness Nadine's not here. Where would we put her?* they ask each other, and then laugh.

When I get home, I shove the front door open so hard it slams into the wall and makes the front hall shake.

My mom appears out of nowhere, creepy-horror-movie-style, with a tray of shrimp in one hand.

"Nadiiiiine," she says in a low, controlled voice, eyeing my bruises and the blood on my shirt. "What's *wrong?*"

"Now you care what's wrong?" I yell, kicking my shoes off so they hit the wall with a thud before hitting the mat.

"*Nadine,*" she says. "Lower your voice. We have a *guest.*"

"Excuse me, then. I guess you don't want ghetto girl messing that up for you." I look past her into the living room. Between the shrimp and the beads of sweat lining themselves up across her forehead, I see Mr. Henderson sitting on the edge of the sofa, watching my dad fiddle with the knobs on our fireplace. He sees me and waves.

I stop yelling, mainly because he's the one guy in the R-C who's stood up for me the whole time we've been here. I push past my mom, and while she's struggling to regain control of the stupid shrimp, I run up the stairs.

"Don't worry about me," I say as I reach the top step. "I'll try not to bleed on the carpet."

I throw my jacket back down the stairs behind me and make a beeline for the bathroom, peeling my clothes off as I go. I whimper as I pull my shirt over my head, then toss it over the railing. I leave my socks in the middle of the hall. My fingers are so raw, I can barely work the button on my fly, but I'm fully undressed by the time I lock the door behind me and turn the shower on, as hot as I can stand it. I just want to get this day off me as fast as I can.

The hot water stings. I wince at the burning, but I'm grateful for the pain. Just for a second, it blocks out the scene that's been repeating in my head all afternoon. Slasher's lacrosse stick on my shin, the sneaker tread on my hand, the hands on my arms, pulling my hair, Winkley lecturing: all of it slowly runs off me, into the drain, and I'm just a puffy, red, thoughtless me for a minute, staring into space while the steam fills my lungs, and everything starts to move more slowly.

Someone bangs on the bathroom door.

I turn the water a little hotter, repeating Public Enemy lyrics in my head. 9–1–1 *is* just a joke.

"Nadine, answer me," says my mother's muffled voice through the door. "Let me in. I want to talk to you."

The lock pops and the door opens with a gust of cold air.

"Mom!" I yell, outraged.

She comes and sits on the toilet beside the shower. I can see her silhouette through the curtain.

"Do you want to tell me what happened?" she asks.

"No. Why don't you just call the school?"

"Actually, Mr. Winkley already called me. I'm asking if *you* want to tell me."

"Why? You're not going to listen to me anyway."

"Is this how you talk to people at school, Nadine?"

"What are you trying to say, Mom?"

A question is never just a question with her. There's always some reason behind it—some reverse-psychology, leading, Nadine-is-wrong reason. She can't just come out and say anything. She has to make me say it, when I don't even believe what she's trying to get me to say.

"Nadine, if you were just more attentive to what other people—"

"I didn't start it, Mom."

"I'm very disappointed in you, Nadine."

She gets up and leaves, closing the door quietly behind her.

Tears fill my eyes and I immediately want to kick my own ass for it.

I get out of the shower, towel my hair, swallow a couple of Advil, get dressed and am back downstairs within half an hour. When I round the corner into the kitchen, I see they are already eating. They didn't even wait for me.

eleven

In the morning, Ms. Bundt is waiting for me outside the gym.

"My office, Durant," she yells.

"It wasn't my fault. I didn't even start it, I—"

"Save it, Durant," she says, holding the door open for me.

This is bullshit. I used to *like* PE. No one at Cuthbert-Deller would have *dared* attack me—not if they ever wanted to play a decent position again. I ran that ish. My parents were always on my back to study more and let other people win sometimes, but I can't see what the big deal was. Do you know how many kids I know whose parents would kill for them to be good at sports? Whose parents practically *are* killing them to be good at a sport?

Besides, as long as I have to be in school every day, shouldn't there be one class I enjoy?

I asked them that. Know what their comeback was?

"The world does not exist for your amusement, Nadine."

Damn if I don't know that already. The world wins. I am not amused.

They think the only reason I win is because I hate to lose. But if that's all there was to it, wouldn't I be running straight As in every class? Wouldn't I be winning *everything* at *all costs,* i.e., studying all the time, changing my clothes to fit in, sucking up to people, basically turning myself into a total follower like Madi the Slasher?

Whose head I see through the wire-reinforced glass of Bundt's office door.

"Ladies," says Bundt as I slump into my seat, "would either of you care to explain what happened yesterday?"

Slasher sits perfectly straight and stares down at her shiny brown shoes, one leg crossed over the opposite knee, manicured hands folded over her pleated skirt. Not even her perfectly highlighted, almost-blond ponytail or the cranberry wool of her sweater moves.

I don't say a word. Bundt isn't going to listen to my side.

"All right," she says. "If you won't talk, then listen. I don't know what this is about, and I don't really care. But it's my job to tell you, if it was about the game, it's not worth it, and if it's something else, then you have to learn not to bring personal garbage on the court with you." She smirks. "Not that much of it, anyway."

"It won't happen again," says Slasher, her voice as polished and friendly as it was that first day of school in the cafeteria. Guess it was fake then, too.

Ms. Bundt takes a gulp from her water bottle and seems to think about it, swishing her water around her mouth before swallowing.

"May I get changed for class now?" Slasher asks when Bundt doesn't say anything.

Another chug. Another swish.

"No," says Ms. Bundt.

Slasher looks cross for a nanosecond, but then takes a deep breath and seems to swallow it all the way down to the toes of her tights.

"I know you've both talked to Mr. Winkley and had some time to cool down," says Ms. Bundt, "but I think he said something to you yesterday about sportsmanship, and I'm not a hundred percent convinced you get what he meant by that."

Something about the way she raises her eyebrows when

she gets to the end of the sentence tells me I'm not going to enjoy what comes next.

Slasher tilts her head and smiles, calm as Jazmin after she's just taken a whiff off a fresh bottle of nail polish. "What do you mean, Ms. Bundt?"

A slow, satisfied smile stretches across Bundt's face. "I mean," she says, lacing her fingers and leaning back in her chair, "community service."

Slasher's smile freezes on her face.

"Does that sound harsh?" asks Bundt. "According to the Safe in School Act, we could *suspend* either one of you. Since we don't really know what happened out there, I suppose we could kick both of you out for a week, but I don't really see what anyone would get out of that."

"What would you like us to do?" Slasher asks, her voice an octave lower than before.

Whatever it is, I'm not even going to react. Bundt is enjoying this way too much already.

"I think I'll leave that up to the office," she says. "You'll find out during detention."

"Oh," says Slasher. "But I can't today. I have Fashion Show practice."

Of course she has Fashion Show practice. Of course this school has a Fashion Show.

"Not today. Today you have detention."

Slasher scowls for a second, then seems to shake it off. "I could do it tomorrow instead."

"Today," says Bundt. "Nadine?"

"No problem."

"Great. Now, since you're going to be fifteen minutes late to class, I expect both of you to give me fifty push-ups before joining us."

—

In detention, no one can hear you think.

Mr. Winkley can make me sit. He can take my books away. He can tell me to put my hands on the desk and look straight ahead. But as long as I don't bob my head in time to the imaginary music, he can't stop me from reliving my best b-girl runs in my head. I can practise even when I'm sitting at a desk.

Step, touch, step, touch; halfsie Brooklyn rock, fake into a turn; bunch of little hops that have no name; a real Brooklyn down to the floor; spin into the third step of a 6-step. CC, CC, pow, pow—

Sean's voice cuts in.

You should be flatter to the ground in your 6-step. Why do you want to go into the move from 2? It's more dramatic on 4.

That's not a coffee grinder. I don't know what it is, but it's no coffee grinder.

My shoulders start to tighten. Imaginary one-armed handstand. Scissor kick, scissor kick, scissor kick, o-oh, o-oh, the crowd goes wild.

I'm just starting to imagine myself doing air flares when Slasher walks in with yo hip-hop guy behind her.

There are like eighty seats empty but he makes a bee-line for the desk right next to mine. I stare straight ahead again, as I have been ordered to. I'd close my eyes and pretend to be sleeping, but then Mr. Winkley would accuse me of not thinking hard enough.

I don't know what yo homeboy thinks is going to happen here. Even if I did think he was hot, which I don't, even if he does have a nice smile, if I so much as breathe in the direction of another human being for the next hour, I'll get my hands cut off. He should follow Slasher's lead and stay as far away from me as possible.

Sean never would have been so obvious. He'd have gone for a seat at the back and let me just wonder what he was thinking. He'd have been cool about it.

A few more delinquents straggle in and head right for the back row like normal thugs.

Mr. Winkley announces he has to go get something from the teachers' lounge. Cigarettes? A drink? Pee break? A clue?

"Don't get any funny ideas about talking or moving or passing notes," he says. "If there are any shenanigans, I will find out and you will regret it. Truly. Deeply." He points at me like he means it.

The second he's out of the room, yo homeboy leans over and whispers at me.

"Hey, you're that girl who breaks, right? You're the one I see practising sometimes at lunch, out back, behind the recycling bins. You're good!"

As if he doesn't know who I am. Like he sat there by accident. How did he even see me back there? I don't even want to know. I don't trust when guys compliment my dancing. They usually just mean one thing, and it doesn't have to do with dancing at all. Not that they give me compliments often. The best Sean could do was congratulate me for not messing up. He never actually told me he was impressed or anything.

Dude smiles, waiting for me to say something. I fight the urge to smile back. I'm not answering him. It's a trap. As soon as I speak, Mr. Winkley will choose that exact moment to come back in the room. I'll get detentions to the power of infinity and they'll make me wear an ankle bracelet and everyone will start calling me Martha Stewart. No way. Those things chafe.

I don't even look at him. But for some reason, he keeps talking.

"Yeah, that's you. I know it's you. You like to practise your 6-step? Your CCs? You like to throw down every now and then?"

Now he's making fun of me. If looks could kill, I'd make him beg for mercy.

"No, no, that's cool. I can support a girl in runners."

Patronizing. Strike two. Seriously, why won't this guy get the message? *I. Am. Not. Interested. I. Have. A. Boyfriend.*

He lowers his voice again and leans closer. "You know, I don't usually come here. Detention's not me. This ain't how I usually roll. I want you to know that."

"Why? I don't care about your life. Leave me alone already."

Of course, Mr. Winkley chooses this exact moment to come back. I practically summoned him. No wonder no one listens to me. I can't even follow my own advice.

"Nadine? What did I say? That's three more detentions."

Yo homeboy leaps out of his seat. "Mr. Winkley, sir, I'm sorry. Don't blame her. It was my fault."

Mr. Winkley sneers at him. "How, Devin? Did you make her lips move? Is Nadine a puppet? Can you throw your voice?"

"No, sir, but you know how I get. She had no choice but to tell me where to go."

Everyone is staring at me now, even more than they were before. I want to sink down in my chair and disappear under my desk but I won't give Devin the satisfaction. I keep staring straight ahead like none of this is happening.

Mercifully, Winkley is done with me.

"Well, Devin, since you want them so badly, I guess it's only fair that I give you three more detentions as well. You kids are going to learn respect for authority if I have to keep you here all year."

"All right, sir, it's a date."

My cheeks burn. Devin sits back in his seat and crosses his arms over his chest like he's impressed with his own chivalry. He whispers out the side of his mouth.

"I guess we'll be seeing a lot more of each other, *Nadine*."

Mr. Winkley's head snaps around.

"Make that four detentions, Devin. Nadine, come to my desk, please. Madison, you too. Awfully surprised to see *you* here," he adds as she comes to the front.

He hands each of us a hall pass.

"Go see Mr. Pitts in the office. He'll be helping you learn the value of team work today."

"What do we have to do?" Slasher asks.

"Everything he tells you to," says Winkley.

Pitts is this tiny old man who looks like he's about 150 years old. He wears a nametag that says Bill, even though no one else in the office wears one. I don't know what his job is. He just seems to do boring office jobs that no one else wants. He's bald, but has all this spooky white hair that sticks out from his sleeves and collar and nostrils. It's creepy to be talking to him after hours.

"Hey there, Mr. Pitts," says Slasher, like she's excited to hang out with him. "We hear you have a job for us!"

I want to remind her that no one is grading her. She can cut the act.

He hands her a huge box of letters, then gives me a giant box of envelopes. "You'll need to alphabetize them before you can fold the letters and stuff them in envelopes."

"How many are in here?" says Slasher, struggling to hold up the heavy box.

"Five hundred and thirty-seven. You can work on the hall-monitor table out in front of the office."

Slasher girl's face goes white. "Are you sure? What about the table in the back room? There's more space to spread out there. We could do a better job."

"No can do. I'm goin' *home*. Can't leave you alone in the office."

"But—"

"Just leave the boxes with Mr. Winkley when you're finished."

He leaves, and Slasher slams her box down on the table out in the hall. "I'll do the letters, you do the envelopes," she snaps at me. "Don't slow me down. I actually have other things I need to get done today."

I laugh at her.

She glares at me. "You think this is funny? You might not care about studying, you might not care about anything enough to actually join in and get involved, but some of us actually want to make something of our lives. I'm not going to let you drag me down."

"Look, bitch," I say, "you're the one who got us into this. Don't blame me."

"Why not?" she spits. "It *is* your fault."

She puts her hand on her hips and puffs out her chest.

I clench my teeth. "No. *You* slashed *me*. Remember? And then you had to go and pretend I'd hit you in the eye. That was low. What did I ever do to you?"

93

Her eyes narrow. "It's what you did to my friend. You hurt her, you hurt me."

I cross my arms over my chest. "That thing with Ashley in the bathroom? You weren't even there. You don't know what happened."

"I know what I saw," Slasher says calmly. "I know what she told me. And I know who I trust."

"And I know she's lying, so maybe you should rethink that."

"*What* did you just say about my friend?"

"Ashley attacked *me*—"

"Now you're the liar," says Slasher. "I mean, *oops*, you always were."

She sits down, grabs a stack of letters and angrily starts alphabetizing.

"You know, it would be faster to just alphabetize the envelopes. If we did that"—I cough—"together"—pause—"it would go faster, and then one of us could just call off the name on the letter and fold it, while the other one found the right envelope. It would take, like, half the time."

She looks up at me slowly, and I half expect her to growl and then snap my head off in one bite.

But she just smiles tightly.

"Fine."

We make piles on the floor for every letter in the alphabet because the table is way too small, and then we each alphabetize a stack, one by one. The whole thing takes maybe fifteen minutes.

I collect all the envelopes in their box, and Slasher starts barking names at me, which I find while she folds the letters.

We actually manage to get a pretty good system going, with her calling out three names at a time, and folding really fast, and no one arguing with anyone, when suddenly, the auditorium door bangs open at the end of the hall.

Jock (actually his real name), Trashley and a whole crowd of Slasher's friends tumble out into the hall. Trashley is riding piggy back on Jock, her jeans sliding halfway down her butt.

Slasher freezes, then dives under the table, as if she's going to tie her shoe—her shoe that has no laces.

But there's no need. Her so-called friends fall completely silent as they walk by. Trashley stares at me like I'm something someone spat out on the sidewalk. Her lips curl into a sneer as she spots Slasher down on the floor. Brittany[4] and Tiffany[3] look away like they're embarrassed to be in the same hallway as us.

Slasher slowly sits up and puffs out her chest, smiling like she's not completely embarrassed to be caught stuffing envelopes with me.

"Losers," I hear Trashley mutter once they've passed us, and her little bitch posse explodes into laughter as they stumble into the stairwell.

"That's who you're doing this for? Great choice," I say to Slasher.

"Shut up," she says, and straightens her pile of letters.

twelve

The ability to take a hint is not Devin's strong point. His latest tactic is to wait for me on the steps out in front of school every day. "How are you doing, Lady Nadine? Cool shoes, Lady Nadine. What are you listening to this morning, Lady Nadine?"

"Can you please stop calling me that, Devin?"

"Why? Is it not your name, Lady Nadine?"

I've tried to get my parents to drop me off at a different door or let me take the bus or bike to school to avoid him, but they're afraid the neighbours will think I have to take the bus, whatever that means.

"I already have a boyfriend," I tell him. An angry boyfriend I have not heard from in two weeks, who I think is screening my calls.

"I'm not surprised," he says, like it's no big deal.

"No? Then why do you wait here every morning?" I ask. He jumps off the railing and runs to hold the door open for me.

"There is this thing called friendship, Lady Nadine," he says, bowing as I walk past. "Perhaps you would like to try it sometime."

Suddenly, I feel insulted. I mean, he's been coming on to me for weeks. He pays more attention to me than my own boyfriend. It stings to be demoted, even if I don't like him back. At all.

The bell rings. I turn my back on him and go to class, but he just catches up with me again in the cafeteria line at lunch, where he tries to show off by sweet-talking the cafeteria ladies into giving him seconds of everything.

"Nadine, would you like a turnover?" he asks, offering me his spare. "It's sweet, like you, and I couldn't possibly finish both of these myself."

"No, that's OK."

"Why?" he asks, and I look at him like he's a freak. "Are you trying to lose weight?"

"No!" I say, guarding my tray a little closer.

"Good," he says. "'Cause you don't need to. You're good the way you are."

"Devin!"

"What? I'm giving you a compliment."

"Well, *don't*."

He leans back against the railing and crosses his arms like he thinks it shows off his pecs. Okay, so maybe it does a little, but it's not like I'm noticing.

"Soo . . . Nadine . . . you gonna get *down* next Friday?"

"Are you memorizing my schedule now?"

He looks confused. "No. I was just wondering if you were going to the dance."

"What dance?"

"The *Halloween* Dance," he says like it's obvious. "You wanna go?"

I roll my eyes. "I told you, I have a boyfriend."

"Bring him too."

I wince. Just what I need, Sean and Devin in the same place at the same time, so everyone can blame Devin's death on me. Sean wouldn't even stick around long enough to hide the body.

At Cuthbert-Deller, only the fundraising committee, yearbook crew, AV club and decorating squad went to dances. The fundraising committee stood behind tables and served fruit punch to the teacher chaperones, who leaned against the walls and supervised basically nothing because the yearbook committee only came to take pictures for the yearbook, the AV kids spent the whole night under the DJ table, and the decorating squad fussed with streamers for three hours.

Tha Rackit Klub never cared about dances. If we wanted to go out, we went to the Friday all-ages jam at the DownRock. We didn't need to make up some lame excuse to dance.

"What's wrong?" Devin asks. "Your mystery man can't dance?"

"He can dance better than—"

No, wait, I don't owe this clown an explanation. I am not going there.

"So invite him," says the clown.

"I think he'd feel weird there without me," I say.

He smirks. "You won't come? Why not?"

"What do you care?"

"Nadine, it's a *dance*. That's, like, your *thing*. How can you not go?"

"I just can't."

"Nadine," he says. "Think about it. Music. Wide-open floor. Forcing people to respect you. I've seen how you practise. It's going to hurt you not to get out there and serve these cats a taste of their own food. Besides, I can't hold the whole dance down by myself. I was counting on your assistance in that department."

"Back off, Devin. It's not going to happen."

He tries to keep his smile, but his eyes narrow, and I know I've hurt him maybe more than I wanted to.

"Fine, Nadine," he says, finally angry. "Have it your way."

He abandons his tray, ducks under the railing and storms out of the cafeteria without looking back.

I look down at his double lunch just sitting there on the counter and suddenly I don't feel like eating either. What's wrong with me? First I get my own boyfriend pissed at me. Now even stalkers can't stand to be near me.

Within a few days, I start to notice the posters in the halls: "Video-Dance! Video-Dance! Video-Dance! Friday! Friday! Friday! In the Gym! Halloween! Dress up!" They're hand-painted on brown kraft paper like a kindergarten project. Some of them have glitter.

Woohoo. Party, party, dance, dance.

I'm not even going to mention it to Sean. It's not like I want to go anyway. I don't want to find out what music the Riverclones like. I don't want to see how they dance. I don't want to watch the Ashleys get drunk on peach schnapps and parade their bunny ears around the football team. I don't want to see the cheerleaders dressed as kitty cats, doing shrooms in the bathroom. I don't want to be anywhere near the building when one of the Tiffanys gets caught wearing a halo and wings and having a three-way in the equipment locker. I see enough of these things every day between math and recess, minus the costumes. My weekends are mine, and they are for hip hop. I'll have a better time watching videos in the basement.

My feet have different ideas though, and geography class is really boring. I daydream about showing up at the Halloween dance with Sean.

Dressed to the nines, we pull up to the door in his car. Someone's car, anyway—it's a little silver coupe thingy. Someone else is driving. Encore? Doesn't matter. He's not staying.

Sean steps out of the car first and offers me his hand. I follow him in slow motion, one glittering sneaker touching down on the pavement, then the other. My $400 Adidas kicks are so fresh, they could make you stop breathing.

Astounded and a little awed, everyone waiting in line turns to stare. They step aside and we float to the front, hand in hand, shoulder to . . . elbow. Sean's about six inches taller than usual and he looks like he could lift a truck over his head.

We are so obviously VIP, the security people melt away. No one asks to see our tickets.

We crash through the gym doors and the music stops. The air gets cold. A spotlight swings onto us and this dry ice foggy stuff surrounds our ankles, making us mysterious and dangerous, like in a music video.

The DJ tosses aside his CD wallet and scrambles to drag a crate of vinyl out from under the table. Rushing to find a worthy song, he puts on some older Gorillaz. It'll do.

A circle forms around us as we dance to the centre of the room. Sean leads the jam, explosive and forceful. His flow is smoother than I've ever seen it. Passion burns in his eyes. All the girls in the room whisper to each other. Even Trashley stares, but he only has eyes for me.

Sean finishes with a backflip and I enter the ring with a handspring. I'm on fire. Every move is smoother and more powerful than I've ever felt it before. I can do no wrong. It's like there's a force field between me and the ground. I'm practically flying.

Sean steps back in as I finish my run, and we dance together, him staring into my eyes the whole time. The music gets faster and the crowd cheers us on and at just the right moment, he lifts me over his head like in *Dirty Dancing*. I somersault out of it and land in an impossible—

Who am I kidding? I have to call him.

I lie on my bed, holding my phone. It weighs 900 pounds.

After the 5,000 times I had to restrain myself from calling Sean in the last couple of weeks, it seems kind of funny that it's so hard to *make* myself call him now. But I know what I gotta do. All that nonsense about dances not being cool enough? Those were excuses. The original b-boys even tried to dance in *disco* clubs. If they could make the most of that, one little high-school dance shouldn't be enough to ruin my rep or Sean's. We're breakers, not scenesters. Who cares where we session as long as we do? We can leave the posing to the Trashleys of the world. The way we move, any joint is hype as long as we're in it.

I'm so nervous, I almost hang up when it goes to voice mail. You'd think it was a year ago and we'd never gone out to begin with. I hope he can't hear it in my voice.

"Yo, Sean, Nadine. There's a dance at my school this Friday. Some Halloween thing. Totally lame, I know. But I thought maybe you and me could go together and show these people what real dancing looks like. Call me. Peace."

I feel better as soon as I hang up. What's the big deal anyway? I can't ask my own boyfriend to a dance?

I stash the phone in my bag, then think better of it and leave it on the bedside table, beside my alarm clock, within arm's reach.

For three days, I hear nothing.

At first I think I must have left the message wrong somehow and he just didn't get it. But then I realize that's stupid. Maybe the phone network delayed the message and he won't get it for a day. But probably not. Probably he's busy at school and his mom needs a lot of help with chores around the apartment.

Then I start to get mad. It's not like we get to talk that often and—

I'm sitting in math class when the text message comes. My phone vibrates in my pocket and it's like my whole right leg catches fire.

I pretend-drop my pencil on the floor, and while I'm hunched over retrieving it, I manage to slide the phone out of my pocket. I peek at the display under the cover of my math book. It's Sean.

When I look up again, Slasher is staring at me from her seat two aisles away. I send her a mean look and she looks away.

My left knee starts to jitter uncontrollably under the desk.

I put up my hand. "Sir, may I be excused, please?"

The teacher looks annoyed, but thankfully doesn't force me to make up an issue about "women's problems." I hurry down the hall, duck into the nearest bathroom and barricade myself in a stall.

I brace myself to read the message. I'm almost afraid to. Why wouldn't he just call? Is he too embarrassed to apologize over the phone? Is he breaking up with me? Oh god, I've heard of people getting dumped by text message. If he ever did that to me, I'd—

I open the message.

"Can da guys come to da dance?"

That's it? I'm sitting here panicking about "the relationship" and he just wants to know about the guys?

"I can only get 1 guest ticket," I text back, totally lying.

"Cant ur friends getem in?"

"U ARE my friends," I pound back.

There's a pause, and I wonder if he's gone. But then my phone vibrates back to life.

"So now Im just a friend?"

"Nooooo. U kno wha I mean."

"Fine," beeps the phone. "Ill come."

"Rly?"

"No," he types. "Psych."

"Sean!"

"KIDDING whatev u want Im thur."

I relax. This is more like it. If he was standing right in front of me, I might even say everything was normal.

"I want U!" I send back.

"Rly?" He asks.

No, psych, I think of texting back.

"Rly."

"Prove it," he says.

"I will."

"How?"

"Cm 2 da dance."

"& den?" he asks.

But now it's my turn to leave him hanging. The bell rings. I stash my phone in my locker and nearly float to my next class, a thousand pounds lighter.

thirteen

My parents get all embarrassing when they find out I'm going to the dance.

"Wonderful," my mother says, clasping her hands together.

She's been in a much better mood since the nausea stopped. She gets excited about everything.

"What will you go as? Oh, we'll find you the most adorable costume! You remember that time when you went out as a mouse? You were so cute—"

"Mom! I was six! Only babies and geeks wear costumes."

She looks hurt.

"Besides, it would be hard to b-girl in Mickey ears."

My dad pulls out his wallet. "How much are tickets?"

"Five bucks."

"Here, have a fruit punch on me, then," he says, handing me a $10 bill as dramatically as if it was a fifty.

"Thanks," I say, taking it slowly, bowing a little, pretending to grovel.

"It's just so nice to see you taking part in a social activity," he says, dabbing at the corner of his eye.

"Dad, are you crying?"

"No."

I wait for the usual pre-dance lecture about abstinence, but it doesn't come. Either they're so happy to see me doing something "social" they forget, or they think that because we're in Rivercrest, they don't have to worry about that anymore.

On Friday I race home after school to put my outfit together. The dance starts at seven. Sean is picking me up at 7:30. I have two hours: almost enough time. I need to look hot, but not in any obvious way that makes it look like I'm trying. I don't need anyone getting the idea that I have dressed up for him.

I go through three combinations before getting it just right. V-neck T—too revealing. Shimmery top with black pants—too dressy. Jeans and track jacket—not dressy enough. Finally, I emerge from my room wearing a tight aqua top with a Chinese-looking collar. The soles of my shoes, my socks, eyeshadow, retro triangly hoop earrings and the piping up the sides of my new black cargoes all match it perfectly.

Because I am not trying to sneak in a flask of anything stupid, I do not have a bag and there is nothing baggy or Halloweeny about me—no kitty ears, no bunny tail, no horns, halo or fangs. I descend the staircase slowly, pausing dramatically on the last step.

My mom looks up from one of the lounge chairs, where she is elevating her ankles. "Aren't you going to get dressed?" she asks.

I look down at my clothes.

"Oh. Sorry, sweetie." She smiles and closes her eyes again.

My dad looks at his watch when I come into the kitchen.

"Shouldn't you be getting going?" he asks. "The dance starts in fifteen minutes. Do you need a lift?" He starts to rifle under some papers for his keys.

"No, I'm good. Sean will be here in a bit."

He almost spits out his Hungry Man stew. "Sean?"

"Yeah. You remember, my *boyfriend*," I say, very slowly, so he'll understand.

"So you're not— You two didn't—?" He gestures some kind of weird together-and-apartness with his hands in the no man's land above his soup. "So he's still on the scene, then?" he finally asks, adjusting himself in his chair as though it just grew something pointy while he was sitting on it.

"Yeah," I snap. No thanks to him, he should know.

"Sean's got the car?" he asks quietly.

"Yup."

I take a Lean Cuisine from the freezer and pop it in the microwave.

My dad sighs.

When the microwave beeps, I grab my food and sit down opposite him, on the last corner of the table that doesn't have work covering it.

"Why aren't you eating with Mom?" I ask him.

"She has a headache," he says, without looking up from his laptop. "The baby is giving her a hard time."

I peel the plastic off the little microwave tray. "Is everything OK between you two?"

He looks confused. I poke my fettuccine towards the sauce in the corner of the box. "I mean, since you're in here, and she's out there, I thought maybe—"

"Nadine—" he warns, a little too loudly.

"What's going on in there?" my mom calls from the living room.

Neither of us answers.

"*Don't* upset her," he warns under his breath.

I hear the vinyl squeak as she eases herself out of her chair.

"Are you two arguing?" she asks, shuffling into the kitchen, giving me the eye that says we'd better not be.

"It's OK," says my dad. "Go back and sit down. Do you need anything? What can I get you?"

"Stop worrying, David," she says, waddling to the fridge "I can get it myself."

"Iced tea?" he asks, leaping to beat her there.

"Water."

"Coming right up," says my dad, turning her around by the shoulders and steering her back to the living room.

"Nadine?" he calls over his shoulder. "Your mother would like some water, please."

I look at the clock as I fill the glass: 7:15. Fifteen minutes till Sean comes.

I hand off the water and go back to my food. I eat every noodle one at a time but it's still only 7:25 when I'm done.

At 7:35, I go to the window. There's no sign of Sean yet. Not that I expected there would be, so soon.

I fix my makeup and double-check that I have the tickets, my keys and money in my pockets. All systems go.

I stretch.

At 7:50, I tell myself there's nothing to be worried about. The later he is, the more chance there is he'll show up in the next thirty seconds. Traffic must be heavy.

I go sit on the front steps outside and count backwards from thirty six times. That gets boring pretty fast. In exactly three minutes, in fact.

At eight, I start to feel nervous. I get my phone from inside and call him. There's no answer. But why would there be? He can't answer while he's driving.

I don't leave a message.

I go inside to fix my makeup again for the trillionth time.

"Nadine," my mother calls before I can make it up the stairs.

"Yeah?"

"Shouldn't you be gone already?"

"No."

"The dance is going to be over by the time you get there."

"No."

"I don't want you walking around in the dark by yourself, and your father has work to do. If you're going to go, get your father to drive you now."

"It's OK, I'm just waiting for a lift."

She props herself up on her elbows. "Really? Who's driving? You haven't told me about any friends from school."

I roll my eyes. "I do have friends, you know."

"Nadine," she says, returning her seat to its upright position, "before you get in a car with anyone, we need to meet them first. We need to know who your friends are."

"Mom, don't worry, it's fine—"

"Nadine—"

My father sneaks up behind me.

"She's waiting for *Sean*," he says gravely.

She closes her eyes and sinks back into her seat.

"What time is he picking you up? The dance started an hour and a half ago."

"Soon. There's traffic and—"

"So that's his excuse this time?"

"It's not an excuse!"

I can feel my dad's eyes burning holes in the back of my head.

"What about that day you were supposed to practise and he cancelled?"

"That was complicated."

"When we moved and he didn't show?"

"That's not true. He came."

"Hours late."

"So?"

"Well, it's your life," she decides. "If you want to put up with that, I can't stop you."

"He's going to come, I say."

My mom rolls her eyes.

"He is!" I yell.

A horn beeps in the driveway.

"See? *See?*" I run to the front hall. I check my reflection and smooth my clothes before throwing open the door.

"Sean!" I shout as I run to the car.

"Hey," he says coolly as he reaches over to unlock the passenger door for me.

I brush a takeout bag out of the way and sink into the seat, which is always lower than I expect it to be. The car smells like pizza, socks and smokes. I lean across the gearshift to kiss him hello. He turns his head so it lands on his cheek. I notice his cologne. It's not the one he usually wears. It smells more of mouthwash than it does of him.

I untangle my seatbelt and we pull out of the driveway.

"So, was traffic bad?" I look over at him, waiting for some big story about how it ruined his mood, but he just shrugs. He's weirdly quiet.

"Listen, Nadine," he says as we pull onto Main Street. "We gotta talk."

The seriousness in his voice makes me sit up a little straighter.

"OK. About what?" He looks annoyed.

"Me and the guys have been talking, and we think that if you're going to keep living here, then you shouldn't be in the crew anymore."

"What?" I grip the door handle.

"If you aren't going to be in Parkdale, you can't be in the crew."

"No, I heard you the first time," I spit. "What I mean is what the hell are you talking about and why are you telling me this right now? What about the Showdown?"

He throws up his hands and the car swerves a little. My stomach lurches.

"It's called the *Hogtown* Showdown for a reason, Nadine," he says, taking the wheel again. "How can you represent if you ain't even in town? Me and the guys discussed it. Breaking is about the street. It's not . . . this." He sweeps his hand around at the wide-open field to our left and the giant sign begging us to go check out the quilting expo at the library.

"It's not my choice, Sean. I can't control what my parents do. I'm doing the best I can."

He shakes his head. "No, Nadine. If you're not going to keep it real, you can't be in the crew. I'm sorry, that's just how it is."

He speeds past a stop sign.

Tears burn my eyes but I crunch my eyes shut to stop them.

"Sean, you can't treat me like this and expect me to still go out with you." I feel dizzy. All I can hear is the blood pounding in my ears. I roll down the window so I can get a little air.

Sean sighs and turns into the far end of the school

parking lot. "That's what I'm saying, Nadine. It's not going to work anymore."

The car squeals to a stop. I freeze for a second, and then I start to shake. My heart pounds. My face gets hot. I look down at my hand, and I'm gripping the door handle so hard, I think I'm going to snap it right off.

Every time I asked what was wrong and he said "nothing" and we should just enjoy the time we have, he was lying. He didn't want things to work out. He's more worried about what his friends think.

He watches me.

I breathe in and out slowly, until my grip relaxes.

"Sorry about the dance," he says, making puppy-dog eyes. "Do you still want to go?"

I summon every ounce of strength I have to laugh. "Yeah."

He turns off the engine and starts to undo his seatbelt. I put out my hand to stop him.

"Not with *you*."

He looks surprised.

"I don't need you, or permission from your poser friends, to go to a dance at my own school."

His nostrils flare.

"Yeah, *Ruckus*. The difference between me and them isn't *the street*. It's that I actually dance. I don't just talk about it."

I get out of the car and slam the door. A piece of rust falls off and lands at my feet. Sean rolls down his window.

"Fine, bitch. Guess I made the right decision."

He slams his foot on the gas so hard he almost leaves half the car in the parking lot as he speeds away. I grind the rust into the pavement with my heel. I think I'm going to be sick.

I turn to face the school and see Trashley stumbling across the lawn, done up like a princess with a pink chiffon dress and three girls following her around, carrying her train. To the right of the front steps, a group of grade niners dressed as the cast of the *Rocky Horror Picture Show* stand in a circle, smoking. I watch a pregnant, bald Britney Spears run up the stairs after a greasy Kevin Federline, and that's when I see him—Devin—in a wine-coloured smoking jacket and slippers, holding what looks like a bubble pipe, and leaning up against some girl in the doorway. She's wearing a Wonder Woman costume. Bald Britney accidentally bodychecks him in the stomach with the baby doll she's swinging by the feet. He sees me at the bottom of the stairs and suddenly jumps away from Wonder Woman. Whatever.

"Nadine!" he says. "I thought you weren't coming."

Wonder Woman touches his cheek and disappears inside, shivering.

The sounds of Hoobastank drift out the gym door. That pretty much seals it.

"I'm not."

Without Sean, there's no point. I never really wanted to go anyway.

"How can I persuade you to change your mind?" Devin asks, puffing into the bubble pipe.

"You can't," I say, flattening a stray bubble under my foot. He winces.

"I'll buy you a punch."

"You sound like my dad."

"I'll battle you for it," he says. "I win, you stay. You win, you do what you want."

He puts the pipe in his pocket, steps away from the door, calmly grabs his right foot in his left hand and does one single ridiculous thread-the-needle, leaping through it with his left foot, before launching into some embarrassing toprock, moving towards me down the front steps.

"Are you making fun of me?"

"No!" he says. "I—"

Without waiting to hear the answer, I dance back with sharp, angry toprock. I burn him with footwork. A smile spreads across his face, but what he doesn't know is, I'm not really battling him, I'm battling Sean—the calls he screened, the way he let his boys badmouth me behind my back, how he couldn't be bothered to find me here, except to fight with me, how he's so afraid of what people think he'd kill us off without even trying. I'm battling my parents and the stupid baby and the whole ridiculous idea of trying to fit in here in the first place. With each step, I'm fighting a lump that's welling up in my throat. I want to pound it into the ground, kick it out of myself and twist the whole school, the crowd that's gathering, my parents and myself into it until there's nothing left of any of us.

Led by Devin, the thickening crowd starts to cheer me on, and they have no idea what they're cheering for. The only one not cheering is Slasher. I notice her standing on the edge of the circle with her arms crossed, watching intently. I wonder for a second why she's not out back following Trashley, but then I push her out of my mind, and instead get it into my head that I'm going to do windmills.

I kick, turn, duck down to the ground and unleash a flurry of footwork, as if it's even possible to build more momentum than I already have. I swing my leg out—

Suddenly a hand clamps down on my shoulder. It happens so fast, I fall on my bad shoulder and land on the pavement before I even realize what's going on.

"Hey!"

I can't see what's attacking me. I have a nightmare moment where I imagine Sean came back to the dance with Rackit Klub and I'm about to be clawed by Jazmin.

"Just what do you think you're doing?" shouts a voice I finally recognize. Mr. Winkley leans over me, his angry face sandwiched between pointy ears and a dark wig.

I jump to my feet.

"I'm danc—"

"Don't give me that. You think I don't know what this is? Someone's going to break a neck. You're going to start a fight."

"I'm not—"

"I don't need any more trouble from you, Nadine Durant. These kids came here to dance and have a good time. They deserve your respect, not some fight. I can't have you bringing violence into this school."

"You're the violent—"

"They call it *break* dancing for a reason, Nadine."

"It's not like—"

"This will go on your permanent record!" he yells so hard his tricorder falls off his belt.

I barely hear him. My shoulder hurts and my outfit is dirty and all I can think of is Sean and Rackit Klub and the Hogtown Showdown and how I never asked for any of this.

I turn to leave and Winkley grabs me by the wrist.

"Let go!" I yank my hand back. "Touch me again and I'll call the cops. Worry about your own record."

His lips tighten. "That's a detention, missy."

"Go to hell!" I yell to no one and everyone and then run as fast as I can across the dark parking lot.

fourteen

My parents are surprised to see me home so early.

"Are you happy now? You got what you wanted!" I yell.

My mother presses her hands to her temples. "What happened, Nadine?"

"We broke up. Congratulations."

"Oh, honey—" She tries to lean forward in her chair, over the baby. "I'm so sorry."

"Sorry? You're not sorry. This is exactly what you wanted. This is why we moved here. Well, good for you, it's working."

My mom makes like she's going to get up out of the chair, but my dad shoots her a look that makes her lie back down again.

"Nadine," says my dad. "I realize you're upset right now, and I'm sorry about what happened with Sean, but you need to grow up and realize that everything everywhere is not all about *you.*"

"No, it's not. It's about how *you* want me to live, and what *you* want me to do, and what *you* want me to be, and who *you* want me to like."

"Nadine—" he warns.

"*You* need to realize that I am never going to be only what you want me to be."

"Nadine," he says. "Your mother is very sick right now, and you are putting her under a lot of stress. This is not the time for your hysterics."

"Dad!"

"Nadine. I mean it. One more word, and you are grounded."

I laugh. "Grounded from *what,* Dad? I have nothing left."

"Nadine, perhaps when you are older you will realize that if you have problems with *everyone* in your life, it's most likely *you* who needs to change."

That same feeling I had as Sean tore away in the car, I feel it again, only stronger. I feel lonely, trapped—like I'm going to be sick.

I shove my feet back in my shoes, grab my jacket and fling open the door.

"If you walk out that door, Nadine, you are grounded. No dancing for the rest of the year."

"You can't do that."

"Oh can't I? Mark my words, I'll—"

"No, I mean you *can't.* There is *nothing* you can do to make me stop b-girling."

"Walk out that door and you'll see nothing but school and the inside of your bedroom for the rest of the year."

"Change the locks if you really mean it," I shout, and slam the door behind me.

The night is cold. I don't know how I didn't notice before. I guess I ran most of the way home. But now I feel that awful chill that seems to come from the inside. I wrap my arms around myself as tight as I can. It doesn't help.

I have nowhere to go. I want to run all the way back to Parkdale. Hitch a ride. Jump a train. Whatever. But then what? No one is waiting for me there, either.

I remember my dad's $10 in my pocket. I can buy myself some time. And some warmth.

Pretty much the only place in town that's open this late is the Breakfast Barn, which never closes. Because you never know when you might have a pancake emergency in Rivercrest. I force myself to jog there because I'm not getting any warmer walking. The place is practically empty, but the waitress doesn't want to seat me because all their tables are booths and I'm by myself.

"I'm just going to sit here, OK," I say, diving for a table about halfway down the first row.

She rolls her eyes and I order the largest basket of fries they have, and a pitcher of water, even though it comes with a free coffee (coffee with fries? Ew) and I eat as slowly as I can, chewing each bite thirty times, while I stare into space with my hoodie still up, blocking the rest of the restaurant from my peripheral vision.

The fries are tongue-burning hot, crispy, and just the right degree of oily-gross. I eat them plain, with no salt or vinegar or ketchup, so it's all about the heat and the thick, crispy edges.

Slowly, as my hands warm up and I gradually burn all the feeling off the tip of my tongue, I start to relax. My body gets all warm and floppy and tired, and every thought in my head just seems to melt away.

I know where I stand now—with Sean, with my parents, with school. I don't need to waste any more energy thinking about them.

I grab a kiddie placemat and a crayon from the cup on the table and start to doodle—little stick b-girls doing little stick moves.

The RHS dance must have let out, because as I get to the bottom of my basket of fries, the Breakfast Barn starts to fill up with freaks in tired, beat-up Halloween costumes—a vampire with half his makeup melting into his collar, a fairy with a broken wand, a drag queen wearing work boots, carrying sparkly shoes in his hands.

I pull my hoodie tighter and try to ignore them, but then, out of the corner of my eye, I see Slasher come in with Trashley and her posse. I shrink down to make myself invisible, but they start to make their way across the room towards me.

Trying to escape as anonymously as possible, I leave five bucks on the table and get up from my seat without waiting for the waitress or my change. As I head towards the back door, Slasher sees me. Our eyes meet. I freeze. I don't need any trouble out here, by myself in the middle of the night, with my parents just about ready to lock me out of the house and pretend I never lived.

Someone waves a hand in front of Slasher's face.

"Hello, Earth to Madi. What are you looking at?"

She blinks and shakes her head. I run out the door.

As I walk by the window with my dark hoodie pulled way down over my eyes, I see Slasher staring down at the b-girl doodles I left behind. She slides them under her menu and laughs as someone blows a straw wrapper at her head from the other side of the table.

fifteen

When I walk in the door, I can tell that something is weird. All the lights are on. But what *isn't* weird about tonight?

I call out, "Hello? I'm home," but there's no answer. I figure my parents went to bed early to make some kind of point.

I wander around the kitchen, opening cabinet doors and not really trying to be quiet about it. I grab a bottle of raspberry ginger ale and take it down to the lounge—the glamorous, glamorous lounge that no one ever sits in but me.

I sit down with all my crew DVDs and sort through them. Every time I come across one that has Sean in it, or even his voice, I frisbee it across the room into the garbage, so it clangs loudly off the side of the can. I make it about halfway through the stack before my eyes start to get heavy and I fall asleep on the couch with my clothes and makeup on.

I wake up early because the phone is ringing. I wait for my parents to get it because it's not like it's going to be for me. They let it ring until it goes to voice mail. I roll over on my face and go back to sleep. It rings again. What's their problem? They never had any trouble beating me to the phone when it was Sean calling.

I try to keep my eyes shut, but there's no denying it: I am awake. I have to get out of here before my parents wake up and try to keep me locked in all day.

I quickly wash my face with cold water in the down-stairs sink, shove my feet in some shoes and grab an extra sweater and my puffy winter vest. The phone starts to ring again as I slip out the door.

It's so early, the moon is still out in the crisp blue sky. I don't think I've ever seen that before on a weekend.

I go to the convenience store and get a stale muffin and some O.J. I slowly make my way to the bridge, scuffing my feet in the dirt. I sit on the bottom step with my breakfast, spilling crumbs on the ground and staring into space.

The tag looks tiny now, in the upper right-hand corner, over the skyline that is definitely Rivercrest and a silhouette that looks like . . . a b-girl doing some kind of flying kick. Fascinating.

My phone rings. It's my dad. I shove it back in my pocket without answering.

I take my time doing some lazy warm-up stretches and then I practise for a while on the cold ground, but my heart isn't in it. I tell myself I'll just do a few mills and call it a day, but I set the first one up and I can't get around more than twice.

I imagine Rackit Klub showing up at the Showdown with some random guy in my place. I can hear the snickers and imagine the messageboard chatter as every crew in the city gossips about how I got cut because I couldn't do the big tricks. I can hear them all clamouring to get on board and say that it's nice that girls try to break, but b-girls will never be able to compete on the same level as b-boys.

On my second try, I smash my hip against the ground so hard, I feel sick.

My phone rings again. It's my dad's cell. Again.

"Hello?"

"Nadine!" he says, out of breath. "I've been trying to get a hold of you all morning. Where have you been?"

"Asleep. Working out."

"We got you that phone for emergencies. Remember that: that is *my* phone. I bought it. I pay for it. You're just using it."

"Yeah, fine."

"Everything's OK now."

"Why wouldn't it be?"

"You didn't notice we're not home?"

"No. Not until now. Where are you?"

"I'm at the hospital."

Whoa. What? I feel a flash of guilt, mixed with confusion.

"Hos—? What happened?"

"Your mother had a scare with her blood pressure and the baby—"

A wave of queasiness washes over me. The last time we talked about blood pressure and hospitals was when my grandmother—

"Nadine? You still there?"

"Yeah."

"She's OK, Nadine. The doctors were worried that it might be pre-eclampsia but we think it's only run-of-the-mill hypertension."

"Oh," I squeak.

"That just means high blood pressure, Nadine. It can be dangerous if the baby has trouble getting enough oxygen. But we're going to take care of your mother and she's going to be OK. She's on some medication and she's sleeping right now. We'll probably be here for a few more hours. The doctors want to monitor her a while longer—just until they can make sure that she doesn't need anything else."

"Is the baby . . . ?"

"The baby's fine. You might not know this but your mom had the same trouble when she was pregnant with you."

"OK. Um . . . is there anything I can do?" My voice comes out all wobbly.

"No," he says gently. "Just stay out of trouble, OK? We'll see you around dinner."

"Kay. Bye."

I close my phone—I mean, my dad's phone—and sit on the ledge staring at it while everything he just told me starts to sink in.

I gave my mom a hard time. What if she had to go to the hospital because *I* stressed her out so much? What if something happens to the baby? I know I say I hate the baby, but I didn't think I could actually hurt her.

My chest starts to tighten.

Breathe, I tell myself.

I press my palms against my eyeballs to keep from crying.

I walk home slowly, the long way.

When I get home, I have a proper shower to help me feel at least a little more human, and then I make myself a peanut butter sandwich for lunch, and some hot chocolate. There's not much else in the fridge because grocery shopping is always my mom's job.

I walk around the house, turning off all the lights my parents left on. I find my mother's bathrobe draped over the upstairs railing and I put it back in her closet, with her slippers.

I run the dishwasher and the vacuum. Then I get some money from the oh-so-secret stash on my dad's dresser and grab my bike and my backpack and head over to the giant grocery store on the far side of town.

When I was really little, my mom and I used to go to the crappy orange Price Slicer store and she would let me sit in the cart—not in the kiddie seat, but in the actual cart—and she would slowly bury me in groceries while we shopped, which was like even cooler than making a fort out of the cushions and blankets in the living room. To keep me from getting bored, we would play this game where I was allowed to choose one treat for the week, and it had to be something in one of the yellow no-name boxes, and I would pretend I wanted everything in the store.

"Yellow boxes, Nadine. You can have *one thing* that's in a yellow box. A mop head? You don't *really* want a mop head."

And then I would giggle hysterically while she filled up the cart with boring junk like vitamins.

Every time I get mad at her, I think of stuff like this, and then I feel bad for it. I wish we could just go back to that and she didn't have to take everything so seriously now. All this *stuff* we have now, I would trade all of it—everything except b-girling—if we could just go back to when we didn't fight about everything all of the time.

I get to the giant fancy grocery store and lock my bike up to the place where you're supposed to get shopping carts. I know even less about cooking than my parents do, so I walk through the aisles aimlessly at first. It turns out that frozen dinners cost, like, a zillion dollars, and all the good ones look kind of salty anyway.

I find a salad-in-a-bag that looks manageable, and then I figure it might go with some pasta. I pick up a box of whole-wheat spaghetti—extra healthy for my mom and the baby—and I manage to track down a bottle of sauce with mushrooms that says "low sodium" on it. I find a salad dressing to match—"Italian" sounds about right—and I pick a super-healthy fruit-salad-in-a-jar for dessert. It all comes to $14 and I have $20 on me, so I go back and get a small bottle of my mom's favourite bubble bath and add it to the bill.

When I get home, I put the salad in a big bowl and cut up our only tomato to make it more interesting. I put the pasta on to boil and set the table. I don't know how hot the stove is supposed to be to heat pasta sauce, so it boils and spits up all over the white stovetop. I am cleaning it up like a maniac, desperately hoping there's still enough for three people to eat, when my parents come home.

"We could order a pizza. Oh no, wait—" I can hear my dad saying through the door from the garage.

I rinse the cloth and leap to put my body between them and the mess.

"Sorry I made a mess," I say, trying to beat them to the punch.

My dad stops and looks around the kitchen, amazed.

"You cooked?"

"Yeah."

"On the *stove?*"

"Yeah."

"Does it work?"

I start to laugh. "I don't know. I think I burned the sauce. Sorry."

My mom looks so tired, but her eyes light up.

"Oh, baby, no, it's wonderful. Come here and give me a hug." She wraps me in her arms. "Oh, baby, I love you sooo much."

I feel like I'm going to cry again, so I excuse myself to go change into a shirt that's not covered in spaghetti sauce.

We don't talk much during dinner, but my mom smiles and my dad keeps looking around the table and sighing like it's the best meal he's ever eaten.

sixteen

I dodge and weave my way through Monday morning, using back doors and side stairwells, avoiding eye contact with everyone.

People from my own grade shoot me the evil eye, and yet, everywhere I go, niners are smiling at me, whispering to each other.

"That's her. That's the girl from the dance."

"She like did this thing where she like kicked and then she was turning, and then she landed in a headstand."

"And she told Winkley to go to h-e-l-l."

"No way."

"Way."

"Well my sister's in grade twelve and she said that girl is a loser."

"Shut up."

"Yeah, Becky, you're jealous. And your sister is ugly. Nadine could kick her ass."

Mr. Winkley finally catches up with me on my spare.

"Nadine Durant, where do you think you're going?"

I say nothing.

"That's right, Nadine. My office. Now."

He marches me down the last twenty feet to his office and throws himself down behind his desk.

"Nadine . . . Nadine, Nadine, Nadine . . . ," he mutters, flipping through the filing cabinet as if he doesn't already know who I am or why I'm there. Finally, after a million, maybe two million years, he pulls out a red folder and places it on his desk. He leans back in his chair and crosses his hands behind his head. He smiles. His moustache is so long, it comes down over his teeth.

"What happened at the dance was unacceptable. I've been doing my reading. I know what happens to kids who breakdance." He reaches under his desk and pulls out a stack of photocopies. "Alopecia. Neck strain. Acute scrotal pain."

Oh yeah. Scrotal pain. That's what I'm worried about.

"If you want to be treated like an adult, inform yourself about the risks of your behaviour, Nadine. Make better choices. Stop hanging around troublemakers like Devin—"

"I don't *hang around* Devin. I don't even like him."

He holds up a hand to shush me.

"I'm not going to argue with you, Nadine. No more violence. No back-talking. Better choices. Those are the rules."

Whatever.

"Do we have a deal?"

He sticks his hand across the desk.

"Fine."

"OK. Then I'll spare you the detention. This time."

He has a damp limp noodle handshake: the worst kind.

I have Media, Youth and Society first period after lunch. Not much usually happens in this class—mostly we sit around watching movies, and everyone sleeps through it except for keeners like Slasher, and then the teacher tries to get people to talk about the movie. I mostly watch, but with my earbuds on under my hair—which is about all they're good for. (Ever heard of *bass*, headphone makers?) Michael Moore movies and old episodes of *Degrassi* come off *way* different with the entire Wu-Tang Clan shouting over top of them.

I'm just turning the volume up, waiting for the teacher, Ms. Finch, to turn the lights down, when suddenly she walks across the room and wheels the TV into the closet. Then she comes back to the front of the class and leans on her desk with her arms crossed over her cardigan, grinning as she waits for us to notice and pay attention. I put my headphones back in my bag and watch her scratch the back of her left knee with her right Birkenstock. Finally, she smoothes out her stiff blue skirt and announces: "We're going to try something new today!"

No one reacts at all.

"You're going to program your own lesson plan!"

There's a nanosecond of silence while that sinks in, and then whiny Britney's hand shoots up.

"How are we supposed to be graded on our *own* plan? This wasn't in the outline."

"Life is about more than grades," says Finch, and then the room gets really noisy. People at the back start planning how their plan is going to be a party at Trashley's house. People at the front plan to stay home and play Xbox. Across the room, Slasher puts her head down and starts writing so hard, I think her hand might fall off. Whiny Britney looks like she's about to cry.

The Finch claps.

"OK, OK, let's have some ground rules before we get carried away. Number one: your assignment is to choose any documentary you like and write an analytical report covering the issues you decide are important. It's open season on everything we're covering this semester: sociology, economics, religion, geographical, political and genera-tional context. It's up to you. Dig deep and show me what you can take away from the film. How do you relate it to *your* environment?"

Everyone groans.

"But how do we know what we're being marked on?" the WB asks again. Finch ignores her.

"This is going to be a group project."

As soon as she says the word "group," everyone cheers except the people who are scowling. Two jock dudes in the back high-five each other. Half the girls in the class start eye-ing each other up, desperately trying to lock down their groups so everyone knows how cool they are and that every-one wants to work with them.

The Finch clears her throat. "Not so fast. I have your groups right here," she says, holding up a list. "There will be no switching groups. No substitutions. No complaining. You will work together. Everyone in the group will receive the same grade."

The entire room groans. WB's arm reaches so high I think it's going to dislocate from her shoulder. Finch ignores her and reads out the groups. Jock, Chodd (his par-ents couldn't choose between Chad and Todd) and Duck (Doug, but he hurt his nose in hockey and when he says his name now, he sounds like a 200-pound bird)—they're happy. Two Tiffanys and an Emma—Emma's going to get eaten alive. A group of four geeks together—they're pleased but no one cares.

It takes so long for Finch to get to my name, I practi-cally fall asleep waiting. What do I care what group I'm in anyway? It's going to suck no matter what. When she finally does call "Nadine," and everyone starts laughing, I look up confused. The only people not laughing are Slasher, some Staci girl who always looks pissed and Marc with a C, who sucks up to Jock and Chodd, even though they make fun of him constantly and keep him around to make him do stuff for them. Slasher presses her face to her hands. Marc goes bright red. Staci rolls her eyes and stares up at the ceiling. This is my group.

Finch gives the signal and all at once everyone rearranges their chairs into groups. Somehow my group just knows to gather around Slasher's desk. She's like a home-work magnet. I drag my chair over slowly, like it weighs a thousand pounds. Staci and Marc shuffle their chairs away from mine, so they're all bunched up under Slasher's armpits. I consider hissing at them just to get a reaction, but I can't be bothered.

We sit in silence for five minutes. Slasher seems to be waiting for someone else to get the ball rolling, and Marc and Staci won't look me in the eye.

Around the room, everyone is hunched in circles, talking. Whiny Britney's group looks like they've already chosen their doc and are divvying up responsibilities. "I want the final edit," I hear her say, bossy. Two Tiffanys are shouting at Emma about being boring. The geeky four are whispering intensely, like they really believe everyone is a) listening, b) seriously going to try to steal their idea and c) not able to predict that they'll choose *Trekkers*. Chodd is telling Jock a joke so dirty, Duck is pretending he wants to puke.

"So . . . ," I finally say.

"Let's get started, then," Slasher says, cutting me off. Taking her notebook out, she looks around her desk at each of us.

"Who has ideas? Staci? Marc? N*adine?*" she says like my own name is an insult.

Staci coughs. Marc rolls his eyes and crosses his arms over his chest.

Without waiting for me to answer, Slasher says, "OK, well, as long as no one has anything, what about *Born into Brothels?* Or *An Inconvenient Truth?*" Marc giggles and looks back at Jock. Staci cleans under her nails with the corner of her student ID.

"Well, if you want to do something else, *suggest* something else," says Slasher, kicking Marc under her desk.

"OK, OK," says Marc, laughing. "Wasn't *Jackass: The Movie* a documentary?"

Slasher stares at him, hard. "This isn't a joke."

"All right," he says. "Chill. What about *The Aristocrats?*"

Staci snorts. "This is so lame."

Another minute passes as Slasher taps her pencil against her notebook, Marc throws wadded paper notes to the back of the class and Staci stares into nowhere.

"Um," I hear myself say as I raise my hand just a little.

I'm not really sure about saying my idea out loud. I know anything I say will probably only make my life worse, and besides, it's not like I'm so awesome at school that anyone needs to hear what I think. But at least I *have* an idea.

Slasher narrows her eyes at me, like she gets to be the boss just because she's the most uptight.

"I know a good documentary," I say, my voice suddenly stronger. "*The Freshest Kids.* It's about b-boying. I mean breakdancing."

There's this weird pause where Slasher looks almost happy that someone said something but then seems disappointed that it was me. The group gets even quieter than before as Staci and Marc practically stop breathing just to show how completely they're not listening to me.

"Breakdancing?" Slasher finally says. "Like in the eighties?"

I can't tell if she's being sarcastic or just clueless.

"Whatever. You'll probably hate it anyway," I say.

"No," she says defensively. "I just don't know what the *broader themes* of *breakdancing* are. How are we supposed to make it relate to *our* environment, as in *Rivercrest?*"

It almost sounds like she's taking my suggestion seriously.

"Well," I say, my mouth going dry as everyone slowly turns to stare me down. "It starts in the sixties. There's lots of scenes from back in the day, but it continues to, like, almost now. It shows how these inner-city kids invented b-boying out of basically nothing, and then, like, everybody added to it and changed it and spread it around the world. There's all this stuff about how trying to make it commercial almost killed it. All the original b-boys were almost our age. We could maybe use that stuff to relate it to RHS."

Did I just say all that? I think I almost sounded nerdy or convincing or something.

"It's not cheesy, is it?" says Slasher.

"No. It's not cheesy."

She chews on her pen cap for a minute until she realizes she's chewing on her pen cap and then looks kind of grossed out at herself.

"Well," she says, sighing. "Since we don't have any other suggestions"—she glares at Marc and Staci—"I'll write it down."

"I can bring it in so we can watch it," I say. "We can give it a test screening."

"OK," she says. "That sounds good."

"It does?"

"Yeah. We can always fall back on *An Inconvenient Truth* if it doesn't work out."

"Is Al Gore your boyfriend or something?" asks Marc.

She ignores him.

"I bet he is. I bet you have his face on a poster on your wall, and you French kiss it every night before you go to bed. I bet you close your eyes and think about Al Gore and touch—"

Slasher slams her notebook shut on her desk. "So does Tuesday at lunch work for everyone? I'll book the AV room, and we'll watch *The Freshest Kids*."

I nod.

Staci has already taken her chair back to her own desk.

Marc points and laughs at Slasher.

"Marc!"

"Yeah, yeah, whatever. I'll be there. Relax."

Take that, Winkley. I may not be allowed to dance on school property, but I'm going to get b-girling in the building one way or another.

On Tuesday at lunch, I track down the AV room. I didn't even know we had an AV room. I have to look it up in my student guide.

Slasher is already waiting, fussing with the DVD player, even though I'm the one with the DVD in my bag.

Marc runs by in the hall behind me.

"Marc!" Slasher yells after him, and he skids to a stop. "You're watching the movie with us now, right?"

"Oh yeah, right," he says, running a hand through his hair. "Right, I'll be right there." And then he takes off, full speed down the hall.

"Any sign of Staci?" I ask.

"Yeah, right," she says, closing the door behind me. "Let's just get this over with, shall we?" She puts her hand out for the DVD.

I find the disk in my bag and hand it to her, sliding the case across the table so she can read the liner notes. She ignores it and slides the disk in the player.

The opening sequence rolls. A guy hits a freeze on the 125th Street platform. A subway rolls over a chain-link bridge. The New York City skyline is blurry in the distance and I feel this incredible rush of homesickness, not for New York—I've never even been there—but for all the things my parents hate about the city, the subway, graffiti, noise, concrete, guys beatboxing out back after school . . .

Slasher sits across the table from me with her skirt tucked under her and one knee crossed over the other, skeptically watching, with her pen ready and her notebook in her lap.

Then the serious dancing kicks in and my homesickness is replaced by jealousy. Before the opening credits are even done, I see five things I'd like to do better and two I can't do at all. I'm like, *oh, THAT's what that move is supposed to look like.* It's depressing and inspiring all at the same time.

Kool Herc drives across the screen in his convertible with the giant speakers in the back, practically inventing hip hop on the spot. I can't believe someone caught that on tape. It's not like every b-boy in town had a camera in his phone back then.

Slasher looks at her watch and yawns.

The video goes through all the different things that different people have added to b-boying—the early uprockers who used to line up to battle each other. The first guys who decided to go down to the floor and dance with their hands, the Latino kids who came up with backspins and stuff, then L.A. heads introducing popping and locking and power.

There's this big battle at the Lincoln Center that the whole world shows up to watch, and then we see this nerdy guy put a crew together just to try to make it commercial, and some b-boys get in movies like *Flashdance,* and then all of a sudden, breaking is at the Olympics, and b-boys are throwing down for the president in these terrible spandex outfits that make me embarrassed to know my parents were alive at the same time as this was all going down.

Dudes are touring Europe, and heads in L.A. are pushing things to the next level and people are pointing out how b-boying is connected to graf, DJing and rap.

I notice Slasher is starting to take a lot of notes now. By the time we get to the part where people start calling breaking a fad, she almost looks worried. But then something beeps in her bag, and she reaches over and pulls out a stopwatch.

"Whoa. Time's up," she says, blinking as she turns the lights back on. "We have to stop here or we'll be late for class."

A stopwatch. The girl carries a freaking stopwatch.

"Do you want to finish watching it tomorrow, or—?"

"Um," she says.

"Oh," I say. "You hate it, right?"

"No. I just don't think we need to waste any more time evaluating it. It's a good film. No one else will choose anything like it. Finch will eat it up. We should just go ahead and use it."

"Really?"

I take a step back and try to figure out if she's just messing with me and I'm about to get the hard end of the mental lacrosse stick.

"What about Marc and Staci?"

She shrugs. "They can be in charge of colouring in the report cover for all I care. If you and I are going to end up doing all the work, we should at least get to pick the movie."

I tense a little at those words—"all the work." Her eyebrows narrow.

"You're going to actually do this, right? I'm agreeing we should go with *your* movie. You *have* to do the work. You're the expert on this stuff! You can't just *weasel*—"

"Hey!" I shout. "I'm here aren't I? Why do you assume—?"

"OK, god, don't be so defensive."

"Don't be a bitch," I say under my breath.

"What?"

"Nothing."

She's not worth it.

"So when can we meet to work on this for real?" she says, organizing everything back into her bag.

I need at least two days away from this chick before I can even think about looking at her again. She's making me nervous with all this stopwatch homework obsessive business.

"I dunno. Thursday after class?"

"OK," she says, making a mark in her dayplanner. "I'll book the room. Don't be late."

seventeen

At lunch on Thursday, my dad calls, and I feel such a burst of panic, I almost don't answer. He never calls me at school. What if my mom's having problems again? What if the baby is being born *right now?* That would make her one . . . two . . . four months early. Can a baby survive that? What would that do to my mom?

But I do answer, and he just wants to know what I'm doing after school.

"I have to watch a movie for—"

"OK, so nothing too important. Wait for your mother and me at a quarter to four."

"But, Dad, it's for—"

"Nadine, don't argue with me. We'll pick you up at the side door."

"Where are we going?"

I figure it's gotta be something awful like family counselling or the dentist or we're joining Scientology.

"We are going to go, as a family, and pick out some things for the baby's room."

Something like that.

"You want me to skip out on a group project for shop—?"

"We won't be gone forever," he says, starting to sound a little annoyed. "You can study after dinner."

"It's a *group*—"

"C'mon, Nadine, you know us old fuddy-duddies have no taste. We need your help."

"You mean, like you needed my help picking out the house? Like how I got to decorate my own room?"

His voice gets lower, like he's on the verge of chewing me out but he can't because he's at his desk in cubicle land.

"Wait for us after school, Nadine. No more excuses," he says and hangs up.

I ditch the rest of my sandwich to go looking for Slasher.

I can't believe this. *I* am looking for *Slasher*. On *purpose*. At *lunch*. My life is not my own.

I take a deep breath, count to ten and make the long walk across the caf to Trashley's table.

Slasher isn't there. There's some new girl in her place—a Britney or someone. Trashley is playing with her hair.

I don't know what to say, so I just stand there waiting for someone to notice.

"What do *you* want?" a Tiffany asks me, sticking her hand out as if to stop me coming any closer, as if the toxic cloud of perfume hovering over the table would even let me.

"I'm looking for Madi."

Trashley laughs. "Like *we'd* know where she is."

"Yeah," says the new popular Britney. "Doesn't she spend all her time with losers like you now?"

Interesting.

I resist the temptation to join in and rip Slasher apart behind her back. It just won't mean as much if she's not here to hear it.

"OK then," I say, faking a smile. "Thanks for your help. Have a lovely day."

But they've already forgotten I'm there, and as fascinating as that was, I'm no closer to finding Slasher.

I go to the library. She's not there. The office—no sign of her. The AV room is empty. She's not in any of the gyms. I don't know where her locker is, so I walk all the halls. But I still don't find her. We don't have any classes together in the afternoon. I hate to say it, but I wish I had her cell number. I could text it in instead of wasting all this time looking for her.

I'm sitting on my bag on the curb after school, shivering and waiting for my parents, who are late, when suddenly the door slams open behind me and Slasher comes storming down the front steps.

"*There* you are! What the hell are you doing? I've been waiting for you—"

"Whoa, whoa, calm down. I've been looking for you since lunch. My dad called. He says I can't stay today."

"But we have the pro—"

"I know. He wouldn't listen."

"Well what are we going to do?" she yells, her voice getting higher.

"We'll reschedule."

"But for *when?* The project is due—"

My dad's car pulls up. His window slides down.

"Nadine! How was your day, sweetheart? Who's your friend?" he asks, putting on his whole happy-family act.

"She's not my friend," I say too quickly.

"Madi Scott-Biggs," says Slasher, sidestepping me to shake his hand. Suck-up.

"We're working on a project together," I say.

"Big project," says Madi. "Worth forty percent of our mark. We were supposed to be working on it *right now.*"

She smiles even bigger and faker than he does, and the setting sun blinds him as it reflects back off her obsessively straight teeth.

"Oh my, that does sound important," says my dad, in exactly the same tone of voice he used to use to tell me my mud pies were delicious when I was five.

"I *told* you."

"Well, Nadine," says my mom, leaning across my dad to yell out the window, "why don't you invite Madi over after school tomorrow? You can do your work then."

"On a Friday, Mom? I'm sure she already has plans."

The last thing I want is Slasher in my house, snooping around, taking notes, judging how lame everything is so she can report back to her pretend friends on Monday.

"No, actually," says Madi. "That would be fine. I really want to get this done."

"There. Don't be silly, Nadine," says my mother. "You'll have fun."

"But we need to use the AV room."

"For what? There's a perfectly good TV in the *lounge*."

"That sounds perfect, Mrs. . . ."

"Just call me Mrs. D.," says my mom.

Mrs. D.?

"OK, cool, Mrs. D.! I'll see you tomorrow."

I'm going to puke.

"She seems really nice," says my mom as we pull onto the highway.

"Where are we going, anyway?"

"The Buy Stuff outlet," my dad says. "It's so good to see you making some real friends finally."

"We're not friends. We have to work on *one* project

together. Why'd you have to invite her to our *house?*"

"Oh, Nadine, don't be like that," says my mom.

I laugh. "God, you're so clueless."

"Well, perhaps if you'd enlighten us—"

"Why? You always hate all my real friends."

"Nadine," says my dad in his warning-me-for-the-last-and-only-time voice, "do not speak to your mother like that."

"Fine. Can we just drop the subject?"

We drive around the Buy Stuff parking lot for an hour, looking for the closest possible parking space to the door, so my mom doesn't have to walk more than necessary. Not that she's not going to walk fifty miles *inside* the store, which is like a giant warehouse of stuff and stuff and more stuff, most of it house stuff.

My parents grab a cart the size of our car and make a beeline for the baby section, which is right beside the paint section. I drag my feet behind them. This store even smells boring.

By the time we leave, eleven hours later, they have talked themselves down to some really basic wood-looking furniture, pale yellow paint, lacy white curtains and some wallpaper border things with pink bunnies on them that I actually picked.

Get it? Hip hop? Bunnies? Haha. Maybe it's too subtle.

When we get to the cash, my mom's debit card won't go through.

"Oh, that's right," says my mom. "The education savings just went through on that account. Do you have your MasterCard, David?"

"It's maxed," he says under his breath.

"I'm saving room on my Visa for groceries," my mom says.

My dad pulls out an Amex card I've never seen before. My mom frowns and twists her gloves into a knot. The check-out girl hands us a ticket to go pick everything up.

"Well, that was fun!" my mom says brightly as we get in the car.

My dad taps his hand impatiently against the steering wheel as she struggles to get her seatbelt done up over her belly and her winter coat.

eighteen

Slasher meets me at my locker after school on Friday. I can't believe this. I have to bring Slasher home with me. I have to walk all the way home with Slasher. She's going to know where I live.

As we leave the school, she keeps looking back over her shoulder and craning her neck to see down the hall, or else she looks at her feet and kind of hides her face in her bag while she looks for—or pretends to look for—I don't know what. Oh right—her reputation, maybe?

We walk right by Trashley and Co., and they don't say anything. They don't even look at Slasher but I *know* they see her. It's like they never even met. We all just imagined the beginning of the year.

When we get outside, I put my headphones on. I'll hear enough of Slasher later while we're working. I wish I'd kept my mouth shut like Staci.

Taking the hint, Slasher trails behind me on the sidewalk, fixing her hair and makeup in the mirror of her pocket compact.

"You don't have to do that," I tell her, turning my music off as we get close to my street. "It's only my parents."

She glares at me and then goes back to fiddling with the compact.

She doesn't need the help. She already looks like something my mom picked out of a catalogue of what my friends should be like. She's wearing a skirt again—brown corduroy, with a high waist. Unlike my cords, which are all worn and stretched and mashed, her skirt is crisp and velvety, like it's never been worn before. Her tights are the expensive kind that are ribbed without being woolly. Her jacket is grey and comes exactly to mid-thigh, with no bulges in the pockets, and she's carrying a flat over-the-shoulder bag, not a backpack. She has fluffy earmuffs instead of headphones. I'm almost positive that under the coat she is wearing an actual sweater set. My mom will faint. She'll ask her to move in. She'll try to hire her to give me lady lessons.

It's Friday. Who dresses up on a Friday?

As we round the corner onto my street, I can see my mom peering out through the curtains, impatiently trying to scope us out. She's probably bored out of her mind after taking the day off work to monitor her blood pressure. If Slasher notices, she doesn't say anything. As we walk up the driveway, she disappears from the window, and by the time I open the door, she has assumed a "normal" position and is acting "natural."

"Madi! Good to see you again! Come on in!" says my mom, with forced cheeriness I haven't even heard her use at work.

"How was your day, darling?" she asks me.

"Just keen!" I practically shout with false enthusiasm.

Slasher takes in the dazzling scene of the front hall as my mom takes her coat. (Yup, I was right, sweater set.)

"You have a lovely home, Mrs. Durant."

"Oh, thank you," says my mom, pressing a hand to her heart. "Are you girls hungry? I made snacks!"

She leads us into the living room, where she has laid out an elaborate platter of cheese and crackers.

"So, Madi, that's a pretty name. Is it short for Madison?" my mom asks, taking a seat at the opposite end of the sofa from Slasher. I grab a chair at the far end of the room.

"Yeah . . . but that doesn't really work for me. It's Madi," says Slasher.

"Oh?"

"Yeah." She giggles as though it might be outrageous. "Once I even thought it might be cool to go by just Mad, but that didn't really work out. Every time I introduced myself, someone would ask me, 'Why? What's wrong?'"

I roll my eyes and my mom shoots me a warning glance.

Within minutes, Slasher has totally bent my mother to her will, going on and on about her father's law firm, running for the cure and so much other bullshit. I lose track until my mom drops the big question—the one that will get Slasher invited over every Friday for the rest of my life if she answers it right:

"So, Madi, what are your plans for the future?"

Sean failed this test by saying how he might miss the game on Saturday because his mom said he had to change the oil in her car. But that's not going to happen to Slasher. She comes out with a big story about saving the world through higher education.

"I want to do journalism at U of T and then maybe law school. My favourite subjects are English and math."

My mom is so thrilled, she nearly faints. "A journalist? My goodness. That certainly is ambitious. Did you hear that, Nadine? A journalist! And a lawyer!"

"Mom, can we go downstairs now? We really have to get to work," I say, shooting Slasher a meaningful look.

My mother smiles at me through clenched teeth. "Oh, of course, listen to me, talking your ear off when you have work to do. Go downstairs! Become journalists and lawyers! Go. Don't let me stop you!"

"Sorry about my mom," I tell Slasher as I lead her downstairs.

"No worries," she says. "Parents are my specialty. Well, not *my* parents, but . . ." She trails off as we reach the bottom step.

"OK," she says, regrouping and taking a seat near the TV. "What's the plan?"

We left off at kind of a depressing point in the movie.

After the big commercial media explosion in the eighties, crews break up. B-boys stop dancing, get jobs, go back to school or hang out with old friends who're into the shady side of things. And then rap gets thuggier, grows bigger than b-boying, and people start to think that all of hip hop is just about MCing.

The b-boys in the movie try to turn it around after that, with talk about going back underground and taking over the world, but the film never gets back to the fun place where it started. It's like all the new b-boys feel a *responsibility* to represent the dance and bring something new and keep it going the right way. No one's just in it to wear nice kicks and get respect at the club anymore. The original b-boys are all amazed at the power of the next generation. They say it's out of their hands.

Then the riot squad comes on screen and breaks up the B-Boy Summit in L.A. Winkley must have called them.

Slasher takes notes furiously, the scratching of her pen almost drowning out the soundtrack.

"So . . . ," she starts to ask me as the closing credits roll, "you *b-boy*, right?" She winces a little on *b-boy* like the word feels wrong to her and she's not sure she's allowed to use it.

"B-*girl*."

"Oh. Right. So . . . were you on, like, a *team* or anything?"

"A *crew*." Did she not just watch the film? They must have said it eighty times.

"Yeah, I was in a crew. With my boyfriend. It was his crew."

"Wait, wait, wait. Your boyfriend? You have a boy-friend?"

"Is that so hard to believe?" I snap.

"No. You just haven't mentioned him before."

Duh. *Because you and I are not friends. We don't talk,* I think, pulling my knees to my chest.

"He still lives in Parkdale?"

"Yeah."

"So with your crew, you would, like, go to competitions and stuff?"

"*Battles.*" Hellooo? I almost want to grab her notebook and see what she's been scribbling this whole time, 'cause it sure ain't vocab.

"Did you win?"

"Yeah," I say a little too fast. "We qualified for the Hogtown Showdown last spring."

"Are you the only girl on the crew?"

"I was the only b-girl in my whole neighbourhood."

"So you were like their secret weapon?" she asks.

"No!" I laugh. "You dance with guys, you just try to keep up. You don't beat them. You don't win. No matter how hard you practise, they don't let you forget you're just lucky to be there."

She gasps as if I just slapped her across the face. "They *say* that?"

"Well, not in so many words—"

"But you *believe* it?" she practically yells.

"You don't understand how it is."

She laughs. "No, I don't *like* how it is. I understand it fine."

"Who are you to judge? You don't even know what you're talking about."

She frowns. "Well, they must be awfully special if you're just *lucky* to dance with them."

"Hey!" I yell. "You are talking about my *crew,* tha Rackit Klub, the future winners of the Hogtown Showdown. A little respect, please."

"OK, OK, sorry. So, your boyfriend, does he ever come to Rivercrest? How come I've never seen him?"

I pause for a second, somewhere between slapping her and kicking her out. But then I think, maybe the fastest way to shut her up is to just answer.

"We broke up," I mumble. "He didn't want a long-distance relationship."

But of course, that's not enough for her.

"Long distance? Don't your parents go into Toronto, like, *every day* for work?"

I shrug. "He had to do what was best for the crew."

Her eyebrows wrinkle together. "Nadine, that is the most awful thing I've ever heard in my life."

I take the disk out of the DVD player and concentrate hard on putting it back in the case so the title is lined up exactly straight, in the right direction.

"Is that why you were so mad at the dance?"

"I guess."

"Your dancing is amazing when you're angry, then," she says.

I slam the box down so hard, it cracks. "Can we just work on the project?"

"We *are* working on the project. It's like they said in the movie, you're the next generation. This is good material. This is how it really is. This is what happens after the movie is over."

"My life is not *material*." My life is not even my life.

"You know, when Winkley grabbed you by the shoulder—"

"Slasher, *please*. Drop the subject."

"OK, fine. Don't call me that."

On Monday at school, it's like Friday at my house never even happened.

For some reason—I don't know what comes over me—I try to say hello to Slasher in the hall, and she completely ignores me.

Well good. I'd rather forget she was ever in my house, touching my stuff, eating my food, sucking up to my parents and asking me a thousand personal questions too. What happens on Friday stays on Friday. Fine with me.

Then, on Tuesday, we're back in the AV room, watching the movie for the 800 billionth time, to make sure we haven't missed anything for the report, when all of a sudden, Slasher puts down her pen and says, "Nadine, what about the b-*girls?*"

"Uh . . . what about them?"

"Well, what big thing have b-girls brought? We saw the old-school years with the black kids and the Hispanic kids, and Brooklyn and Queens and the Bronx, and their different styles, then the commercial age that made everything popular, and the spreading-to-the-West-Coast era with all the spinning and the power, then the back-to-the-underground, slowly-spreading-around-the-planet era, and the new moves that brought. But it's all guys. When was the age of the b-girls? Where *are* all the b-girls?"

"There was never an age of the b-girls."

"Oh." She frowns. "Well, maybe it just hasn't happened yet."

I laugh. "It's hard to even *find* b-girls, let alone expect them to lead some kind of revolution or whatever it is you're looking for."

"Well, maybe other girls already want to break, they just don't know it yet."

I shake my head.

"What if they're right here under your nose and you just can't see it because you're not looking?"

"Yeah, right. In Rivercrest?"

"There are some pretty athletic girls in Rivercrest. What if the revolution begins with you?"

I put my head down on the desk. When I look up again, one teeny clip of Asia One throwing down flashes across the screen. She's practically the only woman in the whole movie—a ten-second blip in an hour and a half of history. I know what I'm up against.

Slasher is still talking.

"I mean, wouldn't that be the best way to get back at those Rackit guys? You *are* going to get back at them, right? Even if you still respect them, you have to go to the Hogtown Showdown. You can't let them think they can just force you out—"

"Don't worry. I'll find a crew. I have a plan."

"I think you should start your own crew."

"Slasher! Just watch the movie and let's get this over with, OK? I don't want to be back in here after class."

"But . . ."

I press Play. KRS1 drowns her out with some theory of his.

nineteen

We finally get to hand the project in. I've never been so happy for a school deadline in my entire life. It must be the most complete report on any documentary in the history of the universe. We have charts and graphs explaining the whole timeline of the history of breaking; Slasher gave Marc a whole bunch of information and told him to make it pretty with his computer. It looks OK-ish. Not exactly pretty—definitely not hip hop—but at least it's organized.

Staci actually did get the job of making the report cover. The b-boy under the title kind of looks like he's melting, and she misspelled her own name, but other than that, I guess it's OK.

"It's what's inside that counts," I tell Slasher before her head explodes.

Even Finch isn't going to care about the cover once she reads the inside.

There's a "Central Analysis" broken down into "Key Themes," a "Breakdown of Journalistic and Cinematic Techniques," an "Opinions and Conclusions" page where Slasher has taken every single theme and found a way to connect it directly to something at RHS, right down to comparing "lunchroom cliques" to "gang warfare," and calling for a "safe place" where "students of different backgrounds can come together and proactively collaborate without sacrificing their unique identities."

Then there are photos of "The Next Generation," a.k.a. me, and the few pictures of tha Klub I didn't destroy, and the words "To be continued . . ." in fancy writing on the last page.

One of the Tiffanys sees the cover as Slasher sprints to the front to hand it in to Finch at the beginning of class.

"Breakdancing?" I hear her say to Staci. "That's so lame."

"I know," says Staci, rolling her eyes. "It wasn't my idea."

"I want to talk to you after class," Slasher tells me as she walks back to her desk.

But as soon as the bell rings, I'm out the door, at my locker, on the street and gone, gone, gone. I run from school to the bridge, head down, earphones on, already warming up and getting my head into the right space. The Showdown isn't getting any further away just because I've been busy with a lot of stupid homework. Nothing can stop me from making it to practice today. No group projects. No shopping trips. No nightmare dinners. No third degree in my own basement. Just me, the bridge and at least an hour's workout before it gets too dark and too cold.

But I have all this doubt in my head.

You're never going to get your mills back. You needed Sean to show you how to do them, and you need Sean to show you what's wrong with them now.

What makes you think you're ever going to find another crew? No one else is going to want you. Tha Klub ditched you for a reason. If you were really good, they would have kept you, no matter where you live.

You're running out of time. You think you can fix this in less than five months? You're as big a loser as they say you are.

I run harder to chase the thoughts out of my head. I crush them into the ground with every step, but my legs feel heavy and stiff, and the harder I try to move, the slower I seem to go. When I reach the bridge, I try to stretch a little, but I'm afraid to sit still, 'cause I don't want to get cold. I can tell my days in this spot are numbered—soon it's going to be winter. Unless I can figure out how to throw down in snow-pants, I'm going to have to find a new spot.

See? You're insane if you think you're making it to the Showdown.

I know how to get past this. Keep the music on. Basic toprocks. Work the beat. Kick it old school. Drop down to the ground, keep it loose, no pressure, just dance. Don't think. Leave the head out of it. The body knows how to dance.

Then why are your knees so stiff? Why are you so slow?

I turn off the music and instead do some handstands against the wall.

Your upper-body strength is crap today. Look, you can't even last thirty seconds without falling.

I do headstands, but my transitions between different poses are like jello.

You call those abs?

It wouldn't be a practice if I didn't do a bunch of 6-steps, so I go back to footwork. Gradually, the evil voices in my head quiet down, take a seat and fall asleep.

See? This is good. Practice is good. You're toughing it out. That counts for something. You can do this.

Coffee grinders, 3-steps, CCs, popcorn, swipes . . . it's all working, finally. Just because it *feels* stiff doesn't mean it *is* stiff.

Just be happy you're working. That's all that matters. It'll feel good later because you're putting the time in now.

I must put in half an hour of pure footwork. Deep down, I know I'm just avoiding mills.

Because you suck at them now, says the evil voice, waking up a little.

Damn. I wouldn't take that from Encore or Recoil. I'm sure as hell not going to start taking it from myself.

You can do this you can do this you can do this you can do this, I tell myself as I set up to try. But I might as well just be crossing my fingers for all the good it does. That feeling I used to have—a natural sense of when to move and where to put my hands—natural because I practised so much—is missing. Gone. It's like I imagined it. Sean took it with him when he left.

I wind up, throw myself into it, and gravity dumps me on my stomach on the cold ground, my arm crumpled under me.

"Aargh!" I yell at the top of my lungs as I flop over on my back and stare up at the underside of the bridge.

I half wish the whole thing would just collapse on me.

I hear a clank at the top of the stairs, and sit up with a start.

Maybe if you sit really still, it will go away on its own, I think, but then a pair of Nikes with the iPod sensor thingy appears at the top of the stairs, followed by Juicy Couture sweats (pale pink—still in style in the R-C even though they've been out at home for decades), a hint of hot pink Lululemon yoga shirt peeking out from beneath a Nike running jacket with reflective strips, little white stretchy gloves gripping the railing, a fleece scarf up to the eyes, fuzzy white earmuffs and a tight honey-blond ponytail.

"Now what?" I ask, jumping up to block her path so she's trapped on the stairs.

Slasher stops, halfway down.

"Am I interrupting?"

"Yes. What do you want?"

She looks hurt for just a fraction of a second.

"Nothing. Forget it. I don't know why I bothered. It's not like you were ever going to say yes."

"To what?"

She clams up and goes back up a few steps. Finally, she speaks.

"I want to learn."

Sound of needle scratching all the way across the record.

"Learn what?"

"To b-girl. I want you to teach me to b-girl."

Stereo system goes dead, shorts out, starts to smoke and blows up in a giant ball of flame. After a long silence, I look her up and down.

"No."

"Not for free or anything," she stammers. "I'd pay you. My dad—"

"I don't need your money."

"I don't mean it like that. I just don't expect you to do it for noth—"

"Whatever. You are so full of yourself."

Her jaw drops. "*Me?* Ha! *You've* been on your high horse since your first day here."

I cross my arms and take a step closer, forcing her to back farther up the stairs. "Fine. You hate me. I hate you. The project is over. You never have to talk to me again."

She grabs her face with her hands. A high, squeaky sound escapes from behind her gloves. "Nadine, no."

"What?"

"Nadine, I *want* to talk to you. Why can't we get along better than this?" she asks. "What can I do?"

Nothing, I want to say. Go home. Get out of my face and my practice spot. Forget you were ever here and tell no one about this.

But my mouth jumps ahead of my brain. Before I can stop myself, I hear myself say, "Well, for starters, you could apologize."

She looks confused. "I did detention for the gym thing."

"So what? So did I." I tear off my wristguards and throw them in my bag. This practice is so over.

"So we're even," she says.

"No, you're even with Bundt and Winkley."

I push past her to climb the stairs. She runs after me.

"Nadine, I only hit you because you—"

I put my headphones on. Her lips keep moving but I don't hear a sound. I speed my walk up to a run and she keeps pace beside me.

"Nadine—"

I'll give her this: she's persistent. By the time we reach the stoplight at Main Street, I'm starting to wonder if she's going to follow me all the way home.

I reach over to push the button to change the light, but she jumps in front of me, trapping me there at the corner.

"You're right," she mouths as I try to dodge around her to get back at the button.

"What?" I yell.

"You're right," she says a little louder, leaning in. I can almost make it out over Lauryn Hill.

"What?" I say again.

She reaches up and rips the headphones off my head.

"You're right!" she yells.

I stick my hand out for her to give me back the head-phones.

"Nadine," she says, blocking me so I miss the light. "I'm sorry about gym. I don't know what I was thinking. I wanted to win. And I thought that Ashley—"

"Yeah, well you were wrong about Trashley. She's been badmouthing you behind your back."

She winces. "Yeah. Thanks. I know. I'm sorry, Nadine. I was wrong. I should have apologized then, and I shouldn't have given you such a hard time, and I should have been nicer to you while we were working on the doc project, and I shouldn't have bugged you with so many personal questions . . ."

She waits for my reaction. She waits a long time.

"And you shouldn't have pretended not to see me in the hall the other day."

"I never preten—"

"Yes, you did. Last Monday."

"No I didn . . ."

I glare at her.

"OK, OK. I'm sorry I didn't see you. I'm sorry I wasn't paying attention."

I think about it. She pulls at a loose thread hanging off the thumb of her glove.

"Well OK, then," I finally tell her, stretching a fake smile across my face. "I forgive you completely. I guess we're *finally* even."

She studies my eyes. "Really?"

"Yeah, sure, whatever. Feel better now?"

She smiles nervously. "So . . . will you think about showing me some moves?"

"No."

I might need a crew but I'm not *that* desperate. I put my hood up and start to jog away. She grabs me by the arm. I have a flashback to Winkley at the dance and I pull it back harder than I mean to.

"Wait!" she yells. "Watch!"

Staring me in the eye, she drops one hand to the ground and kicks up into an L-kick, then she stands up again and nods at me like *so there*.

I laugh. "So you bit a move from me. So what? One move won't make you a b-girl."

"Then teach me more."

"No. You don't get it. You can't just learn a few tricks and then call yourself a b-girl. You have to live it. The guys who invented it needed the escape. They danced on concrete with their bare hands. They didn't wear cute yoga outfits and get their moms to drive them to school every morning. You can't just wake up in the morning and go through your prissy Rivercrest life, throw a freeze on the end of your day and call yourself a b-girl."

She narrows her eyes. "Nadine, *you* do it and *you* live in prissy Rivercrest and *your* mom drives you to school. You didn't stop being a b-girl when you moved here."

"I—"

"No. You're not a b-girl because you were born in the city, Nadine. You're a b-girl because you learned. Someone taught you. I can learn too."

For the longest time, we stare at each other in silence. My breath fills the air between us with tiny dagger icicles.

Finally, Slasher taps a button on her iPod armband and zips her reflective Nike jacket higher. "Fine. Forget I asked." She turns her back and runs off the way we came, into the dark, checking her pulse as she goes.

I hear the guys laughing in the back of my head. *"Rivercrest is lame . . . if you're not going to be real then you can't be in the crew."*

And I start to think . . . when did any of them ever work out when it wasn't comfortable? When did any of them ever apologize for anything? When did they ever stick up for me like Slasher thought she was sticking up for Trashley?

Aw, crap.

I am definitely going to regret this.

As Slasher starts to disappear into the drizzle, I hear myself call out, like I'm having an out-of-body experience.

"Slasher!"

She stops sharply and turns on her heels. "What?"

I take a deep breath. "You need to twist more in your L-kick."

She looks stunned for a second, and then confused, and then a small smile creeps across her face. "OK," she says quietly.

"Meet me after school on Monday. Bring kneepads."

She pauses, waiting for the punchline.

There is no punchline. Me showing her moves: that's going to be the real joke.

"OK. Thanks," she finally says, and runs off, her stupid pink pants glowing in the rain, her ponytail, still perfect, swinging from side to side.

twenty

I've never taught anyone how to dance before. I've just listened to a lot of different guys give me a lot of conflicting
instructions, and watched a lot of tapes, and read a lot of
message boards. How do you describe dancing to another
person? You have to do it to understand it—the position of
your elbow against your abs that lets your arm lock you
into a freeze, the rush when that perfect song comes in and
it's like you're just gliding over the music. The power in
your shoulders. The adrenalin rush that tells you to take it
over the top and pull out that move you've never landed
before.

I'm thinking about this when a shadow falls over my
lunch.

"Is anyone sitting here?"

I look up and Slasher is standing over me with her
cafeteria tray. Skim milk, salad, no dressing, one breadstick,
and an orange.

In my headphones, Gnarls Barkley hums about insan-
ity. I poke at my mashed potatoes.

"No?"

She sits down across from me and unfolds her napkin
in her lap. I keep eating, keep my headphones on.

"So," she finally says.

I take my headphones off. "What?"

She pauses with a cherry tomato stuck on the end of

her fork, looks at me, opens her mouth to talk, closes it again, opens it. "Nothing."

I put my headphones back on. She sips at her milk but doesn't touch the breadstick.

"Um," I finally say, getting sick of the weird silence. "Did Finch tell you when we'll get our mark back from the documentary project?"

"Coupla weeks," she says.

"That's good," I say. I have no idea how to stretch this conversation out. I don't really care about the grade. I just have no idea what to say to her.

"So . . . how's Fashion Show?"

"I quit."

"Oh."

"Yeah."

The bell rings.

"I'll meet you after . . . ," says Slasher, picking up her tray.

"Yeah. After," I say, leaving mine on the table.

I think I might have made a big mistake. I have the Showdown to think about. Training someone else is a big distraction. I know, because Sean always made that really clear when he was working with me.

Madi finds me at the bridge after school. Thank god she doesn't expect to walk there together. I can't handle a rerun of small talk from lunch. When she shows up, she doesn't seem mad that I didn't wait for her. She's dressed and ready to go. Black stretchy pants. Pink puffy vest. Sweater with snowflakes on the sleeves. Toque. I didn't know we were going skiing with James Bond today. I thought we were just going to learn the 6-step.

"Hey," she says.

"Are you warmed up?" I ask.

"Yeah. I ran and stretched already."

"So let's 6-step."

She pulls a tiny notepad out of her jacket and makes a tiny note with a tiny pen. Of course. Not that she's going to need the notes. No way will she be able to forget what a 6-step is by the time I'm done with her.

I drop to the ground and demonstrate. My hands are my centre. My feet run around them, my arms pulling me where I need to go. Six-steps fit like my oldest, best hoodie. I've done probably thousands of them. They're programmed into my muscles so deep, they happen without my even thinking. They flow from me before I even know I'm doing them.

Slasher looks a little panicked. I can't help but smile.

"We'll break it down now."

She puts the notebook down. I turn so we're both facing the same way.

"Crouch like you're going to snap a football," I tell her, bending my knees so I'm low enough to touch the floor if I want to. She folds in half at the waist, keeping her legs pin straight.

"Knees?" I ask, because she's so stiff, I'm not convinced she has any. She checks her position against mine and then bends just enough that she won't fall on her face if a strong wind picks up from behind. Close enough, I guess.

"Now lean forward a little and put your right hand down on the ground," I tell her.

She leans forward just far enough that her fingers graze the platform. Her butt sticks up like she's trying to air it out or something.

"Slasher, seriously, you need to really bend your knees. Bend them so far, you're crouching down, and put like at least half your weight on your hand."

She leans forward.

"Relax!" I yell at her, so loud I startle her, and she stiffens even more.

I shake my head. "Dude, we're not trying to stretch our hamstrings. Bend."

"You mean like this?" she says, trying to make a joke out of bending too far.

"Yeah, that's perfect. Do that," I tell her. She looks insulted.

"All right, now step your right foot forward and put it down between your hand and your left foot."

I put my right foot down where eleven o'clock might be if my hand was at one and my left foot was at seven. Slasher tries to match my stance, but ends up in a sideways crouch with her fingers just brushing the ground again.

"No," I say, trying not to get so frustrated so soon, if it's not already too late. "Your foot moves, not your hand. Leave your hand where it is. Your weight has to be even between your hand and the sides of your feet."

I swat her hand away from the ground. She pulls it back.

"You should fall over if I do that."

She grimaces as she repositions her feet, leaning onto her hand. I let her stay like that, holding herself up until her arm shakes and she starts to look worried.

"Nadine?" she says, her forehead wrinkling, crinkling up her nose like she hopes to use it to help hold herself up.

"Yeah?" I ask, coolly holding the position. It's starting to burn, but I keep my face relaxed just to torture her a little longer.

"Cool," I say, yawning, and cover my mouth with my free hand. "When you're ready, tuck your left foot behind your right knee." I slide forward into a crouching position, with my right leg crossed in front. "This is step two."

She rushes to catch up, practically falling on her face. She teeters between her crossed feet and her hand, unsure if she's allowed to relax.

"Like this?"

"Yeah, but all your weight should be on your left leg now. Collapse into your knee and let your right leg drag there, like it's dead."

She crumples into it, relieved to finally relax a little.

I hurry on to step three, uncrossing my right leg and sweeping it across the ground in front of me as I pick my hand up off the ground. She half imitates me, putting her right foot down beside her left.

She's got it, so I move on, simultaneously lifting my right hand and placing my left on the floor as I sweep my left foot across my right leg.

She follows, no problem.

"Not bad. Now for five, step your right foot back so your weight is on your left hand and the sides of your feet, like the exact opposite of step one."

She starts to look angry as I leave her there, leaning on her arm again. She plasters a smile across her face, refusing to let me see her sweat.

"And then back to our starting position for six," I say, stifling a smile of my own.

She collapses on the floor, breathing hard.

"Nadine, are you showing me hard stuff just so I'll get discouraged and quit?"

"No. Six-step is *the* foundation move for all of breaking. It's what makes breaking look like breaking. It connects moves to other moves, and tons of other moves are built on it. Besides, it builds strength and endurance and agility. It's the minimum. If you don't have a 6-step, you don't have anything."

"Well good, 'cause I'm going to get it. It's going to be perfect."

"Great, then take thirty seconds, get some water and do it again."

I go to my pod and put on "O.S.T." by People Under the Stairs. I love this album. These guys have a flow that sounds to me like a b-boy doing really tight footwork. It reminds me of footage I've seen of one of the originals, Ken Swift, where he's not pushing to be fast or explosive, he's just smooth and creative, and every move flows out of the one before, like he's just doing his thing and it's no big deal, and you can watch or not watch, but either way, he's going to keep dancing.

I would kill to have that kind of technique. I try to practise as if I already do—like if I concentrate hard enough, I can channel the music straight from my ears to my feet.

I start with some threads, weaving my feet through the spaces my arms and body create with the floor, twisting to unravel myself from knots and tie one image to the next.

I flow through a few variations of a baby freeze, tipping into a headstand and using the building momentum of my legs to push up into in a hollowback handstand. Feeling the music, I try to make it look like I'm not pushing into it—like it belongs there naturally—and I twist my torso around into an impossible position, locking my right foot under my left knee.

But I keep twisting and fall right out of it and splat, sprawled out on the floor.

On my second try, I don't get enough momentum to push up.

Then I get up, hold it, but can't force out the twist.

Finally, I give up trying to do it in sequence and just practise the final hollowback all on its own. I kick up, hit it, hold it for a second and then—

At the end of the platform I see, through my arms, upside down, Slasher, not practising her 6-step but standing on her hands in a perfect hollowback—shoulders strong, back arched as deeply as a contortionist's, pointed toes stretching for the wall behind her, holding it as effortlessly as if she was waiting for the bus.

Not that Slasher would ever wait for a bus.

I catch my breath and stumble back to my feet.

"Slasher!" I bark. "Where'd you learn that?"

"Gymnastics," she says, looking up and arching farther to touch her toes to the top of her head.

"Why aren't you practising your 6-step?"

She pops over her shoulders like a flip toy, dropping into a bridge. "I'm bored," she says, sitting up.

"Why? Is it perfect?"

She rolls her eyes as she brings the soles of her feet together for a stretch. "Well, hardly. I *just* learned it. But it's going pretty well."

"Lemme see."

She hops to her feet and stiffly moves through the steps, rushing on two, getting tangled between three and four.

"You can't be so stiff about it. You have to relax and let your weight tell you which step comes next. And stop pointing your toes. It looks weird."

"Sorry," she mumbles. "In gym—"

"Breaking isn't gymnastics. If you go into a battle and dance like a gymnast, no one will be impressed."

"What do you expect me to do? I can't just forget eleven years of training."

"Practise the 6-step."

"Fine. But, Nadine," she calls as I go back to my end of the platform.

"What?"

"Tuck your chin in your handstand and you'll be able to hold it longer."

I pretend not to hear.

twenty-one

I don't see Slasher for a couple days because we don't have media or gym, and I don't run into her in the caf. I don't exactly miss her. The quiet is kind of nice.

That all ends on Friday, when she leaps out from around a corner as I get into school in the morning.

"Nadine!"

I duck instinctively before realizing I'm not being ambushed.

"I have something to show you," she says, clapping her hands together. It is way too early for this much energy.

"Whoa, whoa, chill, man. What is it?"

She fingers her pleated skirt.

"Just something I've been practising."

"Well, you can show me now or you can wait till next Tuesday. It's up to you."

I told her she could only practise with me one day a week.

"I'm not exactly dressed for it. Couldn't I just—?"

I stare at her hard.

"Won't we get in trouble?"

I lead her around the corner to the deserted side of the school. Winkley won't be out here now. It's too cold.

"Oh fine," she says, taking her coat off and checking to make sure no one's around.

When the coast is clear, she takes six small breaths,

rubs her hands together and then ducks down into a crouching football position. She touches one fuzzy grey glove to the ground, counts to herself and does three slow but accurate 6-steps in each direction and kicks up into an L on the last one, her skirt flopping over her hips, hair falling out of its bun.

Her leggings are so thick they could practically be pants. In her white shirt, skirt and ultra-preppy shoes, she looks like something from an ancient tap movie. I half expect Mr. Bojangles to pop out from behind the building and swing her over his shoulder before leading her through a round of donkey kicks.

She jumps back up to her feet, grinning, cheeks flush with excitement.

I pick my jaw up off the pavement and return it to its normal position.

"You practised."

"Duh," she says, smoothing her kilt and twisting her bun back up on top of her head. "So how did I do?"

"Not bad," I say. "You could use more flow and it was kind of slow."

I brace myself for an argument, but she just pulls out her notebook and writes it down.

"Consider it done. I'm going to get good at this," she says, almost like she's warning me. "I'm not going to quit."

"Like you haven't quit gymnastics?" I ask, maybe too quickly. She looks at the ground.

"I didn't quit gymnastics," she says. "I was forced out."

"What? By your parents? And you listened? No one can keep me from—"

"No," she says. "By my surgeon." She kneels down and rolls up her left legging. A long, red scar runs from inside her sock almost to her knee. "I fell wrong out of a vault and pulverized it. I can't do tumbling runs or land anything that starts out fast or high. My coach wrote me off."

"You think b-girling is going to be easier?" I ask her.

"No," she says. "Just closer to the ground."

She waits for my reaction.

"I tucked my chin like you said," I tell her, suddenly feeling guilty for basically calling her a wuss.

She smiles. "I can help you with more of that stuff if you want me to."

"OK," I say carefully. I bet there are all kinds of tricks she knows that Sean and tha Klub have never even thought of.

"Let's see what happens on Tuesday."

"Right foot crosses first and . . .

"Step, together! Step, together!

"Back, together! Back.

"Front, back, Brook-lyn Rock!"

I am yelling dance steps at Slasher over the music, clapping to make it easier for her to follow me. Her flow is backed up worse than the drain in our old apartment the day I decided to flush my grade two science experiment. Under a bridge is exactly where her toprock belongs. In a pitch-black studio, with the lights off, at midnight, I would be embarrassed to be seen in the same room with it. She has rhythm, it's just not the same rhythm that the song has. And she does this thing with her head that makes her look like a pigeon.

It's like someone shoved the gymnastic stick so far up her butt, it hit her brain and killed the part that's responsible for free will and all-around funk. My only hope is that if I lead her, the rhythm will somehow seep into her from the bass to my voice to her feet to her brain, to her soul—if she has one, which I'm still not a hundred percent sure about.

"Relax your arms!

"Bend your knees!

"Stop holding your butt in.

"For the hundredth time," I tell her, "don't point your toes."

She looks at me like I've just dissed her personal god, but nothing wrecks the look of b-girling faster than toe pointing. It's not ballet.

"OK," I tell her. "Forget the steps, let's just bounce in time with the music."

I bounce. She follows, kind of, trying very hard to hit each and every beat precisely.

"Bounce, don't twitch. You look like you're about to have a seizure or something."

She scowls at me.

"Seriously, you've got to just let it go. Relax like no one's watching and there are no steps, and you've just got the radio on and you don't even notice you're doing it."

"I *am* letting go," she says, pointing her toes again.

"Toes!" I yell.

She slams her foot down.

"Nadine, why do you care so much? I thought you didn't even want to teach me. Can't you just show me the basics and let me handle the rest on my own? I'm not going to get it all right away!"

"These *are* the basics. And honestly, I don't want to teach you. But if I'm going to, I want to know that it's going somewhere."

"Well, if I'm going to listen to you, I'd like to know the same thing."

"What's that supposed to mean?"

"I want to be good, Nadine, and I want to be in a crew. I want to battle."

Whoa.

I stare at her, wide eyed. The Showdown is in February—not that far off. What kind of suicide mission—

"Well, maybe you *could* be good . . . ," I tell her, remembering her promise to teach me some tricks from gym, "but not without dancing—really dancing—to the beat, like you feel the music, like you like it and you mean it, and you've maybe even done it before."

She crosses her arms. "Well *this*—you yelling at me—isn't working."

"Well maybe if you—"

She puts up her hand. "I know someone who can help. My friend Alya. She does this hip-hop class at the—"

I sit up straight. "Hip hop is not automatically the same as breaking, you know. We don't even use the same music."

Breakers usually like old funk and classic hip hop, maybe a little electro. Hip hop almost always uses new cuts that doesn't even have the same beat.

"I *know*," she says, like really she didn't. "I've only been to that class once. I don't know what *kind* of hip hop it is. But you could try it and find out."

"*I* could try it?"

"Well, yeah. You could come with me, since you think I'm so unqualified to judge."

I cross my arms. "I dunno."

I hate hip-hop classes. They're enough like breaking that I feel like throwing down while I'm in them, but then because it's a class and you have to do what everyone else is doing, no breaking ever actually happens. And then there's the sexy factor. Some hip-hop classes are actually pretty tight, with cool steps and popping, but then other classes are practically pole dancing. In Rivercrest— I can't even imagine what hip hop looks like in Rivercrest.

"Is it going to be all butt-shaking video stripper moves?" I ask her.

An image flashes through my mind of Jazmin winding her way across Sean's basement with her thong sticking out above her stretch jeans. Shudder.

"No!" Slasher shrieks. "I mean. I don't know . . . I don't think so."

"I'll think about it."

"What's the worst that can happen, Nadine? If it sucks, you never have to go back as long as you live. But you never know . . . Alya really knows her stuff. She might even be b-girl material."

"I *said*, I'll *think* about it."

twenty-two

It's a stupid idea, but *what if* Slasher got good? *What if* Alya or whatever her name is turned out to be b-girl material, as Slasher put it? *What if* I did start a crew? The look on Sean's face if we showed up at the Showdown . . .

It's stupid, but I keep thinking it anyway.

On Thursday, I meet Slasher on the front steps after school, and we go to the big fancy mall in the fancy heart of Fancytown. We grab fancy smoothies at the fancy juice bar on our way in and then park ourselves on the fancy escalator.

Everything about me says I don't belong here. My army pants are worn at the knees. My grey hoodie is all stretched out under my bomber jacket. My Public Enemy hat is probably the only one in all of Rivercrest. I almost feel like my dirty sneakers shouldn't be allowed to touch the fancy floor.

I look around and see people from school hanging out in the food court, taking free samples from the Popcorn Hut, testing out music at the Listening Shack and in some cases, even doing some actual shopping.

"So this is where everyone hangs out after school?"

"You're just learning this now?" says Slasher.

"I never come here. I'm not fancy, I'm street."

"You are such a hermit. I can't believe I'm hanging out with you," she says.

"Hermit? Please. I just have better things to do with my time. Besides, I'm sure you can go back to hanging out with them if you really want to." I point to a pair of Britneys on the lower level playing tug-of-war with an ugly lime green boot. "Don't let me hold you back. I'd hate to make you miss a sale or something."

"And what do you do with your spare time that's so important?"

"I *practise*."

We get off the escalator and walk past a couple of kids who are totally squished up against the railing, making out.

"What about *after* practice? When you're just hanging out? Do you even have a life?"

"You call *this* a life?" I ask as we pass two girls walking side by side, yelling into their phones, trying to drown each other out. "I have a life. I do stuff. In Parkdale, we used to hang out in Sean's building, or we'd go to the club on Fridays—"

"But you're not *in* Parkdale, Nadine."

"Don't remind me."

"You need to get out more."

"The only thing I need is a crew. Somehow flirting with cheesy guys at the mall doesn't seem as important as making it to the Showdown."

"I don't see why you can't have both."

We arrive in front of a large glass storefront with teal carpeting and a big pink neon sign that says "Chloe's" and then "Movement Spa" underneath in small gold letters.

Slasher takes her jacket off and hangs it in an oversized cream-and-gold wardrobe inside the front door. I hang up my bomber jacket and suddenly feel naked.

The studio is really six studios, each one larger than the next. There's a big reception counter, a manicure bar and a cappuccino station and a small, glassed-in dance shop where everything is Lycra and nothing is under $150.

"Do we have to pay to get in? I spent all my cash on that smoothie."

"It's cool. I've got it taken care of," says Slasher.

The receptionist waves us through. We walk down a hall, past rooms overflowing with creepily flexible middle-aged women with scary hair, and one studio that's hot enough to make me break out in a sweat just walking by it.

Slasher laughs.

"That's for hot yoga. Don't worry about it. We're in studio 2."

"How do you know so much about this place?"

"My mom comes here for Pilates, like, six times a week."

We grab a locker in the change room. Slasher's track pants come off, revealing yet another pair of yoga pants. Does she wash them every night, or just start a new pair every workout?

"Aren't you getting changed?" she asks.

"No."

When I took my pledge to become a b-girl superhero, I vowed to be ready for action at *any time.* I don't wear clothes I can't dance in, ever. I stash my bag and my hoodie and I'm ready to go.

Studio 2 is a smaller room at the back of the spa, with mirrors on all four sides and a sound system built right into the wall. I feel like I'm in a Justin Timberlake video, but not necessarily in a good way. I find a spot on the floor and do some warm-up stretches, trying to ignore the sixteen, no, thirty-two, no, sixty-four reflections copying me.

Within five minutes, the studio starts to fill up with perfumed girls in tiny little halter tops. A couple of them are around our age but most of them are college girls, or older. They're skinny and have blond dye jobs—even the one Asian woman in the room, who looks to be about my mom's age. I start to feel pretty weird in my cargo pants and old Tribe shirt, but not as weird as I would feel in a halter top.

I'm trying to guess which one of these girls is Alya, but before I get a chance to ask Slasher, one of the Lycra sisters goes to the front of the room and starts the music.

"Hey, everybody! You ready? OK! Let's! Get! Moving!"

Whoa. That is way too perky. I really must be in the wrong class. Teacher chick is black, about eleven feet tall, with perfect skin and tidy dreds pulled back in a ponytail. She's dressed like the other girls, only maybe a little funkier, with less skin, and shoes that match her hat. She could be a CoverGirl model if she didn't have so much muscle definition.

I stand up a little taller.

The warm-up is fast and furious, with kick-boxing-boot-campy moves and stretching built right into the chore-ography so subtle I almost don't notice I'm doing it.

We step like aerobics and do push-ups like we're in the army.

"Don't stop!" she yells when we start to look tired. "Conditioning makes us better dancers!"

"And you'll look hot!" she adds when that doesn't work.

After the warm-up, the real choreography kicks in: eight counts, four of which involve walking around once in a circle. Step the left foot out, right foot out, left knee in, right knee in, jump the feet together. It almost seems too easy.

But then she goes and adds arms: some overhead claps with the walking, aggressive elbows with the stepping, use the hands to push in the knees, draw the legs together at the end by pulling up on the knees of my pants. OK. Still not rocket surgery, but she makes it look amazing. Her isolations are sharp, and she accents each step with slight popping motions that melt into the smoothest possible transitions.

I'm trying my hardest to match her style, but then she goes and adds another eight counts to the first eight: clap, snap, turn, slide, step, step, ball-change, hop, kick the right heel back and grab it with the left hand, pop the shoulder . . . It's a blur. As soon as I get the hang of the second set, I forget the first steps. Six tries later, I'm clapping when everyone else jumps, and jumping when they bob.

"*This* is a beginner class?" I ask, much louder than I mean to.

Everyone laughs, and I shrink into myself, botching the opening eight again. This is so not me. I'm a b-girl. I don't memorize, I improvise.

Teacher girl catches up with me during the water break.

"Hey, what's your name?"

"Nadine."

"Nadine, don't be so hard on yourself. It's cool. We're going to run through it at least ten more times. You'll get it. Why do you think class is so long?"

"To torture me?"

"You're doing fine. Try to relax and listen to the music. Don't think. Just dance."

There's a screech and a crash like a car accident in the back of my brain. My feet are suddenly glued to the floor. *She's* telling *me* to listen to the music? This might be the most embarrassing moment of my entire life.

I try to relax after the break, but I get distracted watching what everyone else is doing.

Slasher is really struggling to keep up. Anything that involves undulating hips freaks her right out. She is hula-resistant. Then there's this one girl in the front row who picks up the choreography really fast but has no flow. She's sloppy where the hits are sharp and jerky where it's supposed to be smooth. Another girl has decent style but is behind the beat all the way through, until she rushes to hit the ending on time. No one really leaps out as b-girl material.

By the end of class, I'm exhausted.

"Thanks, everybody! Come back next week!" says teacher chick, applauding even though she must know as well as I do that we all stink.

I turn to Slasher. "So where's Alya? She didn't show?"

"You mean you haven't figured it out yet?"

Teach turns the music off and walks over to us.

"Hey, Madi. Did you guys have fun?"

Slasher smiles. "Alya, this is Nadine, the b-girl I was telling you about."

"Whoa. No way!"

"Oh, OK. *That's* why you were so frustrated," says Alya. "You're used to doing all the crazy upside-down stuff."

"*You're* Alya?"

"You were expecting someone else?" she asks, bringing her pinkie to her lip like Dr. Evil.

"No . . . you're just . . ." She seems like she should be about four years older than me—like she should be in college.

"How come I've never met you before?" I sputter.

Slasher cuts in. "Alya goes to Rosewood Academy for Girls."

Alya rolls her eyes. "It's not like it sounds."

"Alya's a genius. She got in on a scholarship."

"A *dance* scholarship. I'm just lucky."

"Well, thanks for letting me take the class," I say. "It was good."

"Thanks. You did good," she says.

We drift down the hall to the locker room, and all the little girls waiting for their jazz class or whatever stop giggling and stand up a little straighter as Alya walks by them.

"Hi, Alya!" they call out, jumping up and down to get her attention.

"Hello, Mackenzie, Nevaeh, Addison, Camryn, Charlotte, Chloe, Zoe, Kaitlyn, Hayley, Emma, Emma, Madison, Madison and Meredith," she says.

Some of them try to hug her legs as she walks by.

"I teach them on Saturdays," she explains, like it's no big deal.

I follow Slasher to our locker, but I feel a little weird, since I have no changing to do. Slasher looks around gingerly before changing her shirt, as if anyone is going to notice, or care, but Alya just keeps talking to us as she casually strips down to her underwear.

"So, breaking," she says to me. "How'd you get into that?"

"I dunno," I tell her. "Just kind of by accident, I guess. I had to teach myself a lot, and then there were these guys on my crew . . ."

"I used to bug my brother all the time to show me

some moves," she says. "He used to break a lot before he started doing whatever top-secret hobby he does now. He always told me, 'No, you're too small and wimpy.' He said he didn't want to hang out with his girly little sister anyway."

I roll my eyes. "Tell your brother I think he sucks. What kind of wuss is scared his little sister is going to be better than him?"

"Ha! I will tell him that," she says, lifting her hand for a high-five.

Madi fixes her hair quickly in the mirror.

"I don't know about you," says Alya on our way back down the escalator, "but I'm ready for some hot chocolate. Who's in?"

"I don't know . . . ," Slasher says. "I used up my treat calories at lunch, and I really need to get home and study for physics."

"Madi," says Alya, "you just did ninety continuous minutes of intense activity. You have the spare calories. It's Friday, and you have all weekend to study. Just come for half an hour."

Slasher frowns. Alya throws an arm over my shoulder.

"Madi, I know I don't have to point out that we'll have less fun without you, but Nadine and I are going to have a good time and you'll probably feel left out later when we tell you how much of a good time."

"I guess," Slasher says, resetting her pedometer.

We power-walk over to the Breakfast Barn, even though I'm so tired, I could practically just sit down in the middle of the parking lot and be happy. Then we wait like three hours to get a table, while the waitresses seat the family that shows up *behind* us first. I think they're hoping that we'll change our minds and just go away. They can smell it on our breath that we only want chocolate.

"So, Nadine," says Alya while we wait. "If you don't mind my asking—"

"Yeah?"

She lowers her voice. "Why do you call Madi *Slasher?*"

"Um . . . It's kind of a long story." I exchange a side-long glance with Slasher.

"It's my b-girl name," Slasher says.

"Your what?"

"You know, like Crazy Legs, or Asia One or whatever," she says, remembering names from our media project.

"Yeah," I nod. "Exactly."

"But why *Slasher?*"

"It doesn't have to make sense," I say with a wave of my hand. "It just has to sound cool."

"OK." Alya shrugs. "So what's your handle?"

"Lady Six Sky," I tell her. "Mayan warrior queen. War lord. Ran things. I found her by accident while researching my ancestors for International Day at my old school."

"Your ancestors were *war lords?*" says Slasher, like everyone's great-great-great-great-grandparents have to be lawyers or farmers.

"Can you prove that they weren't?"

"Touché."

"If I was a b-girl," says Alya, "I would call myself Phat Alya."

"Wait, wait, wait," says Slasher. "You *want* to call your-self fat?"

"Not *fat*. Phat. With a p-h."

"Same thing."

"Nuh-unh," says Alya. "But I don't really care anyway."

"You wouldn't. Your ancestors were probably the Tribe of Skinny People from Six-packonia."

Alya looks at her for a second like that is the most offensive thing she has ever heard in her life, but then she just shakes her head.

"Please, Madi. You have met my aunts and uncles. Mother Africa is no match for Little Debbie and the Hungry Man. Besides, it's not like *you* have to worry about fat."

"Oh, but I do. You might not think so, but my mom pointed out that her ass is getting huge this morning. I have the same genes. I have to watch my back. Literally. Nadine?"

"I'm staying out of this."

Finally the waitress admits we exist and shows us to a table.

Alya orders chocolate cake and hot chocolate with chocolate whipped cream and a basket of fries to share. Slasher gets a mint tea. I order just the hot chocolate. I am not made of money, as my dad would say.

I practically fall asleep in the time it takes for the order to come.

twenty-three

"So did you love Alya or did you love her? She's awesome, right?" Slasher asks at our next practice.

"Yeah. She's cool. I like her. She's funny. She would not fit in at RHS at all."

Slasher laughs. "I knew you'd get along. And she totally told me off for my lame toprock. I should have just stuck with your yelling."

I smile.

"Happy?" she asks.

"Thrilled," I tell her.

"Good. 'Cause I invited her to practice."

"Slash—"

But I already hear footsteps on the stairs. I turn around, and Alya is walking towards us, with her hair buried under her hat, bulky sweaters under her jean jacket, tear-away track pants and warm-looking hiking runners. She is ready to work. But I still want to kill Slasher for giving away my practice spot. How am I supposed to get any work done with *two* beginners hanging around?

Alya walks across the platform, sizing up the environment.

"Wow! I forgot about this place. We used to come here when we were little and pretend to fish. There was nothing in the water but soap suds."

"Oh yeah," says Slasher. "I remember that. Your

brother was always threatening to find a snake and bring it home. But there were no snakes."

"It was a sad excuse for a river," says Alya. "Amazing practice spot, though. I never would have thought of it." She walks to the far end and looks up at the mural. It's so big now, it swallows half the wall. Her forehead wrinkles. "Who did *this?*"

I shrug. "The mystery writer of Rivercrest?"

"This girl looks a lot like you," she says, pointing to the dancer smack in the middle of the mural.

"Uh, yeah. A little, I guess, maybe."

"No. That's you. Look—your hair is identical. And there's Madi in the background."

I look where she's pointing and sure enough, there's a blond figure piking into an L-kick.

Slasher takes a closer look. "That's just weird."

Alya crosses her arms. A skeptical look comes over her face.

"What?" says Slasher.

"Nothing," says Alya, rubbing her hands together. "Let's warm up. I'm getting cold. So how do you do things here, Six Sky? Do you have a warm-up to lead, or do you want me to do mine from hip-hop class?"

"You can do what you want. I do my own thing. Slasher has stretches she likes from gym. Just make sure you warm up your knees, wrists and shoulders along with everything else."

"Oh," she says. "So we're not going to warm up together?"

"It's just a practice. You can do what you want."

She shrugs. "All right. Have it your way. Can I put some music on?"

She puts on some new southern crunk something or other. I let it slide.

"Slasher!" I bark when I'm done stretching.

"Yeah?" She topples backwards out of a headstand.

"Since you brought Alya here, you can teach her the 6-step."

"But—"

"Just do it. If you have any problems, let me know. I'll come give corrections when you've gone as far as you can go."

"Okay . . . ," she says. "I still hardly know how to do them myself. You know that, right?"

"You'll be fine," I tell her. "I have to get these mills back. I need this practice."

"OK," she says finally, looking just a tiny little bit guilty for a fraction of a half of a second. "We'll go work on the other platform, so you have enough space."

"Thank you."

Finally, peace. I take my time wrapping my wrist-guards around my arms. I stretch out my hands one last time for good measure. Then I go to my bag and get out the page I printed off the Internet.

There is nothing original about having problems with windmills. That fact alone is almost more irritating than having lost them in the first place. I did a search online to see if anyone else was having the same problem. A few message boards had some suggestions.

I spit out my gum and use it to pin the advice I printed out to the wall, as inspiration.

Ur prblms wit da collapz, dawg. Y u be fallin is u
gots ta change ur mentality. Rotat ur body 1st

as u go 2 stabb. Rotat lgs as u collapz/roll on2 ur back. Get on2 ur stab and have ur legs ready to kick HARD. U shd just spin round til ur fingers point 2 wer ur head is at. Den turn on2 ur side, and touch da floor wit ur L-bo. U do dat— mad propz.

Honestly? I can barely understand that. I've never been fluent in e-boy. But if this wacko can do it, so can I, right?

The collapz, I think to myself. *The collapz.* Rotat, then stabb. Rotat, then stabb. No problem. Rotat. Stabb. Lgs. I have lgs. I can do this.

I take a deep breath, adjust my wristguards and throw myself into the mill. Once around, no problem. Rotating, check. I stab, check. Legs, perfect. I land on my back, staring up at the underside of the bridge again.

Fine, whatever. I pick myself up and go back to the wall. *Rotat lgs as u collapz/roll on2 ur back.*

Wait, so I'm *supposed* to be on my back? How come I never covered this before? That part just came naturally to me before? Why can't I feel it now?

I throw myself at the ground again. *Rotat. Collapz. Stabb. Lgs-back. Kick HARD.*

It's not working. I just end up flipping myself flat on my face. I taste concrete. Yum.

This is where the instructions break down. *U shd just spin.* Yeah. Thanks, Internet. If I could "just" spin, would I even be reading this? No, I'd be spinning, stupid.

I tear the sheet off the wall, crumple it into a ball and throw it into the "river" as hard as I can. I can hear my grade seven ecology teacher gasping as I do. Yeah. Take that, universe. I'm littering. That's what you get when you take my windmills.

I look over at Slasher and Alya across the platform. Slasher leads Al through the 6-step, once clockwise, then counterclockwise. Alya's not that strong, but she picks up the steps really fast. Slasher is super-patient with her. She makes a game of it, quizzing Alya on the steps, challenging her to do them a little bit quicker each time around. The way they work together, you can tell they've been friends practically since they were born.

I feel a pang. I don't have anyone to help me out right now, but did I *ever* have a friend as close as they are?

There was David, when I was four. Then there was Julie, for grades two and three, but she skipped a grade, and then she was embarrassed to hang out with me because I was in a baby grade and her recess was half an hour earlier than mine. Then Grandma Karina died and we moved and I didn't really talk to anyone for a long time.

It wasn't until years later when I started breaking that I finally got over it for real. B-girling was something to focus on—something to do that meant I didn't have to worry about friends. Something I could be good at—that would make my grandma proud. She was always saying how proud she was that my grandpa gave everything he had to his business even though it was risky and no one said he could do it. I know she would feel the same way about my b-girling if I could make it to the Showdown.

I look back over at the girls. Alya falls flat on her ass and starts to laugh her head off. Slasher helps her up, laughing twice as hard.

"Hey!" I yell. "A little quiet, please. Some of us are trying to work over here."

"Sorry," says Al, cupping her hand over her mouth.

"Whatever," says Slasher, dropping back into position one.

I turn the music up to drown them out, drop the mills and practise footwork until it's so dark I can hardly see my feet.

twenty-four

None of the crews I've tried to get in touch with from back home have gotten back to me. Either tha Klub got to them, or they're being all cagey about their little "brotherhoods," or they're just b-boy disorganized and can't figure out how to answer an email.

I am running out of options. If I ever really had options in the first place.

"So, um, do you want to maybe start practising with me a few more days a week?" I ask Slasher at school on Monday.

"Yeah!" she says. "Sure! I won't be in your way?"

"No. But if you're seriously going to stick with this, you need to start practising *hard*. I need to see some major improvement from you if we're going to keep working together."

"Sir, yes sir," she says, standing a little taller.

"Slasher, I'm serious."

"Oh, I know," she says. "Don't you worry. You tell me what to bring, I will bring it."

I raise an eyebrow, unsure if she's making fun of me. "OK, then. Today. The bridge. Four o'clock."

"I'll be there with Pumas on."

"Bring Alya."

I watch Slasher walk across the platform towards me. There's something *different* about her. Nothing big—she still looks like her usual uptight self, but there are little bits of b-girl winding their way into her wardrobe. She's swapped her trademark yoga pants for what look like last year's stretchy jeans—worn at the knees, but way better for rolling around on the cold, hard ground. She really did trade her high-performance runners for some retro sneaks. She's got gloves and wristbands clipped to her bag, like she doesn't care what it looks like, and she's wearing a bandana under her toque—essential for headstands on concrete. There are no earmuffs in sight.

We warm up in silence while we wait for Alya to show up. It takes her forever to get home from her school, which is practically in the city. Lucky.

"All right, listen up," I say, when she finally shows up.

"What?" She laughs. "Not even a hello?"

"Oh. Hi. So, listen up."

Slasher shakes her head.

"Are you warmed up?" I ask Alya.

"I was born warmed up," she tells me. I stare at her. "No, seriously," she says. "I ran here. I'm good. What've you got for us today, mon capitaine?"

"Freezes," I say.

I hit Play on the iPod and run through a quick demonstration run I worked out last night—Brooklyn Rock down to the floor, two 6-steps, counterclockwise, ending in a baby freeze, tipped over on my head with my hands on the ground, feet in the air, and my elbows supporting my right thigh.

"Whoa," says Alya, starting to look a little freaked out.

"Don't worry, we're just going to do the freeze at the end."

"That *is* the part I'm worried about."

"Well, don't. It's supposed to look hard, but it's not," I say, tipping back onto my feet.

The idea of a freeze is that as suddenly as possible, you stop what you're doing—usually in a position that looks impossible or at least very uncomfortable—and hold it for a few seconds. (Or longer if you can and you're a show-off.) This one is called baby not just because it's easy but because from above, it looks like you're curled up like my future sister. It's usually one of the first freezes b-boys learn.

Slasher and Alya don't look totally convinced about the "easy" part.

"Trust me. Even my mom can do this one," I tell them, crouching back into the starting position to break it down.

I know it's hard to believe, but a million years ago, my parents were actually fun sometimes. When I was three, my dad would annoy my grandma by trying to get me to say "Wu Tang," and once during a study break, my mom even let me teach her a baby freeze. She was good at it, but she looked embarrassed right after. The new kid isn't going to know *any* of this about my parents. It's going to be like we grew up in completely different families.

Help me, Alya mouths at Slasher as they crouch beside me on the floor. I'm kind of glad she's nervous. She picked up the 6-step pretty fast. I don't think I could handle it if she was as good at breaking as she is at hip hop right from the start.

"So to start," I explain as I get into position, "you crouch, plant your hands, and lean on your bent elbows like they're a shelf. Eventually, you'll need to figure out how to do this in the middle of a run, without thinking about it, but for now, this is fine."

I ease my weight onto my elbows and gently tilt until my head is on the ground and my feet are pointing skyward.

"It sounds a lot more complicated than it is," I tell them, upside down, as Slasher's arms slip out from under her and she collapses on the dirt.

Alya tentatively tilts, only to chicken out before letting her head hit the floor.

"Don't be scared. Even if you fall, the ground is only a few inches away."

I use one hand to help her brace her arms at a right angle to the ground and guide her feet off the ground with the other. Slowly, creakily, she lets her head droop. One at a time, her feet leave the ground.

"Eek," she squeals, but then her head gently makes contact with the platform.

"That's it!" I tell her.

"I'm doing it?" she says, relaxing.

"You're doing it."

"I'm doing it!"

"Me too!" Slasher says. "Watch!"

I look over. Not only is she doing it but she has memorized the whole choreography sequence and is playing with the position of her legs in the air.

"Slasher! That's good!"

"Oh my god!" she says, tipping out of it and landing in the splits. "A compliment from Nadine. I never thought it could happen."

Alya sighs and tries her freeze again.

"Maybe I can just specialize in having excellent flow?"

"Nah, you'll get it. Just keep at it."

I smile. I don't know—I'm kind of having . . . fun? It's sort of neat being the expert for a change—having people asking *me* how to do moves, and not being the one following everyone else's rules. I can see why Sean was such a control freak about tha Klub. It's good to be at the top, not taking anything from anybody. But I don't want to be like him and start thinking this actually makes me anything special. In this group, I am the cream of the crap. We all have to get better if we're going to mean anything to anyone else in the scene. Hell, we have to get better just to *get* in the scene.

We keep practising until it's so cold that none of us can feel our fingers or toes. You'd think we were figure skaters, not b-girls.

"Two words," says Alya. "Hot. Chocolate. I'm not hearing any arguments this time."

"This is crazy. We need to find someplace else to practise," says Slasher, pulling a second pair of gloves out of her bag.

"I could try to sneak us into Chloe's," says Alya, "but it's risky. Couldn't be an all-the-time thing."

We run up the stairs to the main road.

"My parents hate it when I bring anyone over to the house," says Slasher. "My mom likes it quiet. But this weekend she has some spa thing in cottage country, and my dad's still in Geneva. I could set up the garage."

"That would be wicked," says Alya. "Nadine, you should see her garage. You could park nine Hummers end to end and still have room to practise."

"It's not that big," says Slasher.

"Whatever you say. But you could harbour a fugitive circus family of fire-eating drummer acrobats in there for a year, with all their gear, and no one would notice. That's how big it actually is."

"Shut up."

The waitresses at the Barn have figured out that the fastest way to get rid of us is to serve us.

"Do you have this in a bathtub-sized serving?" Alya asks when the unsmiling waitress brings her hot chocolate. "I'm so cold, I'd rather bathe in it than drink it at this point."

"See, Nadine," says Slasher, "Al thinks my house is too big, but at her place, they're bathing in chocolate. I hear that the faucets are gold, and so are her fillings."

"That was a one-time thing," says Alya, laughing it off. "I don't even have fillings," she tells me under her breath.

"Show-off," says Slasher. "No wonder RHS was such a disaster for you."

"Yeah. Self-respect makes life kind of rough there."

"You went to RHS?" I cut in.

"Yeah. For like a week last year."

"Nadine," says Slasher, "you should have seen it. By Tuesday, she'd pissed off all the girls, because the guys were following her around like dogs. By Wednesday, the guys were done with her, 'cause she was stealing all the thunder in every single class. On Thursday, she got into a fight with her social studies teacher over—what was it?"

"Racial profiling."

"Right," says Madi. "On Friday, her scholarship came through, so she took the day off. Then she transferred on Monday, and that was the end of her tumultuous one-week career at RHS."

"Those guys were all idiots," says Alya. "What was that one dude's name? Jock? What a joker."

"You never like any guys," says Slasher, rolling her eyes. "Every time, it's like, 'he had a funny walk,' 'his shirt was ugly,' 'I didn't like the way he pronounced his Ss.'"

"Why does my love life bother you, anyway, Madi?" says Alya. "I'm too busy to care about guys. I study. I have my dancing. I have my friends. I'm happy."

She goes back to sipping her hot chocolate and intently studying the dessert menu. Slasher slumps forward and rests her head on her crossed arms. I lean back against the padded booth and close my eyes. As the blood starts to flow through my body again, my fingers and toes start to tingle, my face grows hot and I start to feel like I could just go to sleep right there.

"You guys?" I say, opening my eyes before my whole body becomes one with the bench.

They look up, cautiously.

"Practice today was really good. You're doing good."

"Aww," coos Slasher. "That is so nice."

"Yeah, Nadine," says Alya. "Thanks. It *was* good. Except for the part where I chickened out on the baby freeze."

"And my toprock is still lame," says Slasher, starting to giggle.

"No, you've improved," says Al. "I think we can now upgrade its status from lame to seriously injured, but not critical."

Slasher kicks her under the table.

"Ow!"

"B-girls!" I shout a little too loudly. The wait staff turn to stare at me. "Save it for the floor. Next session, we'll do a practice battle."

"OK, you're on," says Slasher, getting up from the table. "I'm gonna smoke you."

"If you can still breathe after you get a load of the styles I'm bringing," says Alya, counting her change and leaving just enough on the table.

"That's the spirit," I say, herding them out the door.

twenty-five

On Saturday morning, I hop on my bike and pedal across the old, rich side of town. Slasher lives on the nicest street I have ever seen outside the city. Great old trees hide even older stone farmhouses from the road. Each one is separated from the next by a lacrosse field of grass.

I find her house, number 42, and I have to double-check that I wrote the number down right. Alya wasn't kidding. The house is about eleven times the size of mine. It's made of nine different kinds of stone, and the driveway goes on for six kilometres. By the time I reach the doorbell, I need a glass of water and a nap.

As I wait for Slasher to answer the door, I hear a rumbling to my right. I look over and realize it's the garage door. A garage door. There are about twelve of them.

"Hey," she yells from inside. "Over here!"

I walk back down the path to the garage. She's standing behind the fourth door from the walkway, waving at me. Alya is already inside, practising her baby freeze on a large piece of linoleum that's taped down to the floor, over what looks like scrap carpeting. She's doing good.

"Yo, Nadine, check it," she says, switching the position of her legs in mid-air.

"Good stuff," I tell her.

A boom box sits on a workbench at the back of the garage, which is mostly empty except for a somewhat beat-up Volvo the next parking space over, and a white Mercedes convertible at the farthest end from the house. The back seat from an old car is set up as a couch against the wall. A heater hangs from the ceiling, glowing red.

"So? What do you think?" she asks, throwing her arms up.

"It's amazing," I say, putting my bag down. "It's, like, bigger than my family's old apartment."

She looks at me like she's trying to figure out if I'm kidding. When she realizes I'm not, she stops smiling and closes the door.

"OK," I say. "Who's ready for a battle?"

They look at each other and then at me. I wait, but no one answers.

"That ready, huh?"

"You're serious? But I like Alya. I don't want to fight her."

"You don't have to want to fight her. You just have to want to be better than her."

"She's still new," says Slasher, "I *am* better than—"

"Hey!" says Alya, jumping up from her freeze. "*Who's* been teaching you to move, Miss Robot? I'll show you—"

I smile. "See? That's what I'm talking about. You have to be able to look at Al, at me, at anyone, and think, 'I can be better than you.' Then you have to get down and prove it."

"It's true," Alya says to Slasher. "I'll smoke you."

Slasher sticks her tongue out.

"Besides," I say, "if you don't have the nerve to battle each other, how are you going to face some dude three times your size who's been dancing since you were born? Battling is what b-girling is."

Her face falls.

"Don't freak out. It's just a practice thing. There are no pro b-boys hanging around your garage, right?"

"No . . . ," she says like she half expects some dude in a bandana to crawl out from under the convertible.

"All right, then." I rub my hands together. "Who wants to go first?"

Alya concentrates on her hands like she just discovered a hangnail. Slasher pokes at a loose corner of the linoleum with her toe.

"No volunteers? OK then, let's have Slasher versus Phat Alya. Winner battles Lady Six Sky. Loser battles Lady Six Sky immediately after that because no way am I taking it easy on you."

I press Play and James Brown leaps out of the boom box.

Slasher and Phat Alya stand on opposite sides of the linoleum, staring at each other like they're each waiting for the other one to get the battle started.

I pause the music.

"The battle isn't going to start itself."

"How do we know who's supposed to go first?" Slasher whines.

"The person who wants it most goes first. No one's going to hand it to you. You have to take it."

"Okayyy . . . ," she says, wrinkling her nose like she doesn't see how that's supposed to work. But as soon as I put the music back on, Alya jumps into the centre of the floor and lets out a series of sick toprock moves, singing along to the music as she accents it with her feet and body. She gets through her footwork slowly but smoothly, and finishes with her baby freeze. I hardly care that there wasn't much technical difficulty in her run. She has so much style, she could stop traffic standing still.

The second Al steps back, Slasher literally dives into action, somersaulting through the air onto the floor. Her hands and feet race through footwork—dizzying 6-steps, CCs, a coffee grinder. She's been doing her research. But at no point does she do *any* toprock. Al stands on the sidelines, pretending to yawn. Slasher gets psyched out and drifts off beat before finishing with a sloppy shoulder freeze, rolling onto one shoulder and limply crossing one leg in front of the other.

"Alya takes this round!" I announce as Slasher leaves the floor.

"Booya!" yells Alya.

"What?" yells Slasher.

"No dancing, no points," I explain. "And the time to act like you're the shit is on the floor, not now. No arguing with the judge."

"Eliminated in the first round?" she fumes. "Enjoy it now 'cause you'll *never* see that again. I'll be back."

Me versus Alya is an easy win, so I'm up against Slasher in no time.

There's a new look in her eyes—hard, determined. She's done with nervous; now she just wants to win. She charges into her toprock, then leaps into her floor work, pushing her flexibility and strength.

She whips through her footwork at breakneck speed, her concentration carved into her forehead, momentum building as she flies from one step into the next, until finally, suddenly, right before my eyes, so incredibly I can't even believe what I'm seeing, both her feet leave the ground at once and swing up in front of her, then behind, then around, faster and faster.

Holy shit! Girl can do flares! Like hardcore, macho b-boy power-move, gymnast-on-a-pommel-horse *flares*.

I start screaming.

"Whaaaaat?"

The garage seems to move in slow motion around me.

"Yo! Stop the music, stop the music!" I yell, leaping over to the stereo to get it myself. I go through eighty emotions all at once before finally settling on disbelief. I have never seen a girl do flares before, ever. I have been working at this for years and even just my windmills are a total mess.

Madi locks eyes with me and falls out of the move, landing on her tailbone on the floor.

"Ow!"

"Slasher! You've been holding out on me! Where did you—? When did you—?"

"Gym." She shrugs, like it's no biggie. "I used to do them for fun on the horse until my coach told me to give it up and work on something I could use in competition. Some of my floor moves were more important at the time."

I feel dizzy-giddy. I need to sit down. "Well, you win this round."

If we were to take this to the Showdown, tha Klub would lose its petty, stupid head. I almost don't even care that it's not me who has the skill. Almost.

"I need some water or something."

We go inside and make about a bathtub's worth of purple juice drink stuff, then lounge around Slasher's TV room, with Grüv TV on mute.

"So here's what I'm thinking," I say when I've had a chance to catch my breath. "Things are going really well— way better than I ever expected. I think we might really have something. I might be losing my mind here, but I think we should give this a serious go. I want to show people what we can do."

They look at me, not quite understanding what I'm trying to say.

"I want to make a try for the Showdown. I want to put together a crew."

"With us?" says Alya. "I mean, *me?* So soon?"

She and Slasher stare at me in silence while the idea sinks in.

"I know it's risky," I say, "but I want to try. I've been working towards it for so long, and you guys have really surprised me—"

Slasher pounds her fist on the coffee table. "We can do this," she says. "I'm in. Alya?"

"Do yo really think—?"

"Yes," says Slasher. "You're better than you think you are. Am I right, Nadine?"

"Yeah. I'm not saying we can *win*. Let's just try to get there."

Alya nods slowly. "OK, then," she says, raising a juice glass. "To getting there!"

Slasher and I clink our glasses against hers.

"To getting there."

I swallow mine back and it goes down the wrong pipe. I end up in a coughing, spluttering pile on the end of the couch. I try not to take it as an omen.

"Um . . . ," says Alya when I've finally started breathing again.

"Yeah?"

"I don't want to be all negative or anything, but if we're going to enter the *four*-on-*four,* don't there need to be . . ."

"Four of us?" Slasher finishes grimly.

"Yeah. That's going to be the hard part," I say, as if everything about this isn't already hard. "Any ideas?"

"No one from my school lives around here," says Alya. "And no one from my hip-hop classes stands out."

"I would ask around," says Slasher, "but I'm not exactly at the top of the A-list right now. It might do more harm than good."

Behind her, on TV, I catch some video that has breaking in it, and then a giant Hogtown Showdown logo pops up on the screen.

"Slasher! Volume!" I shout, and she scrambles for the remote.

It cuts back to the studio, where VJ Sassy Sam is standing with Jester from Infinite.

"So if you've got a crew, start working on those moves and come show us what you've got in February. The prize is bigger this year than ever. Last year's winners were the Smackdown Posse. They were underdogs—totally unknown. This year . . . we want to see as many new crews as possible come out. It's good for breaking, it's good for hip hop, and hey, you can win a whack of prize money, so why not?"

"You hear that, b-boys?" says Sam. "That sounds like a challenge to me."

"And b-girls," says Moriarty.

"Right," says Sam, like she has no idea what he's talking about.

"Omygod," says Alya as they cut to commercials. "It's on TV? This is huge."

Slasher turns the TV off, the blood draining from her face.

"Does our fourth person *have* to be a girl?" asks Al.

"Yes," says Slasher. "The age of the b-girl begins now. We can hold try-outs. Maybe there's a ninth grader we don't know about yet."

"Except that we can't break on school property," I remind her. "Winkley will cut off my hands."

"It's not like they're already going to know how to b-girl. We can let people audition with whatever kind of dance they already know."

"And we'll just *guess* if their breaking is good?" I ask.

"No. We'll look for strong, tough, athletic girls."

"With rhythm," adds Alya.

I frown. "They have to be people who can follow instructions and don't whine every five minutes that it's hard."

"Yeah," says Slasher. "Kickass girls only."

"And if they could maybe do power, that wouldn't hurt."

Slasher stares at me in disbelief.

"What?" I ask, trying not to grin. "If they're on the crew, they should be good. I can hope."

Slasher frowns but nods in agreement. "I'll get my markers. Let's make posters."

twenty-six

Want to
* Work out? *
* Have fun? *
* Put the power in girl power? *
WE NEED YOU!!!
Hit us with your best shot!
Auditions: Lunch, Thursday, Girls' Gym!

Trashley's slaves tear down Slasher's posters, but the announcement still makes it into the "Daily Bulletin."

On Tuesday, we reserve the gym and a stereo. We set up a table and sign-up sheet. And then we wait.

"How did you get permission to use the gym anyway?"

"I told Ms. Bundt we were doing volleyball try-outs."

The deal is that Slasher will be the nice one with the clipboard, who gets them to sign up and asks them about their dance experience, and my job is to look scary until they're done, and then either big them up or cut them down.

Fifteen minutes before the end of English, we sneak out of class and steal a table from the equipment room in the gym and set ourselves up under one of the basketball nets and go over our plan.

"I passed out flyers at cheerleading practice, volleyball,

lacrosse, dance club, smokers' alley, detention hall and that spot at the mall where girls try skateboarding but not while anyone is watching," says Slasher.

This should be good.

When the lunch bell finally rings, Slasher walks to the door. I sit in my chair and scowl with my arms crossed over my chest.

"All right, here goes," she says as she throws it open.

Her face falls.

I wasn't really expecting *tons* of girls to show up—not like a line all the way down the hall and around the corner or anything—but there is *no one* out there.

Slasher hugs her clipboard to her chest.

"Don't worry," I tell her. "The bell just rang. Give it a few minutes."

She comes back to the table. We sit in complete silence, almost afraid to speak, neither of us wanting to admit that things are in the toilet before they've even begun.

Finally, a girl shows up. A first-year, I think, over-weight, wearing oversize blue polyester basketball shorts and a baggy grey T-shirt.

"So," says Slasher, dramatically sweeping her hair back over her right shoulder. "Tell us about what you're going to do for us today."

"Uh, volleyball?"

"Pardon?"

"This is for volleyball try-outs, right?"

I start to laugh. Slasher glares at me sideways.

"Fine," says the girl. "I don't know why I bother trying out anyway. I never get in." And she runs off before Slasher can even get her name.

"Wait, come back!" Slasher shouts and runs after her.

But it's no use. "This was such a mistake," she says, throwing herself down in her chair.

"It wasn't a mistake, Slasher. I didn't have any better ideas. Besides. There's still fifteen minutes left. People could still come."

But at the end of the hour, no one has even *looked* into the gym except Ms. Bundt, who comes to take away our table because the cheerleading squad needs it to set up for a bake sale after school. We sit there, not talking, table-less, until the bell rings.

"There has to be someone," Slasher finally says, picking up her clipboard. "You came here. I'm learning. We found Alya. All we need is one more. *One.* We can find one. There has to be someone we're overlooking. Someone out there is bound to surprise us."

But by the end of the month, the only surprise that comes is my report card.

Gym: B. Math: C. Biology: C–. Geography: C+. English: B–. Art: B . . .

I'm not doing much worse than usual. Actually, I'm pretty lucky to have that C– in bio because I'm pretty sure I bombed every test, and despite all the time I pretended to be out collecting and studying various kinds of leaves around the neighbourhood, I can't remember actually handing in an assignment. There must be a bell curve involved.

"This is not good," says Slasher. "This is not good at all. What are you going to do?"

She's stressed out because she got a B in physics, which she doesn't even have to take, technically, to get into journalism school.

"How am I supposed to demonstrate that I'm well

rounded if I can't do better than a B in physics?"

"I dunno. Show them your flares? That's all I need to know you've got gravity under control."

The report card says right on it in all caps that I MUST take it home and get it SIGNED by PARENTS as SOON as POSSIBLE (*but no later than January 6*).

When I get home from school, my parents are in "the Nursery," knee deep in bunny wallpaper, yellow paint and drop cloths. It's been "the baby's room" all along, but now that they're decorating it, suddenly, it's the Nursery. It's taken them a month to get around to it.

"So I got my report card today," I say.

"What?" says my mom, straining to stick a piece of bunny wallpaper border into a corner.

"I got my report card," I tell her over the racket of the drill my dad is using to hang bunny curtains.

"Nadine," my mom shouts. "Can it wait? We're a little busy here."

"Yeah. It's only my report card. I don't care."

"OK, sweetie," she yells.

I'm pretty sure she didn't hear a word I said, but that's not a fight I'm in any rush to have anyway. I stick the report back in my bag. They can sign it later. I have bigger things to worry about, like naming the crew—my incomplete crew that only has three members and needs some kind of a miracle to happen if I am to actually take it to the Showdown in—yikes—less than three months.

"I'm going to study at Madi's," I yell.

My dad finally shuts off the drill.

"What?" he asks, wiping his forehead with the back of his hand.

"Madi's. I'm going to go study," I say, running down the stairs.

"That's my girl!" he shouts after me. "Call if you need a ride home later."

I meet up with Alya and Slasher in Slasher's TV room. Her parents never seem to be around, so we practise over there all the time now.

"Names," I say. "We need a crew name. Go!" I say, pointing at Alya.

"Floor . . . Goddess . . . Posse?" she says on the spot, grasping at random words from hip hop and/or feminism. "No. That's awful," she says. "Forget I said that."

"OK, what about Fembots," Slasher suggests.

"No," I say.

"Valkyries?"

"I don't even know what that is," I tell her.

"I thought you said it didn't matter if people got it as long as it's cool."

"Yeah, but by people I didn't mean *us*. If we don't know what it means, that just makes us look stupid."

"I've got it!" says Alya suddenly. "PowerPuff Girls!"

"No!" Slasher and I say at the same time.

I shake my head. "No goddess, no femme, no girl power, no sisters, no chicks, no nothing having anything to do with being an all-girl crew."

"But we *are* an all-girl crew."

"Yeah, but that can't be the only thing that stands out about us. I don't want us to be known for being girls. I want people to respect us for our skills."

"OK, I'm just going to throw this out there to get the ball rolling again," says Alya. "Ill Skillz."

"It's been done," I tell her.

"Footwork Fanatics," Slasher suggests, sucking up a little.

"Taken."

"Born 2 Boogie—get it—with the number 2, so it's like cooler."

"Done."

Alya paces. "We need something that says *who* we *are*."

"The only thing we have in common is this place."

"Rivercrew?" says Alya.

"No way. Rivercrest is not a word you can use to make things cooler. It doesn't exactly have the same ring as Brooklyn or L.A."

"No," says Alya, "but what about something about water? Like, we're the crew that puts the *flow* back in Rivercrest."

"Waves . . . ," she mutters. "Too New Age. Tsunami . . . too grim."

Suddenly, Slasher's whole face lights up. "Hydra Force."

"What the hell is Hydra?" I ask.

"It's this monster water serpent with like hundreds of heads, and if you cut off one of the heads, two more grow back in its place."

Alya flashes a wicked grin. "Feminine but deadly. I like it."

"No kidding," I say. "Mess with us, we'll come back stronger. That's awesome."

"All right, then," says Alya. "We're a Force. All we're missing is one head. No problem."

twenty-seven

Make that one problem: the rest of the force clears right out of the country for the holidays. Slasher's family goes to Costa Rica. Alya goes skiing. That leaves me alone with my parents all day, every day. I'm so excited not to have to go to school for fifteen and a half days, I almost don't realize how much break is going to suck until it's already sucking.

On the first day, my parents set up a brand-new fake Christmas tree that turns out to be too tall for our ceiling, and my dad spends half the day arguing with my mom about whether or not to return it ("This was the tree that was on sale, OK? It was *on sale*") and the other half of the day talking to Mr. Henderson about which of his tools he should borrow to cut it down to size so it doesn't look weird. He and my dad stand over it, whispering, with pliers and saws, like it's a bomb they have to deactivate. My mom sits on the sofa watching them and squeezing her temples.

Day two, they finally get all the branches on the tree and my mom and I are almost done decorating it when we start to notice that the house is like, really freaking cold. I put on a sweater and get my mom her slippers, and then I help her load up the tree with boxes and boxes of shiny red and green presents covered in bows. It's not until after we're done that I notice that most of them are labelled "For: Baby Durant," as in my sister who will not even be born until three months after Christmas.

Day three, they spend all day yelling at each other because it's going to cost $500 to fix the heat pump, $800 if we want it fixed before we all die of hypothermia.

"Why didn't you know this wasn't covered by the warranty?"

"No, why didn't *you* know this wasn't covered by the warranty?"

"Can't we just move back to Parkdale?" I ask, and they pretty much slam their bedroom door on me and go back to fighting.

We never had to worry about heat in the old apartment. Something broke, we called the super. Usually it was too hot all the time, so we left the windows open.

To stay warm, my mom spends the rest of the day in the kitchen, baking four hundred batches of burnt cookies and blaming it on the oven.

Lucky for us, we don't have to do all twelve days of Christmas because break started on like day eight. The fourth day is Christmas Eve, and my mom's belly button pops out as soon as the heat comes back on, so we go out for eggnog to celebrate, and for an excuse to finally leave the house. They joke that they cannot afford the eggnog (or at least I think they're joking) and then they do a special toast to me, "for working so much harder at school this year," and I remember that I still haven't shown them my report card, and then they get mad at me for sulking the rest of the night while they're trying to be festive.

Christmas morning doesn't get under way until almost eleven, which is weird. I know in most houses, it's the kids who want to get up at like three to open all their presents, but I've never been able to beat my parents to the tree.

Usually they're hovering outside my bedroom door as soon as the Internet says the sun is rising. This morning? Not so much.

"Sorry, baby, this baby really wanted me to sleep in," says my mom as she waddles downstairs, rubbing her eyes.

My dad comes out of the kitchen and offers me coffee before remembering he doesn't let me drink coffee.

"On second thought," he yawns. "Maybe I should just drink the whole pot myself."

We gather around the tree, and my dad tries to get the fireplace going. My mom gets all teary as she takes both our hands and tells us how happy she is that this is our "first Christmas as a family in our New Home," and I stick my finger down my throat and she slaps me on the arm.

I watch them open box after box of gifts for the baby. Relatives I didn't know we had send little tiny socks and little tiny sleepers and little tiny T-shirts and a whole busload of toys the kid won't even be able to use until she's five.

My aunt in France sends me Amazon gift certificates so I can read more. I set them aside to buy music and b-boy videos.

When all of that is done, my parents turn to me, beaming, and hand me a red box with a giant gold bow on it. I shake it a little. It crinkles on the inside, and thuds.

"Go on, open it!" they say, grinning ear to ear.

I carefully undo the bow and peel back the tape before sliding the box out of the paper. My dad laughs at me.

"Nadine, what's happening to you? You open gifts like your grandmother now?"

I'm only going so slow because the way things are going they're likely to give me a gift certificate for tutoring or something.

I very slowly and carefully open the lid of the box. It's a shoebox. OK, so far, not bad. I get my hopes up just a little—but inside the box is a pair of shiny hard black shoes with a small heel and metal under the toe.

"We signed you up for tap classes so you can start dancing again!" My mom squeals and presses her hands to her knees. My dad puts his arms around her.

"They were a little expensive, but we know how hard you've been working at school this year, and we think you deserve it."

They wait for me to say something. I slowly fold the shoes back into the box, close it and place it back under the tree.

"I don't know what to say— I—"

But my train of thought is interrupted by the sound of my phone ringing upstairs, mosquito style. My parents can't hear it at all.

I look up in surprise—I'm not expecting any calls— and they give me a strange look, but don't catch on.

I think about it and realize it must be one of the girls calling. After five days in the parentzone, a real conversation with a real friend is the best Christmas present ever. I hope there's a callback number. I'll do chores for a year to pay back the long distance. Or my parents can just take it out of my Showdown winnings. Ha.

"I, uh—have to pee," I say suddenly, because my parents are still waiting for me to finish my sentence.

They look confused.

I smile apologetically and run upstairs, where I grab the phone and duck into the bathroom just to stick to my story.

Sitting on the floor with my back to the wall and my

feet pressed up against the edge of the tub, I look at the last number called.

Now *I'm* confused.

It's not long distance at all. It's a 416 Toronto number I don't even recognize. I brace myself for the disappointment that it's only the wireless company wanting to wish me Merry Christmas and trick me into buying something dumb with my phone, but I wait while the phone connects to my voice mail.

The second I hear the voice in the box, my heart skips a beat.

"Yo, Nadine."

Sean!

Sean?

Sean.

I'm so shocked, I don't even hear what he's saying at first. And yet some ancient, buried part of me forces me to replay the message.

"Yo, Nadine," his voice says again, relaxed, friendly. Where does he get off sounding relaxed while I'm having aneurisms on the floor of my parents' bathroom? I backtrack again.

"Yo, Nadine, I know things haven't exactly been good between you and me lately, but I'm not such a big jerk I can't pick up the phone and wish you a Merry Christmas. So, Merry Christmas. I hope you're smarter than Encore and Recoil, and didn't do nothing dumbass like get your moms a dub of the *Saw* trilogy for Christmas. What else? Just two months left to the Showdown, right? Hope you been practising. Peace."

I hang up and stare at the phone for a minute.

What was that?

What *was* that?

He barely remembered to say Merry Christmas last year, when we were dating. And what was that last bit?

"Just two months left to the Showdown, right?"

Was that a veiled hint? Or a dig?

"Hope you been practising. Peace."

To think, ten minutes ago, I was ready to get all worked up over a pair of tap shoes.

God. What if it wasn't a dig? What if he's, like, *using Christmas* as an excuse to talk to me? Why is he even mentioning the Showdown? Are things not going so well with tha Klub? They still need four people if they're going to battle. Maybe . . .

No way. Sean would never ask me back. Even if he wanted to, his pride would hold him back.

But with a cash prize that big, it would make sense that he would want to go with the best crew he could put together. Maybe even Encore and Recoil are smart enough to figure that out.

Even I would have to admit that would make the most sense—as much as it would kill me.

I don't know what I'd do if that's what he wanted. Maybe Slasher and Phat Al could even come as spares and enter the two-on-two, and like start a new generation of tha Klub.

I toss the phone back and forth from hand to hand for a couple of minutes, trying to figure it out.

I decide I'm not going to be that girl who spends Christmas break trying to guess what some guy is thinking.

I hit the call-back button and it rings twice before an all-too-familiar voice that isn't Sean's answers.

"Who is this? What do you want?" Jazmin snarls.

My mouth makes word shapes, but no sound comes out.

"I *know* my man dialled your number. You better tell me who you are," she shrieks. "As if I can't already guess."

I almost hang up right then and there, but then there's a rustling sound, and Sean comes on the line.

"Nadine?"

"Sean?"

"Nadine, why do you *always* have to go making a big deal out of nothing? Yeah, so I called you, OK, but so what? I just wanted to wish you a Merry Christmas. I didn't ask you to call back."

I play his message back in my mind on high speed. Jerk. Christmas. *Saw III.* Showdown. Practise. Peace. (As if.)

I'm a little embarrassed to have already memorized the message, but yup, he's right, he did not actually ask me to call back, like most people expect you to when they leave a message. How specific of him.

"Oh right, like I read *so* much into it," I say. "*I'm* the one making a big deal right now. God. Your ego is so huge. I was just trying to be polite."

"Yeah, righ—"

"Goodbye!" I yell, and press the end-call button as hard as I can. It so sucks that you can't slam a cell phone to hang it up.

I hear my parents calling me from downstairs. They probably think I've died in the bathroom. I stand up, take a deep breath and flush the toilet. It makes the same sound as the lurching feeling in my stomach.

"Nadine, what's wrong?" my mother asks when I go back downstairs, clutching my stomach.

"I dunno. Nothing. I'm just not feeling well."

I spend the next three days asleep in the basement.

twenty-eight

Alya and Slasher finally come back from their glamorous family vacations. I don't really feel like doing anything, but on New Year's Eve day—the coldest day in the history of forever—I get bundled up from head to toe and my dad drives me to Slasher's house for what my mom keeps calling a "sleepover party."

"Whew," he whistles as we drive down and then up her driveway. "This place is amazing."

He puts the car in park, undoes his seatbelt and makes like he's going to get out of the car.

"Dad, what are you doing?"

"I'm going to meet Madi's parents," he says, sitting down again.

"You don't have to do that," I say.

"No, but I want to," he says.

"They're not going to be home right now."

I don't want him meeting Madi's parents. Number one, *I* have never met Madi's parents. Number two, I have no idea what she's told them about me. I don't need this b-girl stuff coming out right now.

"If they're not home, I don't want you staying overnight," he says.

Oh, crap.

"Dad," I say, thinking as fast as I can, "her dad is like this crazy lawyer guy. He'll be working. Her mom will be shopping or at yoga. They'll come home by dinner. Why do you think I'm allowed over in the first place?"

"All right," he says, eyeing me suspiciously.

"It's Madi, Dad. It's fine."

I jump out of the car and slam the door before he has a chance to change his mind.

He waits in the driveway with the motor running as I ring the front doorbell. I wave goodbye, but he keeps sitting there until he sees the front door open. Finally, he starts to back away.

"Hello?"

When I turn back to the door, it's not Slasher standing on the other side but her mother. At least, I think it's her mother. She has crazy blond hair, fried from too many dye jobs, all piled on top of her head in a big, messy bun. She's older than my parents, but her skin is shiny, with no wrinkles. Her eyes are done up with gloppy black mascara, and her weirdly lumpy lips are frosted with thick pink lipstick. She's wearing what looks like one of Slasher's yoga outfits, with poofy feathery slippers, with a small heel.

"My husband pays the newspaper bill online," she says, looking me up and down with razorblade eyes.

The warm draft from inside the house melts the ice on my eyelashes a little.

"Is Madi home?" I ask in a small voice. Whoever this woman is, I bet even Encore and Recoil would feel about six inches tall standing in the cold with her looking down on them like this.

"Oh," she says with a wave of her hand, and wanders off, leaving me standing outside with the door still open.

"Madison!" she yells as her slippers click-clack down the hall towards the garage.

Since the door is still open, I let myself in and stand in the entrance, which is like something from an old movie, with a big turny staircase and a chandelier and a floor made of marbly stuff.

I close the door, take off my coat and hat and wonder what I should do next.

There's some kind of weird New Age music playing upstairs.

Finally, I hear Slasher's mom click-clacking back. I breathe deep and try to smile.

"She's in the garage or wherever," she says, walking right up the stairs without looking at me a second time. "My meditation is *ruined*," she mumbles to no one I can see.

Man am I glad my dad stayed in the car.

I take off my boots and walk down the hall in my sock feet to find Slasher in the garage. Or "wherever."

I've never been through the house this way, but wherever the garage is, the music is loud enough that I can follow the bass down a long hallway, and down a short flight of steps, past the TV room.

Slasher and Alya don't hear me at first when I open the door. I find them lying in a heap on the floor, laughing their heads off.

"Hey!" I yell. They look up at me guiltily before one of them looks at the other, and they start laughing again.

"What's going on?" I ask.

"She started it," says Alya, pointing at Slasher. Slasher starts laughing again.

"Started what?" I say, starting to feel left out on the joke.

"Nothing," says Alya, laughing harder.

"Yeah, nothing," says Slasher, punching Alya in the shoulder.

Slasher laughs so hard through her nose, it comes out as a snort.

"Whaaat?" I ask, seriously getting frustrated now.

Alya shakes her head, tries to stand up, but then falls over again, hysterical.

"Hey!" I yell, clapping my hands together. "Snap out of it! This is important. I've been waiting for you for practically two whole weeks. It's almost *next year* already. The Showdown is scary-soon. We're still short one head. We have to get some serious work done."

"OK, OK," says Slasher, wiping her eyes. "Relax. It's still supposed to be fun, right?"

"Yeah," says Alya, catching her breath. "It's New Year's. Party now. Worry later."

"Don't you get it? This *is* later."

"Whoa," says Slasher. "*Someone* needs a vacation."

Her words hit me like a slap in the face.

"You're right," I snap. "I'm sorry I forgot to be rich like you. Next year, I'll tell my parents to save up."

Slasher looks embarrassed.

"It's not like my parents paid *cash* for our trip," says Alya quietly.

I think of the baby furniture and my parents' forty maxed credit cards. I don't even know how to have this fight. I'll give tha Klub this much: when Encore and Recoil spend their whole paycheque on one pair of shoes or new rims for the rust bucket, at least they know how many pizzas they had to deliver to make it happen, and how many more DVDs they'll have to move out of the trunk of said rust bucket to replace the cash.

"Look, can we just practise already?"

"Whatever you say, El Presidente," says Alya, turning

the music up so loud she can't hear my reaction.

After all that, practice basically sucks. Even though Slasher claims to have spent her entire vacation swimming her ass off and Alya hit the slopes every day, they're both stiff and out of practice. Alya can't make it through a single 6-step without giggling for no reason. Slasher insists she's forgotten how to do them entirely and spends all her time in headstands and backbends.

While I'm on the floor, they sit on the couch, chatting it up over the music. Slasher won't shut up about some lifeguard she's pretty sure flirted with her. Al keeps re-enacting how her brother got stuck on the chairlift the first day he tried snowboarding. They don't even *ask* how my break was. I don't try to tell them.

The house is dark and empty when we finally give up and go inside. Slasher's parents already left for their New Year's party without saying goodbye.

We turn the lights out on centre court and head into the kitchen to drink an entire pitcher of OJ before throwing ourselves down on the couch in Slasher's TV room with a stocking full of candy she got for Christmas but won't eat, and the year's worst video countdown on Grüv TV.

"So what are we going to do now?" says Alya, helping herself to an entire chocolate orange from the top of the stocking.

Slasher shrugs as some guy with a guitar-shaped keyboard does the swim against a spacey rainbow background on the TV.

"I dunno. Order a pizza and watch *Stick It?*"

Alya pouts. "I'm all hyper now. I feel like doing something New Yearsy."

"There's champagne in the basement," says Slasher.

"I want to go *out*," Alya says.

"I think one of the good Tiffanys is having a house party."

"I'm tired of Rivercrest parties. Let's go downtown."

I raise an eyebrow.

"How are we going to get away with that?" Slasher asks.

"How are we *not* going to get away with it? Your parents are out already. Me and Nadine are sleeping here."

Slasher sits up a little taller. "Where would we go?"

"Six Sky," says Alya. "You're from the 416. Where can we go?"

I have a sudden flashback to Trashley begging me for "stuff" in the bathroom at school.

"Oh I don't know. Are you sure you want to do that?"

"I don't need to sneak out to walk over to Burger King. If we're going to do this, let's *do it!*"

"How are we supposed to get there?"

"Easy. My brother will dr—"

"I dunno, you guys," I say. "You have no idea what it's like trying to get in anywhere at the last minute on New Year's. Everything's like fifty bucks just to get past the door, and then it's like not even as good as normal, and everything's packed with idiots from the suburbs . . ." I remember where I am and who I'm talking to. "Well, anyway, it's not worth fifty bucks."

"We don't have to go to a club," says Slasher. "Let's just go somewhere fun and hang out—like the fireworks at Nathan Phillips Square or something."

"Yeah!" says Alya, jumping up. "Bershawn Sera is playing at eleven. Omygod! I love his voice."

"Guys," I whine. "I thought we already had a plan."

"Sitting around *here?*"

"I thought we were going to watch videos and—"

Some woman on the TV climbs out of a cake and starts showering herself in grape juice. OK, bad timing, maybe.

"It's two against one, Nadine," says Alya.

"What?"

"It's two against one. I want to go. Madi wants to go. I guess you can stay here by yourself if you want."

"Slasher—," I say.

"Do you want the first shower, Nadine, or do you want to just wait until after we're gone? You'll have the whole house to yourself."

"Fine," I say, throwing myself angrily into the couch. "I'll go. But don't blame me if it's stupid."

They're not even listening to me. They're already running down the hall.

"Omygod, I'm going to wear your white pants!" Alya yells.

When I step out of the bathroom, Slasher and Alya are already dressed. Slasher is wearing brand-new pants she just got for Christmas, with brand-new boots she just got for Christmas and the brand-new white puffy coat with fake-fur-trimmed hood she bought with her Christmas money this morning because she was jealous of Alya's. Her hair is down for maybe the first time ever, and she's wearing a shade of lipstick that for once is not exactly the same shade as her lips.

Alya is glowing under what looks like a pound of bronze powder, but knowing her, it's totally possible that's the skin she was born in and I just never noticed. She's wearing Slasher's coat, in black, with one of Slasher's scarves wrapped around her head.

I have no funky outfit to change into. If you were to multiply Alya's pant size by Slasher's, it would still be a size too small on me, and I don't exactly want to show off as much cleavage as one of their shirts would expose on my body.

I stuff my feet back into my Timberland boots and pull on my extra hoodie and my jacket. I guess I'll put on some lip gloss in the car or something.

The doorbell rings.

"Yes, yes, yes," says Alya, running downstairs to get it. "I cannot believe *I'm* going to see *Bershawn* live in less than two hours. This is the best New Year's *ever*."

The doorbell rings again five times, just for fun.

"Devin, stop," says Alya as she swings open the door.

Needle scratch.

He is wearing crisp khaki pants, boots like mine, only new and clean, and a crispy-new black puffy jacket. His head is freshly shaved. I can smell his cologne all the way from upstairs.

"Slasher," I say, jumping back out of view, but unable to look away from the tragedy that is unfolding in front of us.

"Yeah?"

"Why is *Devin* here?"

"*Be-cause* Alya is his *sis-ter?*" she says, like I should have known from the get-go.

"Why didn't you *tell* me?"

"I thought you knew! You didn't notice the resemblance?"

"What? Like there can't be more than one black family in Rivercrest?"

"You could look at it that way if you wanted to be a bitch about it," she says, taking a step back. "But I meant something more along the lines of they have the same eyes and laugh alike."

I snort. "Well excuse me if I haven't exactly been *gazing* into Devin's eyes."

She eyes me suspiciously. "Why are you being so *touchy?* Do you *like* him or something?"

"Um, hello? No."

"Then why do you hate him so much?"

"I don't, I just—"

"He's always nice to you," she says, getting louder. "At that dance when Winkley—"

"Slasher!"

"I thought Devin was going to punch him," she says, loud enough for him to hear. "I've known him since I was seven and I've *never* seen him that angry. He must really like *you.*"

"Slasher. Shut. Up."

"Whatever." She flips her hair.

I hate my life.

I follow Slasher downstairs.

"Nadine, what a pleasant surprise," Devin says with his teasing half smile.

I study his face, trying to figure out if it was really a surprise for anyone other than me.

"Ladies," he says, holding the door open, "your chariot awaits."

I pull on my ugly toque—the one with the ear flaps—and storm past him.

He winks at me. Gag.

I drag my feet down the walkway after the Force, and

notice there is weird blue smoke seeping out from under the chariot.

"Is that normal?" I ask, stopping at the end of the walkway.

"Yeah, no worries. It's 'cause it's cold out. I only left it on 'cause I was afraid if I turned it off, I'd never get it to start again."

"Great. I feel totally safe now."

Devin opens the front door and pushes his seat forward. Alya dives into the back. He pretends to stuff her into the car with his foot. Slasher piles in behind Alya, laughing. I realize, too late, this leaves me sitting in the front seat beside Devin.

"Watch your seatbelt," he says, running around to open my door. "You have to really tug it to get it on."

"Great," I mumble again, and slap his hand away as he tries to pull it loose for me.

Devin jumps into the driver's seat and puts the car in gear with a loud grinding sound. We start to roll-slide back down the driveway.

It's dark out now, and every house in Rivercrest has its Christmas lights on. I stare out the window as we drive, so I don't have to look at Devin, who's humming and tapping the steering wheel along to the beat on the stereo, which is probably five times as powerful as the car itself.

"Yo, what *is* this?" I finally ask, when the music gets too lame to take.

"Bershawn Sera!" Alya and Devin say together.

"God, Nadine, even *I* knew that," says Slasher, kicking the back of my seat.

"That is *not* something to be proud of," I tell her.

"Ooh, dis!" says Devin.

"Hell yeah," I say. "This music sucks."

"It does not. Bershawn is our boy. He's from TO."

"That only makes me hate him worse," I say. "I don't want my city being known for this."

"And what music do *you* enjoy, Nadine?"

"Why do you care?"

"Pick something," he says. "I bet I've got it in here. Al, hand me those binders."

We pull onto the highway.

"Devin—"

"C'mon, pass them up front."

Alya leans forward and hands me three heavy binders full of CDs.

"Go ahead," says Devin. "Pick something."

I refuse to open them.

"OK," he says, "let me see if I can guess." He reaches over and opens the top binder without even looking at it.

"Shouldn't you be concentrating on driving?"

He flips through the pages, still without looking. "Aha, yes, I've got it," he says.

"Right. I'm sure every disk in this thing is solid gold."

He pops Bershawn out and tosses him carelessly onto the dashboard. The new disk slides into the player and a familiar intro starts: horns, Spanish guitar, then the bass kicks in. Damn. "The Creator" by Pete Rock & C. L. Smooth. I *do* like that song.

We listen for a minute, Devin glancing over at me periodically and smiling to himself.

"So," he says. "How'd I do?"

"It's OK . . . I guess," I say, shrugging as much as my seatbelt will let me. As soon as I start to lean forward, it goes out of control and snaps back so hard, it practically strangles me.

"Hahaaaa!" he says. "You love this song. I know it. I can tell. You can pretend you don't care all you want, but I can see you sitting there trying not to bob your head."

"We should add this to our practice mix," says Slasher.

"I'm not trying not to bob," I say. "I am trying to keep this stupid seatbelt from killing me. Where did you get this car anyway?"

"Hey!" he says. "No disrespecting the car." I can't tell if he's serious or not. "I'll have you know this is the first car my parents bought after I was born. This car and I have *history.*"

All of a sudden, Devin's little piece of history makes a funny sound. Or rather, it makes a funny non-sound. Everything gets really quiet and then the car starts to roll slower and slower. Devin pumps his foot on the gas and jiggles the keys in the ignition.

"Nadine!" he says, pulling over into the breakdown lane. "You jinxed the car."

"Nuh-unh," I say. "I blame Bershawn. Car couldn't take it anymore."

Devin tries the keys again, but the car won't go. The engine turns and gets smoky, but not smoky enough to move us forward.

"Shit!" says Devin, slamming his fist against the steering wheel. Then, "Sorry," in a quieter voice.

"What are we going to do?" Slasher whines.

"Give me your phone. We'll call CAA."

"What's wrong with yours?"

"This was your trip. I'm not using my minutes."

"Fine," she says, digging the phone out of her bag. It's cream coloured with a dangly pink beaded wrist strap. Devin takes it from her delicately between two fingers, leaves the car and walks twenty paces down the highway.

We watch him gesturing as he leans into the phone, his free hand on his head. Finally, he hangs up and stands on the side of the road, staring down the highway.

"I'd better see if everything's all right," says Alya, unbuckling her seatbelt. Slasher jumps out of the car after her. I slowly untangle myself and follow.

"Dev," says Alya. "What's the story?"

He sighs. "They're going to come tow us, but it's going to take like forty-five minutes."

"Forty-five minutes!" says Alya. "I'm going to miss Bershawn."

"We're going to die of hypothermia before then anyway," says Slasher.

Devin shrugs. "It's New Year's. They're busy. What do you expect?"

I look around. I don't even know where we are. Scarborough, maybe?

"Isn't there *anything* you can do?" Slasher asks Devin.

"Like what?"

"I don't now. It's your car. Can't you, like, look under the hood and see what the problem is?"

"Madison, I know two things about how this car works: I can turn on the stereo and I can call CAA. I've already tried everything I know."

"Well, as long as the car is dead anyway, I'm turning the radio back on," says Alya. "I'm missing Bershawn, I'm going to make my fun any way I can."

Slasher starts to do jumping jacks to warm up. I jog in place beside her. Devin pulls the collar of his jacket up and blows on his hands. Seconds later, the sound of Pete Rock & C. L. Smooth blasts out over the roaring of the highway. Slasher hugs her arms to her body and looks around like maybe the sound is going to disturb someone driving by at 120 clicks.

"All right, make some room, people," says Alya, running back towards us.

"Room for what?"

"It's called the breakdown lane, isn't it?" she says. She ducks down, plants a mitten on the asphalt and launches into the footwork she couldn't seem to remember at practice this afternoon.

A passing car honks as she kicks into an elbow freeze.

"Oh!" says Devin. "Oh, oh, *oh!* It is *on,* sister, it is *on.*"

And with that, he launches into a jerky, bouncy set of toprock steps.

"I am not seeing this," I say, burying my face in Alya's shoulder.

Slasher covers her mouth and giggles.

"You call that b-boying?" Alya shouts. "That's the best you can do?"

He drops to the ground and proceeds to lay down a set of proper, by-the-book footwork, most of which I miss because I turn my back to him and cross my arms over my chest while I wait for him to finish. I turn back around to see him coming out of a basic crab freeze.

"All right, Nadine, you're next," he says, standing up and pointing at me.

I laugh. "I don't battle beginners."

"Lady Nadine! I'm hurt," says Devin. "This is one hundred percent Devin freshness, finely honed, and refined with age."

"You really shouldn't steal your sister's style like that."

He kisses his teeth. "I used to break all the time. My sister has simply reinspired me. Admit it. It was good."

I shrug. "It was okay, I guess. For a guy."

"Your footwork could be a lot faster," says Slasher.

"Your transitions aren't smooth enough," says Alya.

"Haters," he mumbles, and launches into a handstand with scissor kicks, to make a point.

Just then, flashing lights finally show up on the horizon, and the CAA truck pulls up. A middle-aged guy in jeans and a puffy Gore-Tex jacket gets out and walks over to Devin.

"You call for roadside assistance?" he asks.

"Yeah, that was me—you, uh, got here faster than we thought."

"You been drinking at all, son?"

"No, sir."

Alya and Slasher start to giggle so hard, I think they're going to fall over into the snowbank.

"What are you kids doing out here by yourselves?"

"Trying to get into town to check out the fireworks, sir."

"You shouldn't be horsing around on the side of the highway like this. Dangerous."

"Just trying to keep warm, sir."

The roadside guy goes over to the car and pops the hood like Devin didn't. He gets a toolkit out of his truck and spends about ten minutes poking around.

"I can't fix this here. I'll give you a tow, but only to a garage, all right? You gotta get this thing looked over before taking it on the road again."

"Yes, sir."

"So we're really not going to see Bershawn?" Alya whines.

"Al," says Devin, "don't even start with me."

A cab comes to take us home. Devin rides in the truck to the garage, and Slasher, Alya and I pile into the back of the cab.

"You know," says Slasher, "Devin isn't half bad."

"I know," says Alya.

"Interesting," says Slasher. "Don't you think so, Nadine?"

"No. What are you getting at?"

"Oh nothing," she says. But then she sighs again.

"*What,* Slasher?"

"Well," she says, "it's just that the Showdown is only how many weeks away now?"

"Nine."

"And we still haven't found a fourth—"

"We are not letting Devin into the Force, Slasher."

"What? No! Wait, I didn't say *that* . . . ," she says.

"It's not the worst idea," says Alya, closing her eyes and leaning back against the seat.

"Yes, it is," I say. "It's a terrible idea."

Slasher makes a face. "Nadine, even if we found a fourth girl, nine weeks isn't long enough to train her from scratch."

A knot tightens in my stomach. "You guys, we are not quitters. We will find someone else."

"Nadine," says Alya, "have *any* of the b-girls you called gotten back to you?"

"Not yet . . ."

"So what's this really about?"

"I seem to remember a story you told us about how Devin doesn't even think girls should break."

"Not *girls*. Me. His sister. To get on my nerves. It's in his DNA to do everything he can to piss me off."

"I still don't want him in the group."

"Why not?"

"It doesn't feel right."

"Why? Do you *like* him or something? Does he make you *nervous?*"

Apparently pissing people off is in her DNA, too. It's like a family thing.

"Ha!" says Slasher. "I said the same thing."

"Shut up!" I yell, pressing my hands over my ears. "I don't. He's just annoying."

"Well, duh. He's my brother. But is he really so annoying that it's worth missing the Showdown?"

"I don't think so," says Slasher.

The car stops. We get out and continue the argument all the way back up Slasher's driveway. I can tell from the snow on the driveway that her parents are still not home. Girl is practically an orphan.

"I thought you were with me on this, Slasher. The *all-girl* idea was yours to begin with."

"That was then. Things are different now. I think we should give him a try."

"Me too," says Alya.

"It's two against one," Slasher says for the second time tonight.

I clench my hands into fists.

"I can't believe you're doing this to me," I finally say, kicking my boots off. "I thought we were crew."

"We are *friends*," says Slasher. "And friends don't let friends risk months and months of work on some petty grudge you're going to regret later."

"It's not only about you," says Alya. "We've been working our asses off for this too, you know."

"And besides," says Slasher, "Devin can drive."

I laugh. "Not in *that* car."

She shrugs. "It's two against one," she says again.

I stare at each of them, leaning on opposite sides of the front doorway, grinning down at me, smug.

I have to walk between them to get in the door.

"You know what? I think I'm just going to call my dad to come get me. I've had enough of this."

"See?" says Slasher. "You can't even have a mature discussion. It's always your way or nothing."

"Don't worry about that anymore. I'm done. I'm out."

I grab my phone out of my pocket and speed-dial home.

"Nadine!" says Slasher, putting her hand on my wrist to stop me. "Come on. Over this?"

I tear my hand away. "Dad," I say when he answers. "I feel sick again. Can you come get me?"

"Fine, be a big baby," says Slasher. She turns on her heels and storms upstairs.

"I can't believe you, Nadine," says Alya, following her.

The door upstairs slams twice, then opens again, and my backpack comes tumbling down the stairs. The door slams again. I'm left to wait for my father alone in the dark, surrounded by the cold marble of the grand foyer.

twenty-nine

"Honey, how are you feeling this morning?" my mom asks at breakfast.

"Crappy," I say.

"Were you having a good time before you got sick?"

"No."

"What were you doing?"

"Nothing."

I stab at my cereal. It tastes like dust. It's getting soggy in the milk.

"Why did you come home early?"

"I told you, I wasn't feeling well."

"You look OK to me," says my mother, pressing her wrist to my forehead. "You're eating. You don't have a temperature."

"You are *going* to school tomorrow," says my father.

"I know."

They look at each other over my head, like *what? What am I supposed to do with this?*

"Well, I hope you're not planning to spend the whole day down—"

I don't hear the rest because I'm halfway down the stairs with my breakfast already. I don't know why I brought it. I'm not going to eat it.

I sit on the sofa, surrounded by mountains of blankets. I try to watch TV but it doesn't take my mind off anything. I can't stop thinking in circles. *When* exactly did everything go to hell, and *how* did I not notice until now? I'm sure Slasher would say it was when *I* wouldn't let Devin in the Hydra Force, but I think it was before that—maybe when I agreed to go to Chloe's stupid Movement Spa. Sean never would have set foot in that mall. Or when I let Slasher hang out with me at the bridge. I never should have showed her my moves. This "two against one" crap is just tha Rackit Klub repeating itself all over again, dressed up in pink Lycra.

It's my own fault. I didn't get the message when Slasher hit me in lacrosse. How desperate did I have to be to miss a sign like that? They're just spoiled Rivercrest girls. They pretend you're on their team until they get what they want, and then they're done with you. I should never have expected them to stay on my side. What do they need with me now that they know a few moves? Traitors.

I get down on the floor and stretch a bit. I feel like garbage. I do a quick chair freeze. Total crap.

What the hell am I supposed to do now? Show up at the Showdown alone? Shake my bootie for a pat on the head and a new pair of jeans? The Force knows how important the Showdown is to me. I can't believe they'd use it against me.

I want to punch something. I want to scream.

I sit back down and go to sleep for four hours.

I change all my routines so I don't have to run into Slasher. I go in through the back door in the morning. I walk through the grade nine hallway to get to homeroom.

"Hey, it's that Nadine dance girl," one of them announces to the whole hallway.

"Get out of my way," I say as I shove him to get to the door.

I go through my classes like a robot, not really thinking about anything. Everything that was hard at the beginning of the year seems even harder now. I get called to the board in math and I can't even understand the information in the first half of the problem, let alone how to solve it. In geo, I can't care about, let alone remember the name of, every fish in Lake Ontario.

Eventually, Slasher and I have media studies together, but she doesn't try to talk to me either. She sits at her seat, trying to engage Staci in conversation about Christmas break. It's like trying to draw blood from a stone. She notices me notice and tries to look away, but I stare at her hard. I look right through her.

After class, she actually tries to catch up with me.

"Nadine—"

I walk away and refuse to turn around.

At the end of the day, as I'm running home the long way, my phone rings. It's Alya. I block the call and then delete her number from my phone. We have nothing to talk about.

When I get home, I try to practise, but there's still not enough room in the basement. It's still the most ridiculous practice spot ever and the practice is maybe the worst I've ever done. But what does it matter anyway? What's the point?

I take all my b-boy videos and I put them in a box, then bury it at the back of the storage room, behind my dad's skis (He skis? Who knew?), under the gardening stuff. I don't need to be reminded of everything I'm never going to do. This is the end of the line for me.

When I come upstairs, my parents are rushing around the house. My dad is still in his suit and my mother is wearing her most motherly maternity dress, clicking around the kitchen in her sensible pumps. She fusses in the hall mirror, trying to make her jacket hang right over her belly. I catch a whiff of the perfume she only ever puts on for important things that happen in the evening. She never wastes it on work.

"Argh!" she huffs, giving up on the jacket. "It is so hard to look professional while pregnant! This is not doing anything good for my blood pressure."

I think she wore track pants the whole nine months when she was carrying me. Maybe that explains my fashion sense now. If that's true, the new baby is going to pop out wearing a pantsuit.

"Oh, Nadine, good, you're home," says my dad. "Where were you?"

"Downstairs."

"This whole time?"

"Yeah."

"What were you doing?"

"Nothing."

"What about your homework?"

"I did it at lunch."

"OK," says my mom. "Dinner's in the fridge, just nuke it in the micro. We're late. We'll be back in a few hours. Do your homework."

"All right, already."

She kisses me on the head and they disappear into the garage. It's not until after they're gone that I realize I don't know where they're going.

thirty

In the morning, I wake up in the basement, and it takes me a minute to remember where I am. I can hardly unfold myself, I'm so stiff from sleeping crumpled up on the couch again. The TV is still on. I hear quiet footsteps in the kitchen and I creep upstairs, hoping that if I move quickly and quietly enough, I can make it to the shower without getting questioned about my homework or having my mom force breakfast down my throat.

But my parents don't even look at me when I pass by the kitchen. My mom is staring out the window, with her arms folded over her belly, not eating her bagel. My dad's face is hard and angry. He's reading the business section.

They get like this sometimes when they're fighting.

I get dressed and we drive to school in silence. I can barely hear my mom when she says bye. My dad does not tell me to have a good day.

During homeroom, I get called to the front of the class.

"Ms. Durant, Mr. Winkley requests your presence in the office."

I look around the room and see a sea of raised eyebrows. How much trouble does a person have to be in to get called to the office before class even starts? And to the guidance counsellor. Did someone die? Do I have an eating disorder? Does Winkley have some new research to show me about how breaking somehow causes mad cow disease?

Everyone watches as I gather my books, trying as hard as I can to act normal.

"Nadine!" says Mr. Winkley, leaping out of the office to meet me. The papers on the bulletin boards rustle after him. "I had a *very* interesting conversation with your parents last night."

I freeze. So does my brain. "What?"

"At parent-teacher night, Nadine. Last night?"

So that's where they went. Uh, oh.

Winkley smiles and begins to walk me back down the hall towards his office. The receptionist frowns at me over her glasses. "You know, Nadine, some of our students volunteered to run the refreshment stand last night at parent-teacher night. Some of them spent a month learning the school song to sing last night at parent-teacher night. Some of them made special projects to present last night at parent-teacher night. If you were one of those students, Nadine, then you would know that last night was parent-teacher night." He holds open his office door and waits for me to sit in a scratchy grey chair opposite the desk.

What am I supposed to say to that? So I didn't know it was parent-teacher night. Am I a parent? No. Am I a teacher? Not here. After what happened at the dance, I somehow doubt that he wants me to show up at P-T night and do battle cries in the foyer.

"Good thing I called your father at the office, or he might not even have known to come. They care about you, you know—your parents," Mr. Winkley drones on. "They're worried about you. Frankly, I'm worried too." He closes the door and sits down across from me. Ugh. Alone with Winkley.

"If my parents have a problem with me, let them tell me."

"That is exactly what I'm talking about," he says, pointing. "You're angry, Nadine. We can all see it. And you think you have us so fooled. You know, all this time, your parents think you've been spending your afternoons at the *library?*"

I roll my eyes.

"Did you think you could hide your report card forever?"

"I *tried* to show it to them. They were too bus—"

"They're very confused as to why your grades aren't better. I mean, your grades are fine, Nadine. Nothing to panic about. You can still get into community college someday if you don't care what your major is."

He opens a book, flips to some chart and runs his finger down a list. "As long as you can live on . . . eight thousand dollars a year, Nadine, you don't need to do anything differently. I hope you enjoy living with your parents."

I say nothing. He throws up his hands. Not like he's actually frustrated. More like he thinks it looks cool. I'm supposed to think he's in the driver's seat or something.

"OK, Nadine. You don't want to talk? That's OK. Maybe there's something going on that even I don't know about. And that's all right. I understand. It's tough being a kid, isn't it?"

This is getting stupid.

"You know what I think, Nadine? I think we've just had one big misunderstanding, all year long. But I'm a great guy, and you just might be a good kid under there somewhere. The way I see it, what we need here is some cooperation. So I'm going to make you a deal. You tell me what you've been doing every day after school, and I'll go easy on you."

I cross my arms over my chest. "It's none of your business what I do when I'm not here."

"Is it drugs, Nadine? Have you been hanging out at those pit parties?"

"No!"

"Are you sure? How do I know you're not high right now? Look me in the eye. Have you been smoking? Let me see your hands."

I pull my hands back and hug my knees to my chest.

"Be honest with me." He lowers his voice. "It's Devin Merchant, isn't it. You drive around in his car, maybe park at the mall . . ."

"Ew! No!"

Can't he get fired for talking to me like this?

"Well, Nadine, I'm at a loss. What could you have possibly been doing with your afternoons this whole time?"

"Nothing."

"Nothing?"

"Yeah. Nothing. Before I was dancing. But that's over."

"Dancing? I thought we had a talk about that."

"Yeah, well, you wi—"

"Nadine. That's enough. I've discussed this with your parents already, and mark my words, things are going to change, young lady."

My parents pick me up from the office immediately after school.

"What's all this about dancing?"

"What did Winkley tell you?"

"Is *that* what you and Madison have been working on together all year?"

"Well, we *were*, but—"

"I thought we were very clear that this year you were to focus on your schoolwork, not this clowning around," says my mom.

I cross my arms and stare at my knees.

"Winkley only showed you my worst tests. I have better ones. Besides, Slash— I mean, Madi—"

My dad shakes his head. "That's not enough, Nadine. You're a smart girl. You shouldn't have *any* grades like that."

"You're focused on the wrong things, you're still running with the wrong crowds—"

"I'm not!"

"And you lie to us."

"Mom—"

"Don't Mom me. *Mom,* we're going to the library. *Mom,* I was working on my media project. You should be ashamed. What do you have to say for yourself?"

"It's not clowning, it's b-girling."

"Whatever you want to call it, it's not taking the place of your studies anymore."

"I know. I qui—"

"There will be no more sleeping in the basement."

"No more videos instead of homework."

"I don't even *watch* those videos any—"

"You're grounded for a month."

"No dancing until the end of the year. We don't like what it does to you."

"I am *trying* to *tell you,*" I yell, "*it's already over!* How can you ground me? It's over. Done. I'm finished."

"Nadine," says my mom, "I don't *care* what you're trying to say. You have lied so much already, how can we believe you?"

"You're moving your computer to the kitchen," says my dad before I can argue. "I'm suspending your phone privileges."

"Am I allowed to close the door when I go to the bathroom? What about my privacy? What about my rights?"

"From now until June, Nadine, you don't have any rights. Your world is as big as school and this house."

"Now go downstairs and get your books. You have five minutes."

I hate myself for it, but my first instinct is to call Slasher while I still have my phone. Luckily, my mom follows me down the stairs, waddling as she grips the railing, so it's not even an option.

"Take everything you need," she says, "because this is your last chance. From now on, if I find any evidence that you've been hanging around here after school . . ."

"Good luck thinking of something to take away, Mom. I already told you. There's nothing left."

I have got to stop looking for other people to rely on. I have to learn that it's me versus everybody and no one is ever going to change that.

thirty-one

This is my life for the next four weeks: every day, I get driven to school—from the garage to the front door. At the end of the day, I sit in study hall for two hours until my parents come get me and drive me home—front door to garage. I finish my homework in the kitchen with my parents looking over my shoulder to make sure I'm not using email or downloading b-boy videos or—shock—using email. As if I have anyone to message. I'm in bed by 10:30. And then the whole thing starts over the next day.

On Saturdays, I study in the kitchen, with my parents watching over my shoulder all day, making sure I read every page and answer every question and call for help the second I don't understand something.

"If it kills me, Nadine, you are going to catch up on your schoolwork," says my dad.

Sundays are Family Days—a.k.a. getting-ready-for-the-new-baby time.

"You're an important part of this family, Nadine. We want you to really feel it."

They make me go with them to birthing classes at Chloe's, where the only thing I feel is humiliated. I am the only odd girl out in the whole class. Everyone else is a couple. No one else is under thirty. We help my mom practise breathing techniques, and we learn stretches and massages, and how to support her in all these different weird squatting positions. It's gross.

As if that wasn't bad enough, I have to see Alya every week. She's always hanging around the lobby or lurking in the change room where she can hear every humiliating word my mother says to me.

"Nad—," Alya started to say to me the first week we went, but I just looked away.

"Who was that?" my mom asked instantly.

"No one," I said, loud enough for Alya to hear.

"Is she your friend?"

"No."

Alya doesn't try to talk to me anymore.

The weather finally warms up, not that it's anything to get excited about. One weekend before the Showdown was supposed to happen, we have one of those freakishly warm weeks in February, where it's hotter than spring and I'm like *Canada? my ass,* and all anyone can talk about is global warming—global warming and patio season. But the weather gives my mom headaches, and then she has to take her maternity leave from work over a month early because her blood pressure is so-so and the doctors want her to rest. That means she's home *all the time.*

My dad is so obsessed with the idea that something horrible is going to happen while my mom's napping in the R-C and he's downtown at work, he draws up lists and charts of emergency procedures.

"Nadine, can we run through this again?"

"Yeah, whatever."

"Your mother's suitcase is—"

"Packed and ready to go in your closet upstairs."

"The numbers for the doctor, hospital, cabs and ambulance—"

"Are on the fridge, by the phone."

"If your mother goes into labour *or distress of any kind* and I am not home—"

"I am to activate the escape procedure and contact you via text message once the target has been set in motion."

"I don't appreciate your sarcasm. What will the text message say?"

"B-A-B-Y!"

"You will follow this text message up with?"

"A phone call. But, Dad—"

"Nadine, concentrate. What's my work number?"

I tell him. "But, Dad—"

"If you are not home and I call, what will you do?"

"I will stop what I am doing and come directly to the hospital. But, *Dad*—"

"*What,* Nadine?" he barks, like I'm being difficult on purpose.

"Can I have my phone back?"

He reluctantly hands it over.

"This is not a licence to run wild."

"No kidding."

If the new baby knows what's good for her, she'll stay where she is. I'd think twice before shoving my way into this family.

On Saturday morning, the impossible happens: when I wake up, my parents are still asleep.

My mom had a rough night—I could hear her getting up every other hour to pee or get a glass of water. Through the papery walls of our glamorous Rivercrest house, I could hear my dad asking if she needed anything, and her getting irritated with him asking. They must not have finally fallen asleep until long after I did.

I guess a good daughter would be worried, but all I can think is: *no 9 a.m. math quiz!*

I don't even *want* to go anywhere or do anything, but animal instinct kicks in and I find myself stuffing my feet into my shoes, grabbing my jacket and running out of the house in my pyjama bottoms.

I guess, technically, it's an amazing morning. The sun is rising right in my eyes. The sky is blue. Little patches of snow glisten as they shrink from muddy lawns. A smell like rotting milk hangs in the air. There's a bird out somewhere, making a racket. Spring is kind of disgusting, now that I think about it.

I walk for a long time in no particular direction. This town is so small and empty, there's almost no point having a plan. As soon as I get close to anything, I pretty much have to turn around and start walking away from it anyway. I walk not in the direction of the school. I avoid the mall. I try not to pass too close to the Barn. Eventually I get bored and start running. I don't even notice I'm doing it at first, and when I do, I make myself stop. But my legs twitch, so I pick it up again.

Before I know it, I am standing on the bridge.

A knot tightens in my stomach. I haven't been here in months—not since it got too cold and the so-called Force moved its practices inside. It's familiar, but different—like someone came into my house and moved all my stuff. There's snow piled up at the base of the railing, flattening down the grassy bushes that usually hide it. The entrance to the stairs is covered with snow, and littered with leaves and branches.

I stand looking out towards our crappy subdivision. There's an empty desert of snow between me and it. I take a deep breath. It smells muddy-fresh—no grossness out here. I imagine my parents waking up in house #63988 and losing their minds when they don't find me in the kitchen working on my English essay and I feel a sudden surge of . . . happiness? No, that's not it. But my nerves quiet down. It feels good to have time to myself, and a place to go where no one who's looking is ever going to find me.

But when I brush the debris away from the top of the stairs, I find out that the staircase is missing. It's been replaced with some cheap fencing stuff.

As the knot in my stomach reties, I step onto the half-thawed grass and slowly squelch my way across the bank, until I'm low enough that I can crawl down to the platform.

The platform is surprisingly clean under the bridge—almost totally clear, except for a few muddy workboot footprints and some construction-orange lines spray-painted at either end of the platform. My heart beating faster, I turn to look up at the mural. It's been totally painted over, bright white. No more flying b-girl. No skyline. No Slasher in the background. Just bright white paint in ugly, sloppy roller streaks, all the way across the wall. And then, like a final insult, big orange Xs slicing through it.

"Oh—"

A small squeak escapes my throat. I feel winded. How many hours did I practise in front of this graf? And I never even found out who did it. Now it's gone and I'll never know, and it's like the whole beginning of the year has been erased.

I step forward and touch it, like I'm expecting it to tell me something. Who did this? I thought this was the bridge Rivercrest forgot—

I hear footsteps on the hill above my head.

Instinctively, I throw myself to the ground and slide over the ledge into the trench. I land on my butt with a squelch.

Nice going, Nadine, nice, I think as I catch my breath, adjusting to the new, soaking-wet state of my ass.

The footsteps stop.

I sit perfectly still, butt sinking deeper into mud and melting snow.

Brilliant, Nadine. Awesome.

The footsteps start again. I hear someone walk down to the platform and stop almost exactly where I was standing seconds before. There's a pause. Then I hear a sound like a bag being dropped on the ground, with a thud and a metallic clank.

"Dammit!" says a voice that is a little too familiar to me.

"Dammit!" it says again. There's a sound like a sneaker kicking the wall.

Then, after a moment of silence, the bag shuffles. Something rattles. There's a pop, like a plastic cap, then some spraying—

Slowly, I push into the mud with my feet and slide my back up the wall. The sound stops. Dude stands perfectly still. I don't even think he's breathing.

I hold my position until my legs start to shake. Eventually he gives up and starts spraying again. Carefully, on my tiptoes, I ease myself along the wall to the far edge of the platform, where the drop isn't as high.

Gripping the platform for balance, I edge up the steep bank of the trench, until I can just see over the ledge.

Blue shoes, paint speckled.

Blue track pants, paint speckled.

Blue track jacket, paint speckled.

Blue cap, paint speckled.

Blue do-rag, paint speckled.

Concentration on his face. Paint on his hands.

Devin.

I stare, motionless, unsure what to do next. I'd like to tiptoe away and sneak home through the trench, but my curiosity gets the better of me.

Gradually, I soften my grip and pull myself over the edge. Still crouching, I carefully ease my way across the end of the platform until I get to what's left of the bottom of the staircase. Devin is concentrating so hard now, angrily spraying over the construction-orange Xs in broad red strokes, he doesn't hear me creeping along.

I reach into my pocket so slowly, I think it will be sunset before I make my move. Ever so carefully, I close my fingers around my keys. Then, in one smooth, lightning-fast motion, I whip them out and crash them against what's left of the railing from the old metal staircase.

The sound rings out so loud, it surprises even me.

Devin drops the spray can and spins around, lifting his hands and throwing his back up against the wall. We blink at each other for a moment, locked in a quick-draw situation that neither of us realizes is over already.

When he sees that it's me, a change comes over him. The concentrating, scared writer melts back into Devin, the doofus from school, who grins at me and points his hands like he's holding revolvers.

"Well, well, as I live and breathe, Nadine. Or should I say, *Lady Six?*" With his heel he nudges the can under his backpack, like I'm not going to notice. "So, you come down here to get a little practice in?"

"No. Just wandering around."

"Really? Isn't the big Showdown just around the corner?"

"Yeah . . . ," I say cautiously. "But I'm not going."

"What? Haven't you been working towards it for months? I thought Al said—"

How could he not know what happened? Is this some kind of a trick?

"I haven't talked to those girls in over a month. They didn't tell you we had a fight?"

His jaw falls open like he's trying to catch more gossip with it.

"No. What happened?"

"You really don't know?"

"Oh . . . ," he says, that little half smile, half smirk slowly spreading out the left corner of his mouth. "I get it. Random Girl Drama."

"No!" I react too loudly. Like his dimples are going to make his opinion matter. "We just . . . We needed to enter the four-on-four, and we only had three people and . . . the crew was a dumb idea. It was never going to work."

His smile drops. His eyebrows shoot up like they're going to blast right off his forehead.

"That's it? You needed one more body to fill a spot? Why didn't you just ask me? I would have helped."

I shake my head. "No, thanks. I've heard enough of what you think of girls breaking."

"What?"

"I think you already know."

"What? What did my sister say about me?"

"More like what did *you* say to *her?* Something about us girls being too weak. Ring any bells?"

He starts to laugh. "Nadine, I was like thirteen when I said that. I just wanted Al to leave me alone while I hung out with my friends."

"Riiiight," I say, "but you've *totally* changed. You'd *never* say anything like that now."

"Of course not," he says. "You'd hurt me. Plus, my friends *want* Al around now. They think she's hot."

"Devin!" I slap him in the arm. He fake-overreacts, his smile spreading into a grin.

"I don't get it," he says. "Couldn't y'all just pretend not to be fighting until after the Showdown? You know you're just going to be friends again in two months anyway."

"And what are you doing here, anyway, Devin?" I ask, turning the inquisition on him.

"Oh," he says, starting to swing his arms, "I'm just, uh, out for a, uh, run . . . and stuff. You know."

"Really?" I ask. "What kind of stuff?"

"Oh . . ."

I make a dive for his bag. He tries to block me. I grab his hand. The second my skin touches his, he freezes. I grab the red spray can and give it a shake. His eyes dart back and forth as he tries to think his way into some other excuse.

"What's wrong, Devin, or should I say *Typ0?*" I ask, releasing him. "You think I'm going to rat you out?"

"No. I just know you probably think it's . . . stupid."

The comeback I was preparing dries up on the tip of my tongue.

"Are you fishing for a compliment?"

He looks at me like I'm mental. Maybe I am.

"Actually, *Typ0,* if I have to tell you, I liked the mural. I'm sorry it's gone."

"Thanks," he says.

We just kind of stand there, looking at each other for a minute.

"So, uh," he says, picking red paint out from under his nails, "do you want to go grab breakfast at the Barn or something? My treat?"

"Can't," I say. "I'm grounded. I'm not even supposed to be out here right now."

"At ten a.m.?"

I nod.

"Ouch. That's harsh. In that case, let me give you a lift home before your folks freak out."

I raise an eyebrow. "Do you still have the same car?"

"It's fixed," he says. "Even the seatbelt."

I think about it. It's getting kind of late. I probably should have been back at the house a long time ago if I wanted to save my own ass.

"OK."

We climb back up the mushy hill.

"Nice pants, by the way," says Devin, pointing to my muddy pyjama bottoms.

"Shut up."

thirty-two

"We need to talk."

Slasher grabs hold of my desk and shoves it so hard, it screeches against the floor until it slams into my rib cage.

"Whoa. Cool it, psycho. I've got nothing left to say to you."

"Whatever. Come with me."

She picks up my bag and starts to walk with it.

"Class is starting in like two minutes," I say, sounding unbelievably lame, even to myself.

"Whatever," she says.

"Oh, so now you're some kind of rebel?" I grab for my bag and miss. I get up and follow her out the door. We pass the Finch on the way out.

"Mr. Winkley asked to see us in the office," Slasher tells her, rushing past.

Finch looks confused, but she doesn't stop us.

"Listen," says Slasher, leading me into the bathroom. "This has gone too far."

"You're telling me."

"You owe us an explanation."

"*I* owe *you* an explanation?" This should be good.

"Yeah, Nadine. I leave town for ten days, and when I get back, it's like the whole last semester never happened, and I have to convince you to be my friend all over again. You're pissy, you're mean, you don't listen to anything Alya and I have to say. You insult our clothes, you insult our music, you find something wrong with every fun thing we try to think of doing, and then, at the end of it all, after we spend the whole night trying to get along with you, you just get up and leave, and then you give me the silent treatment at school. We were supposed to be friends, Nadine. What gives?"

"Friends? Ha! You don't respect me. You don't even like me. You were just using me for my moves the whole time."

"What? Where the hell do you get that?"

"You and Alya are always trying to force everything down my throat. Whatever you want, it's always two against one, two against one, two against one."

"That is so not true. You're the one who needs to have everything your way."

"It's not my way. It's the way b-boying—"

"You wouldn't even let Alya run a *warm-up.*"

"What's it to you what Alya does? This is exactly what I'm talking about. The pair of you are a two-headed monster. When you get together I don't even know why I need to be in the room. Did she put you up to this?"

"No, actually. For your information, it was Devin."

"What?"

"I hear you haven't been practising this whole time."

"Great. There you go, trying to drag Devin into this again."

"Don't try to change the topic, Nadine. This has nothing to do with Devin and you know it. Why can't you focus on what's important?"

"And what is that, exactly?"

"The Showdown, Nadine. The crew."

"Well, there is no crew, so there is no Showdown. It's that simple."

She shakes her head. "Wow. I totally misjudged you."

"Why? What did you think I'd do when you tried to force some random dude into the crew, like the decision was already made?"

"I didn't— I for sure didn't expect you to *give up* just like that," she says. "I thought you'd be mad for a few days. I thought we'd talk once you calmed down. I thought we might come to a compromise. But no, there is no compromising with H.R.H. Lady Six Sky, drama queen of the G.T.A."

"Congratulations, then. You're free now. I don't tell you how to dance. I don't try to make you practise. You don't have to work with me. You don't have to worry about the Showdown."

"That's where you're wrong, Six Sky."

"Don't call me that," I say, weakly.

"Al and I are going to the Showdown. We've been practising."

"Figures. Dumping Nadine is all the rage this season. Who you gonna replace me with? Hmm . . . oh, let me guess, Devin and some random buddy of his who wants to get with Al? Wow. Way to stick up for the girl power, Slasher. Way to stand up for your cause."

"Hey!" she yells over me. "Stop jumping to conclusions, will you?"

I cross my arms and stare at her.

"The fact is, Nadine, you are not replaceable. We still want you with us at the Showdown, but if you won't come, we'll enter the one-on-one."

My mouth falls open. "Is this your way of *inviting* me? Do you think you need to *invite* me to a battle in my own hood?"

"Arghh!" she shrieks. "Fine. Do what you want. I don't care. Just take this."

She presses a DVD into my hands and pushes through the bathroom door into the hall.

"What's this?" I ask, following her.

"Watch it and weep."

She strides back to class, her skirt and ponytail swishing from side to side, making her look a little horsey from behind.

I use a plastic ruler to pop the lock on the AV room and sneak in at lunch, covering up the windows with my math and geography books so Slasher can't tell I'm watching her stupid DVD.

I don't know what she thinks is going to happen here, but we are not going to just suddenly turn into best buds again because of some stupid video. And if she's trying to make me feel bad or something, she's got another thing coming.

I slide the disk into the player and put my feet up on the table.

There's a menu screen that says "The Freshest RC Kids: Hydra Force Sessions, January." Great. So they really do think they can use the name all over the place without asking me. Some team.

There's an opening sequence with a shot of cars zipping by on the highway, and then Slasher doing a freeze outside the Barn, and a blurry shot of the mall. Alya does toprock up and down the escalator. Then there's a montage of Slasher doing flare after flare all over town—in the garage, at Chloe's, down by the bridge. Clips of Alya drilling footwork are spliced in between shots of Slasher working her flares until she can finally get four or five full rotations.

Then the video cuts back to Slasher's garage.

"Now that we're all warmed up, it's time to move on to the main event. We've been working on a little something. It's a surprise. But first . . ." She ducks down, off camera, and when she stands up again, she's wearing a baby blue trucker hat with *Slasher* spelled out across the front in Typ0-style graf letters. "Just a little something to get into the crew spirit. Yo, Al, come over here, show off your new threads."

Al sticks her head in the frame. She's got the same hat, in black, with *Phat Al* stencilled across the front.

"That's the sickness," she says, pointing to it.

"And last but not least," says Slasher, "we got this one made for Lady Six, but she's not around, so we'll just set it down on the studio floor here, as a reminder of where she's supposed to be."

She turns the camera around to where a red hat is sitting alone in the centre of the room. She zooms in on it, and I can see it says *6 Sky* in fat letters.

"OK, we're going to be a little lopsided without her, but here goes. You ready, Phat Al?"

She turns the camera on Al. Al salutes. Then the screen goes black for a second while she puts the camera down.

"Hit it, Al."

Alya pushes a button on the stereo. James Brown's "Give It Up or Turn It Loose" comes on. They run to the centre of the room and take their positions.

"Remember, this is where Six Sky would be if she was here," says Slasher, pointing at my hat.

Alya counts in. "Five, six, five, six, seven, eight—"

In perfect sync, they throw down the toprock I showed them, plus some hip-hoppy moves that must be Alya's. I have to admit, Slasher's flow is looking a lot better. I can see

Alya's help in how much more relaxed she is. Not that it matters anymore.

I check my watch. How much longer is this video going to run? I don't have better things to do with my lunch hour?

They do some almost-in-sync footwork, Slasher slowing down so Alya can keep up. Then they jump up and link arms behind their backs, Slasher bends forward, lifting Al off the ground, and Alya does a cutesy pose, freezing on Slasher's back.

Slasher crouches down and Al does a little somersault backwards over her head down to the floor. Then they let eight counts of music go by with Slasher mimicking the same movement on the opposite side.

"It looks kind of dumb with just two people," Slasher yells to the camera.

Phat Al leans into the camera.

"You listening to this, Six Sky? We need you back."

The screen goes black, and then there's a shot of the Hogtown Showdown flyer, with a picture of a warthog in a do-rag and Pumas kicking over the CN Tower. Did they put that in there just to torture me? Are they trying to make me guilty or jealous? Either way, it's not going to work.

I eject the disk and zing it into the wastepaper basket.

thirty-three

No matter how hard I try, I can't fight off this twitchy feeling in my legs. It's been too long. I need to dance. I was lying when I said I could stop. It's not right that those girls are out there practising my moves, going to my battle with my crew, while I'm stuck at home, not allowed out, not allowed even to stretch in the basement.

My dad is riding me harder than ever on the home-work tip. He's stressed out because the doctor ordered my mom to bed rest.

"Did you finish yet?"

"Almost. I have one left."

"Why have you only answered the even-numbered questions?"

"Because we were only assigned the even-numbered questions."

"Not at this table. Do them all—"

"Daaad—"

"Nadine, I warned you."

"If Mom's the sick one, what's your excuse for being bitchy?"

"Nadine!"

Someone's going to lose an eye if we have to stay cooped up together much longer.

—

The night before the Showdown, I'm so mad, I hardly sleep. I see my alarm clock at one, two, three, five and six a.m. Finally I give up and crawl out of bed to stretch on my floor. It's not bad, actually. Why didn't I think of this before? I could have a double life if I just gave up sleep.

I'm just reaching for my toes with both hands when a set of heavy footsteps comes down the hall, and there's a quiet knock on my door.

"Nadine, what are you doing in there?"

He *heard* that?

"*Trying* to get back to sleep. You're not the only one with issues, you know."

"Cut out the nonsense and get back to bed."

Without the Showdown to work towards, what is the point of putting up with this? What is the point of *anything* without b-girling?

Someone else is going to go to the Showdown today and qualify to win $5,000. Someone else is going to win the chance to move out, make his life over, escape Rivercrest and live by his own rules, and instead, he is going to spend it all on kicks, smokes and video games.

It's just wrong.

When I finally fall asleep again, I dream that I am at the Showdown, but instead of faces, everyone has targets sitting on their shoulders. The Force is there, with targets under their trucker hats. Encore and Recoil are there, with targets under their do-rags. Sean has the collar of his jacket turned up so it hides half his target. Jazmin's corn rows are stretched tight across her target. I'm the only one with a face. I jump into the battle without waiting to find out whose turn it is, and when I drop to the floor, I kick out as hard as I can, trying to hit those targets. They dodge back. I get madder and madder, and kick harder and harder. Suddenly, I notice, I'm doing windmills. I'm doing windmills, and I'm not falling flat on my face, or smashing my hips. I'm not even touching the ground. As soon as I notice, the targets melt away and the people disappear. I wake up.

Eight o'clock. Time to eat breakfast and do more homework, and do anything I can to distract myself from the fact that there will be no actual mills for me, no Showdown, no second chances.

I get dressed and take my time on the breakfast part. Missing the most important event of my life calls for some kind of celebration, and nothing says party like pancakes from a box with sausages from another box. I'm halfway done stirring when my dad comes downstairs.

"What are you doing? Why are you making a mess? I thought I told you—"

"Well good morning to you too. Remind me not to ever make *you* pancakes again."

He frowns and reaches for the coffee. "Just don't let it take all morning. I want you to get to work as soon as possible."

"OK," I say, slowing down my stirring to a crawl.

He storms out of the kitchen the second his coffee is done.

"Oh well," I call after him. "More for me, then."

I mess up the first batch—I think the pan isn't hot enough. Then I burn the second set. By the time I sit down to eat, with my geography book open in front of me, it's almost ten.

Slasher will have Devin and Alya warming the car up by now. She'll have printed thirty maps off the Internet and planned out exactly how much money they need for admission and parking, and she'll have the whole trip to the Showdown planned down to the second, with probably an hour to spare.

I take a big bite of pancake, drumming my pencil against my notebook with the other hand.

My dad comes back in the kitchen.

"Nadine! Why are you so jittery? And why is this place such a mess? As soon as you finish eating—"

"I know, I know, I'm going to do the dishes."

"I don't want you taking all day. You had better memorize your geography homework. I'm going to quiz you at—"

"Dad, I *know*. I'm doing it. It's under control."

"Then why are you making this so difficult?"

"I'm not! If you weren't in my face every ten—"

He throws up his hands, turns and walks out of the room. "I swear, between the women of this house . . ." I hear him mumble as he goes.

He comes back with his keys ten seconds later. "I'm going for a drive. Get your work done. Get the dishes done. Be good to your mother."

The door to the garage slams, I hear the garage door go up, the car revs and within seconds he's gone. Finally, everything is quiet.

I finish eating and head to the sink, grateful for the excuse to get away from memorizing every type of rock or mineral anyone ever yanked out of the ground in Ontario. I rinse everything really well before loading up the dishwasher.

Eleven o'clock. By now, the Force will be on the highway. They'll listen to Bershawn Sera and sing along, and everyone will think in the backs of their heads how awesome it is that I'm not there to ruin their little karaoke party.

Meanwhile, tha Klub will still be fast asleep, since they only live five minutes away, and they're going to show up half an hour late anyway.

I sit down to my geography homework. Aurostibite, arsenohauchecornite . . . Should I even bother trying to remember that one? I'm never going to be able to spell it on a test anyway. Cerianite, dadsonite . . . Oh, so he *is* made of stone . . . Hastingsite, playfairite . . . I feel my eyelids start to droop. I shake myself awake. I get up, jog in place as quietly as possible for thirty seconds, then sit right back down. Don't want the dadsonite to come back and catch me playfairite-ing around. He'll aurostibite my head off.

Michenerite . . . paracostibite . . . No. This is seriously not working.

My head gets heavy. I rest it on my textbook. Just for a minute . . .

A loud smack on the window wakes me right up.

"I *am* working," I yell, sitting bolt upright.

But when I look out the window, it's not my dad but Devin staring back at me.

I stifle a scream.

He motions for me to open the window.

"What are you, crazy? What are you doing here?" I mouth at him, checking behind me to make sure my mother hasn't somehow magically floated down from bed, just to catch me in the act of speaking to another living human under the age of thirty.

Open the window, he motions again.

I slide it up, just a crack.

"Devin," I whisper. "What the hell are you doing here?"

"I'm giving you a second chance."

"Since when do I need second chances with you?"

He smiles, but almost in a way that says he's making fun of me. "Not with me!" he says. "To get to the Showdown. Get your ass out here."

"Um, hello . . . I'm grounded."

"Why do you think I came to the *window?*"

"I don't know, but you have to leave. I'm not getting in any car with those Hydra skanks."

"You won't have to. They're already at the battle. I had to come back for Al's other shoes. Thought you might have changed your mind. It just didn't seem right not having you there."

I cross my arms over my chest. "Oh, so they *didn't* want me to come?"

"Look, Nadine, I can't tell you what to do, but this is what *I'm* going to do. I'm going to park my car at the end of the street and wait in it for the next fifteen minutes. You can get your ass out of the house and down the street and make it to the Showdown. Or you can sit here and worry about . . ." He stands on his toes to see past me into the kitchen. "What's that you're working on? Minerals? Watch out for arsenohauchecornite. That one almost killed me in Grade 10."

"Is that all, Devin?" I lean forward to shut the window.

"I'll be in the car," he says, and stalks off across the lawn.

I throw myself back down at the table. I can't believe his nerve. Like he's just going to pick me up and haul me back there like some old pair of shoes.

I look back down at my work. Stupid arsenohauche-cornite.

I picture Sean's face, grinning as he realizes I'm not there.

Whatever. I'm not travelling all that way just to hang around in some dingy club, booing the two lamest crews in the b-boy universe. Nothing can make me—

I hear the rumbling of the garage door that tells me my dad is back—back to test me on my geography homework, tell me I'm breathing too loudly and make sure I'm not spending too much time in the bathroom.

Next thing I know, I'm running to the front door. I'm not even thinking, I'm just stuffing my feet into the nearest, flyest shoes in the front hall. I'm grabbing my jacket and my bag without even checking to see what's in it. I'm slipping out the door as quietly as I can, and I'm hoofing it down the street as fast as I ever have.

I make it to Devin's car, totally out of breath, with seconds to spare. I bang on the window just as he's getting ready to pull away. He leans over slowly and lets me in.

"All right, Typ0," I say as I jump in, "you win. So drive. We don't have much time."

I'll figure out what to do when I get there.

Unlike Rackit Klub's mini battles at Broderick Community Centre, the Hogtown Showdown always happens at the Colossus, a huge, ancient ballroom down on the water that's been half abandoned for years. Back in the day, when the whole area was like a beach town, it used to be a big band swing club. But then after the highway plowed through, the building was abandoned. Then ravers rediscovered it and named it Colossus. Then the city outlawed the big warehouse raves, so it got dropped again. Now big Broadway-style shows rent it for rehearsals sometimes, and Infinite takes it over once a year for the Showdown.

As Devin barrels down the street and onto the highway

at roughly twice the speed limit, my mind goes blank. I, Lady Six Sky, am going to the Hogtown Showdown. I haven't practised in a month. I have no crew. I have no idea what I'm supposed to do when I get there, and no one there wants to see me there anyway. No problem.

I grip the door handle and try to breathe. Is it hot in here? Suddenly I feel like my T-shirt is trying to strangle me.

I flip down the sun visor and check myself out in the mirror. What a disaster. I'm wearing some faded old blue shirt, dingy cargoes with almost no fabric left in the knees and my beat-up Nikes. My hair is sticking out all over the place. My jacket is black with an orange lining—totally mismatched. I have no makeup, no earrings, not even a belt. I'm not dressed to represent anything except the wrong side of the bed.

I close my eyes and lean back in my seat, trying to get my heart to beat at a normal speed again. It's not like I can just change my mind and jump out of the car in the middle of the highway.

"You might not think so, but they're going to be happy when they see you."

"I'm not going to battle with them."

"That's your choice," Devin says. "I'm just letting you know."

He doesn't try to talk to me more than that. He concentrates on the road. The scenery whips by. We sit in what might be a comfortable silence if I wasn't so panicked.

As we get closer to the city, it's like moving day in reverse. The traffic gets thicker and the lights get brighter. The skyline appears at the end of the highway.

"Um . . . ," I say, clearing my throat. "Thanks for coming to get me, Devin."

He glances over at me. "No place like home, huh?"

"This is the first time I've been back," I say, almost in a whisper. I can barely believe it.

He nods, and then we hit the Jameson off-ramp. The car swings southward, back over the highway, towards the water, which is all thrashy-cold and frozen at the shore.

I show him the secret parking space behind the deserted warehouse lofts.

I get out of the car, stretch my legs and take a deep breath. The air might not smell fresh, but it does smell like home.

"Ready?" Devin asks.

I nod. Ready as I'll ever be.

We squeeze through the hole in the fence and run around to the front of the Colossus, where there's a symbolic line of spectators on the sidewalk—girls in heels on tiny pink phones, a bunch of big guys dressed too gangsta for actual dancing, even a couple of moms and little kids waiting to get in.

We hurry past them, up the steps into the front alcove, where some bored girl with blue hair is mindlessly fiddling with her eyebrow piercing and waiting for the last straggling b-boys to put their names down for the four-on-four.

Devin shows his wristband and I slam down a twenty. I get frisked by a giant blond bouncer who looks like she can crush walnuts with her biceps. I lose half the contents of my pockets to a big cardboard box. There are no sharp objects allowed in, no bottles and nothing in which you could hide any kind of drug, even a cough drop.

My heart jumps into my throat as I run down the last hallway. I am actually here. Now what?

thirty-four

I step through the doors. A light flashes in my eyes. I feel like I'm in a gladiator movie. The disgraced warrior queen invades the ring . . . and no one notices.

Just this once, that's OK. I pause inside the door and try to get my bearings. There's an old chandelier hanging from the arched ceiling. Half its crystals are missing and a disco ball hangs from its centre. In the semi-dark, with coloured lights spinning everywhere, you almost don't notice the purple paint peeling off the walls and the missing ceiling tiles.

The whole club, as big as an airport hangar, is alive with hip hop. DJs are taking turns spinning everything from old-school funk to fresh cuts from last week—anything with a decent beat. Crews are practising anywhere they can find space. In the centre, where the battle will happen, around the sides behind where the audience will stand, even out in the hallways, b-boys are making their own ciphers. Half practice, half pissing contest, these mini faceoffs are almost as important as the battle itself. Some crews only get to meet up once a year. Some of them are friends, some of them are . . . not. Some get schooled on the sidelines. Others sharpen their claws, hoping to run up against each other at centre court, where they'll have an audience. People are high on adrenalin and energy drinks. Everyone is repping their brand-new sneakers, fresh out of the box—the mark of an important hip-hop event if ever there was one.

I can't believe that just this morning, I was rotting away with my homework. I wonder for a second if my dad is losing his mind, searching the neighbourhood for me, but then I chase the thought out of my head. That's what phones are for, and he hasn't called.

Barlog, from Furry Feet, sees me and waves. Spotting a friendly face makes me relax a little. He's one of my favourite b-boys in town but I've only spoken to him a few times. Sean and tha Klub hate him. He's six feet tall, with a gut like MF Doom, and they laugh at the way his man-boobs jiggle when he does power, but dude can hold it down.

"Lady Six! Where've you been?" he says in his deep voice. "We've missed you."

"Rivercrest."

"Oh, snap."

"Are your boys here?" I ask.

He calls the guys over. Furry Feet are basically a bunch of North Toronto sci-fi/fantasy geeks who also happen to b-boy. There's Skeletor—he's freaky-flexible and weighs less than one of my legs. Then there's Hal, who specializes in the robot, and finally this quiet guy, Owen, who just goes by 0/1. They showed up to a battle once dressed like characters from *Star Wars* and they were so good, no one even tried to kick their asses. They must totally kill at sci-fi conventions.

"Yo, we were just about to start a cipher," says Barlog. "Join us?"

"Yeah, totally," I say.

My nerves melt away. I didn't come this far for nothing.

Skeletor smiles and widens a space on the floor before jumping into it with his toprock. Barlog starts clapping along to the beat and the rest of us join in, urging him on as he runs through a loose warm-up. He ends with a tip of his hat to Hal, who jumps in with the locking and the popping and the popping and the locking.

Then I leap in to beat the next guy to the centre.

"Whoo, whoo, whoo," Barlog cheers, pumping his fist in the air.

Everyone laughs. Riding high on their energy, I pull out my basic tops with a little Nadine twist. It feels good—a little rusty, maybe, but decent. I slide down into some footwork and it's good to be on the floor, getting my cipher legs back. I'm almost starting to enjoy myself, when the two voices I've been dreading most yell out, "Yeah, Nadine! Go Six Sky!"

Slasher and Phat Al. Suddenly it's like I've got lead for legs. I do a quick, sloppy elbow freeze and get out of there as fast as I can, running to hide on the opposite side of the circle.

I size them up as I pretend to retie my shoes. Slasher has taken her inner Rivercrest geek and hugged it so hard, it's exploded all over her body. Two blond pigtails frame her face under a baby blue bandana and her "Slasher" hat from the video. A crisp white collar and pink tie stand out from under a blue and beige argyle sweater vest. Slim brown and beige Pumas peek out from under the cuffs of her stretchy camel cords. I can just make out the faint outline of volleyball kneepads underneath.

Phat Alya is wearing the skinniest tight black jeans I've ever seen, with black-on-black Adidas runners, a tight black tank, tight black hoodie, black hat and gold earrings as big as her face.

"Everyone," I say begrudgingly, when there's a break in the music, "this is Slasher and Phat Al, from Rivercrest.

They *were* part of a crew called Hydra Force. Take it easy on them. They're new."

"Hey!" says Slasher, taking the bait. "Don't listen to her. I'm not looking for easy props."

"Let's see what you've got!" says Barlog.

Slasher steps forward to meet his challenge. The circle cheers.

Suddenly, someone shoves me hard from behind. I trip over myself and land on my knees, crashing into Slasher as I fall.

"What the—"

"Yo, yo, yo, *what* is *this?*" says a voice behind me. I turn around and see a pair of angry new fluo-green Pumas striding towards me. "I thought we made it clear you weren't welcome in Parkdale anymore, Lady *Bitch* Sky."

I scramble to my feet and find myself eye to eye with Recoil.

"What's going on, Six?" he says, looking around the circle. "You bring your princess friends to try and get with some fresh ghetto meat?"

Slasher's smile sours.

Behind him, Encore forces a laugh, and then the laugh turns to a giggle, and soon he's snorting through his nose, slapping his thigh, shaking so hard he can hardly stand straight.

"You little girlies going to do some damage today? Tear Parkdale a new asshole?"

"No," I say. "Between you and your boys, I think Parkdale already has enough assholes."

He takes a step forward like he's going to hit me, but out of nowhere, Devin wedges himself between us.

"What's *your* problem?" says Encore. "Dancing with girls? Can't get into a real crew? You a fag or something?"

"Would I scare you if I was?" Devin answers, growing taller.

Recoil takes a step back, shrinking into his desperate-cry-for-attention shoes.

That's when I notice Sean leaning against the wall near the door, watching, with Jazmin hanging off his arm.

Jazmin comes forward, sticks her chest out and snaps her fingers in my face. "Don't you get it, bitch? You're replaceable. Go home."

"I *am* home."

"Oh yeah?" She sneers. "All right, it's on. Let's go."

Jazmin strides into the circle, hips swinging. She takes the floor with her own special brand of hip hop, grinding and twisting, and working herself into seven kinds of splits. She's wearing a short halter top that's cut off one shoulder and tied at the waist, baring so much skin that there's pretty much no normal floorwork she can do without getting floor burns.

A small crowd starts to gather. Guys cheer her on, but not the same way they cheer for each other. Half of them are laughing at her. Half of them want to get with her. But the more they cheer, the further she goes, waving her ass in the air, rubbing her crotch against the floor, shaking her AA-cup breasts in my face.

I dance against her like I would anyone in a battle-cry situation, stepping left as she leans to my right, leaning right as she shimmies to my left. She won't get out of my face to let me onto the floor, so finally, I drop to the ground and slide through her legs, somersault backwards into the middle of the circle and land in a crab freeze. As the crowd cheers for real, she scowls back over her shoulder, while Slasher shakes her own shoulders back at her, mocking.

Jazmin ignores my run, of course, while she unties and reties her shirt, finally taking it off and parading around in her bra, like she's so hot from twenty seconds of dancing in a drafty club.

But Sean is staring hard from the corner with his arms crossed over his chest, even as Encore and Recoil shout insults after each of my moves.

As I complete my run, the MC comes over the loud-speaker.

"Last chance to register for the four-on-four battle. The Showdown will begin in ten minutes. Last chance to register."

The circle dissolves as everyone rushes to get a good seat. Jazmin gives me the finger. "Grab a seat, Bitch Sky, and see how it's really done." She runs off after Encore and Recoil.

Out of the corner of my eye, I see the Force hanging back, waiting for me. I duck out in the opposite direction, when someone catches me by the wrist and pulls me back.

I fall back, tripping into him.

"Sean!"

"Nadine."

I catch my balance and pull back my hand.

"Lady Six Sky to you."

"Can I talk to you in private?"

"If you have something important to say, say it here. I'm not leaving this room."

"OK," he says, and leads me back behind a speaker, out of sight of Jazmin and tha boyz. "Nadine, you've improved. I don't know who's been helping you, but you're stronger than you were when you left. Either that or you were holding out on me before."

"I told you I was going to keep practising."

"Listen, Six, I don't want to fight. You've made your point. So what would you say if I gave you a second chance?"

"What?"

"Come back and battle with tha Rackit Klub today."

"Excuse me?"

"Come on, Nadine, don't make this hard on me. You know the guys are already going to give me a hard time."

"That's funny," I say. "I didn't know you had a vacancy. I count four of you already. Only three real b-boys maybe, but four bodies."

He lowers his voice. "I'll pull her. I'm serious."

His breath on my neck sends a shiver down my spine.

I look out across the room. The Force is still watching me intently.

"*Do you need help?*" Alya mouths.

Sean's thumb traces a circle on the back of my hand.

"You were my girl, Nadine. That wasn't for no reason. I know we've had rough times, but who's to say we're done forever? Give this a try and . . . who knows?"

I think of the props I would get if we won. I think of the money. I imagine looks on the guys' faces, and especially on Jazmin's if I showed up with Sean ringside to give her the boot.

But when I look back into Sean's eyes, they are empty. I don't see any of Slasher's bull-headed dedication, Alya's poise or Devin's total refusal to leave me alone. All I see is my own reflection bounced back to me. I see how after all his promises, Sean always put me last in the crew, and how fast he hooked up with Jazmin after dropping me. I see how I've had to start all over on my own without him, and how Slasher, Phat Al and Typ0 are *still* standing on the sidelines waiting to give me a *real* second chance, after everything we've been through.

Like Kool Herc said in *The Freshest Kids,* b-girl—break-girl—has nothing to do with a beat or a dance. It means you've been to your breaking point. Sean and tha Klub may play it tough. They may pretend you need to be from the city to break. But I was never really broken until I moved to Rivercrest. Tha Klub tried to break me. My parents tried to break me. My school tried to break me. But I'm still here. I'm not giving my power back to anyone.

I pull my hand back. "Sean, I'd rather come *dead last* without you."

"Don't be like that, Nadine. We're crew."

"No," I say, looking across the room at the Hydra Force. "I already have a crew."

He follows my gaze and his face turns ugly—his nostrils widen, his lip curls and his eyebrows grow together as he sneers.

"You're seriously going to dance with those . . . *girls* when you could be up there with tha Rackit Klub? I never thought you'd be such a traitor, Nadine."

"Save it for the battle, *Ruckus.*"

He storms across the club, grabbing Jazmin's ass as he rejoins tha Klub on the side of the floor.

I've got some serious explaining to do.

The MC's voice comes on over the loudspeaker.

"This is absolutely the last chance for four-on-four crew registrations. Last call. Going once, going twice—"

I race across the club to the registration table, where the Force is waiting.

"Wait!" I yell. "One more crew! The Hydra Force."

I turn to the three of them—my crew, if I dare call them that. "I'm so sorry. Can we do this?"

They blink at me for a second, and then a smile starts to grow across Slasher's face.

"Yessss!" says Alya, pumping a fist in the air.

"Nadine!" says Slasher, drawing me into a group hug. "I knew you'd do the right thing. I knew you'd come."

"Really? Just like that? You're going to let me come back?"

"We didn't send Devin all the way back to Rivercrest with that ridiculous shoe story for nothing," says Alya.

"You tricked me!" I yell.

"That's what friends are for," says Slasher.

"Um, *excuse* me," says registration table girl, waving her pen and clipboard at us. "Can we get on with this, please? I need your names."

I smile. "Sorry. Lady Six Sky, reporting for battle."

"Phat Al."

"Slasher."

"And don't forget Typ0," I say. "We are the Hydra Force."

"Uh, yeah, thanks, I got that," says registration girl.

thirty-five

The club has really filled in since we started warming up. People are standing on benches and sitting on one another's shoulders to see over each other. There's a square taped off around the dance floor for crowd control, but people treat it more like a suggestion, edging farther and farther over the line between each qualifying battle. All around the front row, people have video cameras surgically attached to their hands. The Showdown will be on VideYou before it's half over.

We're up against some random crew of kids who've chosen to call themselves the Asian Mafia. I wonder how long that'll last. I recognize this one girl, Meagan Van Dai, from my old school. I didn't know she was into b-girling. She was a skater last year. I wave at her. She nods back, already getting her game head on.

The music stops and the first battle is over. One crew is already pissed off at how things went and refuses to shake the other crew's hands. The second crew demands an immediate rematch, outside in the parking lot, even though the winner has yet to be announced. Boys.

The judges signal the MC, who calls us to the floor.

We dive into a quick huddle.

"We've come a long way," I tell them. "After all we've been through, this battle is nothing. We've already won today. The Hydra Force is *unstoppable.*"

"Yeahhhhh!" they shout in unison.

"Have fun, dance for yourself, and the Force will support you."

Slasher sticks her hand into the centre. Alya follows suit. I cover her hand, and Devin covers mine.

"Hydra Force!" we yell.

We take our place in the centre, shoulder to shoulder opposite the Asian Mafia.

The music starts up again, and our crews kind of shuffle back and forth, daring each other to go first. Normally I would just jump in, but I'm not feeling the song.

The Mafia isn't feeling it either. Finally, their leader, a spiky-haired Korean kid, steps forward and offers to toss a coin for the honour of going first. I step forward like I'm going to accept it, but just as I do, the song changes, and I recognize the killer first line to "Mama Said Knock You Out," by LL Cool J.

I've never felt a song more in my entire life.

I look at the coin in the b-boy's hand, fake like I'm going to take it, but then spin around on my heel and explode into my toprock, mouthing the lyrics as I dance, punching in time to the music.

I *am* going to knock you out.

Coin boy looks dissed and steps back in line with his crew, who watch me with their hands on their hips, looking for any kind of error they can seize on, but the crowd cheers, getting into the song with me. It feels amazing. I Brooklyn Rock down to the floor. My footwork flies furious, my legs like helicopter blades. The room swirls around me. The cheering gets louder.

But then, over the crowd, I hear, "Boo! You suck!"

The Mafia looks around, confused, as if to demonstrate that it wasn't them who brought the haters, but I just ignore it. I already know exactly who it is. I'm really battling two crews—the one in front of me and the one hidden in the crowd.

"Yeah! Go Six Sky," another voice yells, even louder. It's Barlog. The crowd cheers back, drowning out tha Klub. The support makes me smile, makes me grow an inch taller, a hundred pounds stronger. And then something happens to me. That something that's been missing—my confidence, my inspiration, that feeling of how to move without thinking—with every shout of my crew and the crowd, it starts to come back. And I think to myself, *It's now or never.*

It might be risky. It might be bad battle strategy. It might be just plain stupid, but I launch into my windmills.

"Yeahhhhhhhhhhh!" Slasher loses her mind on the sideline.

"Go Nadiiiiiine!" Alya shouts.

And it's like I'm so caught up in the moment, I forget to mess up the move. One, two, three, four times around—I'm flying through it. I don't ever need to stop.

But I do. I twist out of my windmill and land in a final shoulder freeze. Then I jump back up to my feet and finish with a smirk in my b-girl stance. Or rather, I try to smirk, but my smile is way too powerful, and I just stand there beaming, almost stunned by what I finally achieved.

The Force totally loses it, jumping up and down and cheering on the sideline.

Meagan goes next for the Mafia. She pulls off a decent run for a beginner, but nothing really original.

The second she's done, Slasher leaps into the circle like she's been waiting for this chance her entire life. With the confidence of a veteran, she holds her head high and looks everyone at ringside in the eye, like she's letting them in on a secret. With her jerky style, she has to fight for her toprock, but by the time she hits the floor, she has their support.

Rackit Klub tries to give her a hard time, but the more they boo, the harder she fights. When she finally lets loose her flares, the whole room gasps, and I look up to see Encore and Recoil picking their jaws up off the floor, while Ruckus and Jaz glare at her, tight lipped.

I am floating on air.

The spiky-haired Mafia kid goes next, and shocks us by diving into a run in which his feet never hit the floor once. He does the whole thing Spider-Man style, swinging his light body around at the ends of his arms, leaping from hand to hand.

"Can you even call that *foot*work?" Alya asks under her breath.

"I don't think it matters what you call it. I got nothing to match that," says Devin.

"Can we invite them to practise with us later?" Slasher wonders.

"If there's anything left of them by the time I'm done," says Devin, grinning.

And just like that, we're back in the game.

He drags himself onto the floor by his arms, getting a big laugh from the crowd, then proceeds to do his whole run as if moving in reverse, starting with freezes and threads, backing into his footwork and ending with his toprock. I have to admit I have never seen anything like that. Neither have the judges, I assume, from the way they nod and whisper to one another.

The next guy the Mafia sends up is a popper who twitches and clicks through half a minute of poses before losing the floor to Alya, who wins more than her fair share of whistles for her smooth, flowing style. For all of Jazmin's forced attempts at baring her midriff, she never looks half as hot as Al does fully clothed.

By the time the MC calls the battle done, the energy in the building is more than twice what it was when we started.

We shake hands with the Mafia, one by one, and they clap us on the back, thanking us for a good battle.

People everywhere take pictures. It may only be a qualifying round, but it tastes like victory to me.

Slasher pulls us all into a group hug, and in the middle of it my cell beeps. I actually don't hear it at first because it's on the ground and Slasher is screaming right next to my ear.

"You guys! That was awesome!"

But then it beeps a second time. I grab it out of my bag and see that there's a text message from my dad.

"B-A-B-Y!"

Oh. My. God.

I have no idea when he sent it. What if—

The phone rings while I'm holding it. I run across the room and duck out one of the side doors, into a quiet hallway.

"Dad? Don't be mad. I have something to tell you," I blurt, trying to beat him to the chase.

He's deadly silent for a minute.

"What?" he says, through gritted teeth.

"I'm at the Hogtown Showdown."

Even longer pause. *"Where?"*

"The b-boy battle. In Parkdale."

I hear him breathing heavily on the other end of the phone. I can practically see the veins in his neck starting to pop out. He starts to speak a few times, then stops himself.

"N— Na— Nadine?"

"Yes?" I ask in a tiny voice, bracing myself for the avalanche of shouting.

But when he finally speaks, he's almost frighteningly calm.

"Did you compete already?"

"What do you mean?"

"At the Showdown. Did you battle?"

"Yeah."

"How did you do?"

I'm so startled, I laugh. "Um . . . We killed?" I answer, unsure where this is going. I am so dead.

Finally, he sighs. "Good girl."

"So you're not mad at me?"

"We *will* talk about this later, but you are not to breathe a word of this to your mother. Do you understand me?"

"Yes."

"Do you have a way of getting home?"

"Yes."

"Then come to the hospital. Now."

"I'm on my way."

"Hurry."

I hang up and see the whole Force creeping down the hallway, listening in.

"What's going on?" says Slasher.

"My mom's having the baby."

"Oh my god! Now?"

"Soon. She's in labour."

"What are we going to do? What if we make it to round two?"

There's a moment of silence where we all stare at each other, our eyes growing wider and wider by the nanosecond.

"What are we waiting for? Let's go!" says Devin, jingling his keys.

I look to Slasher and Alya.

"But you guys have worked— I don't want— I can take a cab—"

"We'll find out how it ends when we come back next year," says Slasher, pulling on her coat.

"Are you sure?"

"Totally," says Alya, grabbing me by the arm and walking. "Let's do this."

We run down the hall, feet pounding, Devin's keys jingling, our coats and bags flapping behind us.

"Where's the fire?" one of the bouncers calls after us.

"Rivercrest," we yell back.

"Ew," I hear one of them say. I'd laugh if I wasn't running so fast.

Adrenalin pumping, I run after Devin, down the hall and out the doors. I fly right over the stairs, landing on the sidewalk with the thud of an elephant. Alya bounces down the steps after me, and Slasher slides down the railing.

"Whoo!" she yells, as she makes a ten-point landing.

"Wait here. I'll bring the car around," says Devin.

As he vanishes around the side of the building, the doors burst open again. I look back, expecting to see a bouncer, or maybe Jazmin come to get one last dig in about quitting.

I'm almost shocked to see Ender from Infinite loping down the stairs.

"Lady Six!" he says.

"Yeah?"

I'm surprised he even knows my name.

"Hydra Force, right?" he says, pointing at Slasher and Al.

"Yeah . . ."

"Where are you going? That was wicked."

"Family emergency," I say.

"Birth of a new b-girl, in t-minus . . . now," says Slasher knowingly.

"Whoa. No way. I won't keep you, then. But, dudes, the guys all thought you were great."

The guys? As in *Infinite?* I don't even need to pinch myself for him to know that I think I might be dreaming. I'm sure my eyes are as big as dinner plates right now.

"We do these semi-closed sessions once a month," he says, like I haven't been trying to get into them for three years. "You should totally come. Here's my card."

"Thanks!" I say, trying to be cool. "We'll try to make it."

"All right. Good luck!" he says as Devin pulls up beside the sidewalk. "See you later."

The girls don't even wait until he's back in the building to start screaming, and they don't stop until we're practically at the hospital. Even Devin.

thirty-six

My dad is waiting for us on the steps outside the hospital. The first thing he does is give me a hug.

"Is everything OK, Dad?"

"Fine," he says. "Your mother kicked me out of the room a minute ago, so your timing is good."

Alya laughs.

"Dad, this is Alya and her brother, Devin."

"Do you go to RHS?" he asks, shaking their hands.

"Devin does, but Al goes to *private school*," I tell him, faking a British accent.

"Wonderful," he says.

Even at a time like *this*, he cares about *that?* Amazing.

"We brought a present for the baby," Slasher says as they follow us into the elevator.

"Oh, really?" he says.

Alya digs into her bag and pulls out an energy drink and a green visor with the EnerSpree logo on it that she got free at the battle.

"Thanks. I don't know about the baby, but I know I could sure use *both* of these," he says, putting on the visor and turning it to the side. He pops the can open. "A man can only drink so many hospital coffees before his wife calls him hyper and kicks him out of her hospital room."

Slasher and Alya laugh.

When we get to the eighth floor, my dad disappears

down a hallway to "beg" my mother to let us in.

The Force throws itself down all over the chairs in the waiting area.

"You guys don't have to wait," I tell them. "Go. Celebrate. Get hot chocolate at the Breakfast Barn. Torture the waitresses for me."

"We have hot chocolate right here," says Alya, snuggling up to the vending machines.

"It could be a while. You're going to get bored."

"We will read magazines," says Devin, reaching for *Your Breasts and Breastfeeding*.

Slasher covers her mouth with both hands to keep from laughing out loud.

"We'll behave," she says. "I'll keep them quiet. Promise. But we're not going anywhere. Even if I only get a tiny glimpse, I want to be here when they wheel her by."

I give them each a hug and then hurry down the hall to find my father.

My mother actually looks relieved when I tiptoe into her room. For a second I worry that my dad might have told her about the battle after all. But she just stretches her hand out to me and says, "Nadine, thank goodness. Come here, your father is driving me crazy."

She grabs my hand, and I think she has a contraction at that exact moment because she squeezes it so hard, my knees buckle.

I remind her to relax like they told us in class, and then a nurse comes in and tells us she's dilated to six centimetres—no turning back now. It's almost time to push.

My dad puts down the EnerSpree and comes to hold her other hand.

I run down the hall to get her a glass of water.

When I get back, the nurse hands me the chart and lets me write down that she's dilated to eight centimetres, and then that she's ready to start pushing.

I stay up by my mom's head, fanning her and keeping her hair out of her face, and my dad darts back and forth between her head and the bottom of the bed, where he reports that he can see the top of the baby's head, and then the shoulders, and then the whole baby. I turn my head when it happens, because no way do I need to see what's going on down there.

The nurse hands my mom the baby, and she's all wet and screamy and the cord is still attached.

"Hello, my little girl number two," says my mom to the wiggly red blob, and I take a step back, nervous because it's hard to tell that she's even human, let alone a girl.

Mom closes her eyes, and the nurse takes the baby away to clean her up.

My dad finally relaxes into a chair. I fall asleep with my head on his shoulder.

I wake up as the nurse is bringing the baby back into the room, all cleaned up and sleeping.

"Have you thought of a name?" she asks my parents.

"Karina."

My breath catches. I didn't think of it before, but my sister is going to grow up without ever knowing our grandmother. It almost seems impossible. She has a deluxe crib and more toys than I ever did, but there are so many things she's going to be missing—the city, and how my parents used to be.

"All right now. Who do we think baby Karina looks

like?" the nurse asks, looking back and forth between my mom and dad.

There's a pause while they examine each bit of her, trying to figure it out. Then they look at each other and back at the baby, and up at the nurse.

"Nadine!" they both say, at the same time.

The nurse laughs and lays Karina down in her bassinet.

I lean over and take a closer look. Giant hair, bigger than my mom's, that cannot be contained by the little pink hat they've tried to force on her head. Almond eyes, more slanted than my dad's. Her nose, narrower than Dad's but more pointed than Mom's. Full lips, squeezed down into an angry frown.

Suddenly she blinks and lets out a giant scream, demanding to know who dragged her into this place and why these bossy parent people are staring at her. She struggles against her swaddling blankets, twisting around like she'd nail a chair freeze already if only we'd unpin her arms.

"Those are definitely my lungs," I say.

Everyone laughs.

I pick her up and bounce her gently in the cradle of my arm, while my parents' eyes get wide, like they're afraid I'm going to drop her.

"That's cool, K. I get it," I whisper to her. "You just let it all out."

Shout-Outs

This book was made possible by the dedicated work of my tireless agent and friend, Sarah Heller, and my first editor, Lara Hinchberger, who each recognized what I wanted to say and helped me shape it into something other people might like, too. Many thanks also to Kristin Cochrane, Amy Black, and everyone at Doubleday.

Thank you shebang! crew & associates: Blazin', Dalia, Jennrock, Mae Hem, Ms. Mighty, C4, Chrisa, mecc, myssfit, Psyche and Skribbs for their friendship, inspiration, and for volunteering themselves as models for the line drawings used throughout this book.

The Greater Toronto Area was more than just a backdrop for this project, and the Toronto Arts Council was a big help too.

Finally, love all around to my my partner-in-crime, Les Seaforth (Emcee More Or Les), my supportive family—Trasks and Murrays and everyone in-between, and three life-saving English teachers from my days at Royal West Academy and John Abbott College: Doug Floen, Keith Wilkinson and Larry Weller.

ABOUT THE AUTHOR

Jill "2-left" Murray dances when no one is watching. A web designer and theatre school graduate, she travels between Toronto and Montreal with her partner in crime, emcee More or Les. *Break On Through* is her first novel. She is working on her second, about an R&B group gone scandalously wrong. You can find Jill Murray online at www.jillmurray.com.